Illegally Dead

DAVID WISHART

Illegally Dead

HODDER &
STOUGHTON

First published in Great Britain in 2008 by Hodder & Stoughton
A division of Hodder Headline

A Hodder & Stoughton Book

2

A CIP catalogue record for this title is available from the British Library

ISBN 978 0 340 84038 2

Typeset in Plantin by Hewer Text UK Ltd, Edinburgh

Printed and bound by Clays Ltd, St Ives plc

Hodder Headline's policy is to use papers that are natural, renewable
and recyclable products and made from wood grown in sustainable
forests. The logging and manufacturing processes are expected to
conform to the environmental regulations of the country of origin.

Hodder & Stoughton Ltd
A division of Hodder Headline
338 Euston Road
London NW1 3BH

To Sue and Swati, with thanks

DRAMATIS PERSONAE

(Only the names of characters who appear more than once are given.)

CORVINUS'S FAMILY AND HOUSEHOLD

Alexis: the gardener
Bathyllus: the major-domo
Lysias: the coachman
Marcia: Perilla's courtesy aunt
Marilla, Valeria: Corvinus and Perilla's adopted daughter
Meton: the chef
Perilla, Rufia: Corvinus's wife
The animals mentioned are: **Corydon,** a donkey; **Dassa,** a
    sheep; and **Placida,** a dog

Acceius, Quintus: Hostilius's lawyer partner
Bucca (Gaius Maecilius): Lucky Maecilius's elder son
Castor: Veturina's brother
Clarus: Marilla's boyfriend; Hyperion's son
Cosmus: a slave-boy belonging to Hostilius
Faenia: Fimus's wife
Fimus (Marcus Maecilius): Lucky Maecilius's younger son
Fuscus: Acceius and Hostilius's clerk
Gabba: a barfly
Habra: a Bovillan woman

Hostilius, Lucius: the dead man; a Castrimoenian lawyer
Hyperion, Publius Cornelius: the local doctor
Libanius, Quintus: head of the Castrimoenian senate
Novius, Publius: a lawyer in Bovillae
Paulina: Hostilius's ward
Pontius: owner of the wineshop in Castrimoenium
Renia: a Castrimoenian housewife
Scopas: Hostilius's major-domo
Seia Lucinda: Acceius's wife
Senecio: Habra's brother (her other brother was **Lupus**)
Tascia: Acceius's first wife
Tuscius, Marcus: a Bovillan slave-dealer
Veturina: Hostilius's wife
Veturinus: Veturina's father; owner of a wineshop in Bovillae

I

Valeria Marilla gives greetings to her adoptive parents Marcus Valerius Messalla Corvinus and Rufia Perilla.

Hi, how are you? Thanks for the books you sent, especially (Clarus says to be sure to tell you) the replacement for his father's *Rhizotomica* that Corydon ate. Everything here is much as usual. Aunt Marica has had a bit of trouble with her knee again but she says the liniment Clarus brought round is working really well; also Laertes's piles are improving, although I'm not supposed to mention them. Dassa caught another cold at the end of last month (!), but Clarus and I have been feeding her hot grain mash and giving her regular chest rubs and an evening cup of mulled Caecuban so barring the usual croaking and sneezing she's not too bad. Placida's settling down nicely after that unfortunate business with Cloelia Secunda and the topiary hedge, although you've still got to watch her with next door's mastiff and both households now keep a bucket of water handy for what Aunt Marcia calls their Mutual Bouts of Unacceptable Behaviour. Clarus is still working on her flatulence problem (Placida's, not Aunt Marcia's), since the charcoal pills I mentioned in my last letter don't seem to be having the effect he hoped for, quite the reverse – Clarus says this is a pharmaceutical anomaly, but there you are. On the positive side, now we've fenced off the pig run the rolling problem seems to be under control. More or less.

Oh, and by the way, please could you come down here as soon as possible? Clarus thinks there's been a murder.

2

So there we were, in Castrimoenium, three days later, in the atrium of Aunt Marcia's villa: me, Perilla, Marcia, Marilla, young Clarus and Clarus's father Hyperion, the local doctor and pharmacist.

I don't go much for doctors, myself, especially at the dinner table where after the third top-up they tend to lie glowering at you over their lettuce and making snide remarks about an imbalance of humours, but Hyperion's okay. For a start his full name's Publius Cornelius Hyperion, and despite the Greek bit on the end he's as Roman as they come, or Latin, anyway: the family've been settled this side of the Adriatic for over two centuries, since his great-whatever-grampa was handed the citizenship by a grateful Senate for curing General Scipio of a nasty boil on the bum just in time to let him fight Zama in comfort, thus giving us Carthage and a large slice of Africa. Or at least that's what their family tradition says. Which meant a refreshing absence of facial hair and a ditto presence of good Italian common sense.

I could take young Clarus as well, which was lucky because over the two years that I'd known him he and Marilla had become a permanent item: a quiet-spoken, serious kid streets away from the fluff-brained lads-about-town we got in Rome. Good-looking, too. Certainly Marilla thought so, from the way she couldn't take her eyes off him, and the attraction was obviously mutual.

'Right.' I held up my wine cup for the hovering Bathyllus to refill; as usually happened when we came to visit, Marcia had sent her own ancient piles-afflicted major-domo Laertes to stay with her freedwoman in Baiae for the duration. 'So tell me about this murder, then.'

'*Possible* murder.' That was Aunt Marcia, from her usual stool – stool, mark you, not chair: no decadent back rest for Perilla's Aunt Marcia – beside the portrait bust of her late husband Fabius Maximus. The old girl might've been in her eighties, but mentally she was needle-sharp, and where accuracy was concerned she didn't take prisoners. 'Please bear the distinction carefully in mind, because Hyperion has no actual proof of foul play. Do you, Hyperion?'

'No. None at all.' Hyperion shifted his lanky six-foot body on the guest-couch he shared with Clarus. 'The man was a patient of mine by the name of Lucius Hostilius.'

'Senior partner in a local law firm.' Marcia again. '*The* local law firm, in fact.'

'So how did he die?' I said.

'He was poisoned,' Hyperion said. 'At least, I think he was.'

I leaned back against the overstuffed cushions and tried to keep my expression neutral. Bugger! Well, that explained the guy's reluctance to make the accusation formal and why he'd go Clarus and Marilla to fetch me from Rome, anyway. If you were a dead man's doctor then bringing up the question of poison was juggling with razors. Where cases of poisoning were concerned, doctors were the first suspects in line.

'Not *exactly* poisoned, Dad,' Clarus said.

Hyperion grunted. 'Quite right. I'm sorry, Corvinus, I stand corrected. No, there was no actual poison involved, not as such. But I'm very much afraid that I supplied the means of death myself.'

Oh, hell; this did *not* sound good, not good at all. To break the eye contact, I lifted my wine cup and took a slow sip. It was Marcia's best Caecuban, or what Dassa the oenophilic sheep had left us of it anyway.

'Perhaps, Hyperion,' Perilla said carefully; 'you'd better explain things from the beginning.'

'Yes. Yes, of course.' Hyperion touched his own cup on the table beside him but took his hand away without lifting it. The guy was clearly worried as hell, and in his position I didn't blame him. 'Well, then. I was treating Hostilius for chest pains and palpitations, and had been for several months. The medicine was in a bottle near his bed, a ten-day supply which I'd renewed only two days before. Five days ago – late morning, to be exact – one of his slaves knocked me up to say that his master had suffered a fit and would I come at once. By the time I arrived it was too late and the man was already dead.'

'You're sure the death wasn't natural?' Perilla said.

'No.' He shook his head. 'No, I'm not sure, not at all. That's just the problem. When I began treating Hostilius my initial prognosis was that although the condition was fatal in itself with appropriate medication and strict attention to diet he might live for another two or three years, perhaps even twice that. However' – he paused – 'the signs showed that he had died from a seizure typical of the final stages of the disease, so that prognosis could have been wrong. Could *well* have been wrong, because the gods know we're not infallible.'

'But?' I said.

'Oh, yes. Certainly there is a *but*. After I'd inspected the body I checked the medicine bottle. It was almost full, as it should have been, but the medicine was a clear liquid. When I tasted it it was water.'

Uh-huh. 'And if Hostilius had drunk the original contents – all of them – the effect would've duplicated the seizure?'

'Yes. More or less exactly.'

'So you think someone gave him the full dose and refilled the bottle?'

'Yes. At least, that's what I'm afraid of.'

'Would that have been possible?' Perilla said. 'Practically speaking, I mean?'

'Oh, yes. Hostilius took the medicine in spiced honey wine, so what taste it had was masked almost completely. He wouldn't have noticed all that much difference from the usual, especially if he gulped it down, which he normally did. The effects wouldn't be immediate, either.'

'But you didn't tell anyone about the bottle at the time?' I said.

'No, Corvinus, I did not. And I won't.'

'If Dad reports it,' Clarus put in, 'all the slaves'll be tortured for their evidence, maybe even killed if the torture leads nowhere. That's the law.'

Shit. Yeah, right, that is the good old Roman law, at least technically, and I'd done Hyperion an injustice because the guy wasn't worried on his own account at all. Where the master of the house dies under suspicious circumstances his slaves are automatically assumed to be hiding crucial information about the death; information that, to be deemed valid, has to be extracted under torture. And if that doesn't produce results then as presumed accessories before, during and after the fact the whole household – men, women and children – are liable to execution. On principle, and to make sure that any other slave thinking of murdering his master or covering up for a pal who does gets the point. Roman law doesn't play games with slaves gone to the bad; it can't afford to.

'How many?' I said.

'Twenty-one,' Hyperion said. 'And I couldn't even be sure I was right.'

Marilla, perched on a stool of her own next to Clarus, hadn't spoken, but her fingers touched his arm.

'The medicine'd been switched, so *ipso facto* it had to be murder,' I said. 'You can't get past that.'

Hyperion looked even more unhappy than ever. 'Oh, but I can,' he said. 'Too easily, I'm afraid. You know slaves, Marcus. If they don't always act as we would in their place that doesn't mean they're stupid, only that their priorities – and their fears – are different from ours. The bottle was on the table in open view, and it had a loose-fitting glass stopper. Let's say one of them knocked it over accidentally while he was cleaning. It's quite within the bounds of possibility that to cover up the accident and save himself a beating he would replace the contents with water. In which case, of course, Hostilius wouldn't have drunk any of the medicine at all.'

'Yet he died. You said yourself—'

'I *said* that I wasn't infallible; that my initial prognosis could have been wrong, and that the perceived symptoms, both as they were described to me and as they showed themselves after death, point neither one way nor the other. Also, if the liquid in the bottle was only water then Hostilius could have missed two of his doses, which in his condition would be crucial. I repeat – and I must stress this – I've no *incontrovertible* proof of deliberate murder. Only the suspicion of it.'

'But—'

'Corvinus.' He leaned forwards and put his hands palm down on the table. 'Listen, please. I'm afraid there *are* no buts, not in this regard. If you're ready, for your part, to wager twenty-one innocent lives that the facts show otherwise, then I am not. And I'd think the less of you for it.'

'He's right, dear,' Perilla murmured. Marilla nodded, a brief, sharp bob of the chin.

True. I wouldn't think much of myself over a bet like that,

either. I sighed. 'Okay, pal,' I said. 'Assuming the thing was deliberate, let's see where we are and what we've got. You say the medicine bottle was on a table in Hostilius's bedroom. So in theory, given the proper opportunity, anyone in the house could've had access to it, right? Slave or family?'

'Yes.'

'Fine. We'll come back to the who in a moment. Hostilius took the medicine in wine. When?'

'In the morning, before breakfast. At least, those were my directions. Whether he followed them, as a general rule or on that occasion, I don't know.'

'Did he dose himself? Or was the dose mixed in front of him? Or was it left ready-mixed in the cup?'

'Again, I don't know, you'd have to ask Scopas. All I know is that the cup and stoppered wine flagon were sitting together on the tray with the medicine bottle.'

'Scopas?'

'His major-domo.'

Bugger; and if Scopas had been the one responsible? 'Fine. So let's shelve the how for later consideration and think about the who. Forget the slaves, what about the family? Was he married?'

There was a slight but noticeable pause. Out of the corner of my eye I saw Marcia's chin lift and Clarus and Marilla exchange a brief glance.

Uh-oh.

'Yes,' Hyperion said. 'His wife's name is Veturina.'

'Hyperion,' I said wearily. 'If you don't tell me I can't help. Separate bedrooms, was it, or something worse?'

This time the pause was longer before Hyperion said carefully, 'The first. But I don't think you should—'

'It isn't quite as simple as what you're thinking, Marcus,' Marcia cut in. 'Or what I assume you're thinking. Oh, I know nothing of Hostilius's private life – I scarcely knew the man personally – but I do know that there was a . . . *difficulty* about him. He was a very difficult person, and not only where his wife was concerned.'

'You mean he didn't get on with people?' I said.

'I'm afraid there was more to it than that,' Hyperion said. 'The problem was clinical, it first showed itself some eighteen months ago, and it was becoming progressively worse. Hostilius would suddenly take it into his head that people were cheating him, or injuring him in some way and then make accusations which were completely unfounded and made no logical sense.' He must've seen the look on my face because he held up a hand. 'Corvinus, I am not stupid, and I do understand the implications there if we're considering murder. Nevertheless, I'm speaking not only as the man's doctor over the course of many years but as a lifetime resident of Castrimoenium. We're a small community, and we may have secrets but – small communities being what they are – they don't stay secrets for long. In Veturina's case, the accusations were predictable, in the clinical sense: that she was stealing his money and that she was having affairs behind his back. He made them to me himself, sometimes in her presence; he made them to everyone. Believe me, both are nonsense.'

I glanced at Marcia. Like I say, Marcia is no one's fool, and if she wasn't a lifetime resident herself she'd spent more time up here in the Alban Hills than most of them had clocked up.

'Hyperion is right,' she said. 'Again I don't know Veturina sufficiently well personally to give an absolute opinion, but I know nothing whatsoever against her. Quite the reverse. Despite the differences in their respective backgrounds by all accounts she's been a loyal, honest and devoted wife, latterly under extremely trying circumstances.'

'The differences in their backgrounds?' I said.

'Her father kept – still keeps, I understand – a wineshop in Bovillae. She and Hostilius had been married for over thirty years.'

'Children?'

'Two, but they died in infancy. They have – well, I suppose you'd call her a stepdaughter, although there was never a formal adoption. The orphaned child of Hostilius's cousin. She'd be about Marilla's age now, or slightly younger.' Marcia must've noticed my expression, because her lips tightened. 'Marcus, listen to me. I do realise that when a husband is poisoned the wife is an obvious suspect, and I don't wish to seem dogmatic or seek to prejudice you in any way. But I do think that if you jumped to that conclusion without careful thought you would be making a very silly mistake.'

Yeah, well, maybe; certainly I took the point. All the same, despite Marcia's five-star encomium and Hyperion's caveats if we were talking murder here then we'd be fools not to consider this Veturina, especially given the ostensible family circumstances. And some people are good at keeping secrets. Still, that was for the future. 'Okay,' I said, 'we've got a wife and a stepdaughter. Anyone else in the house? Family, I mean?'

'Just one,' Hyperion said. 'Veturina's brother Castor. Hostilius took him on a few years ago as the law firm's jack-of-all-trades.'

'Her *brother*? He doesn't have a place of his own?'

'No. He isn't married, and the house is one of the biggest in town. When Castor moved from Bovillae Hostilius gave him the use of the east wing.'

'What's he like?'

'Youngish, much younger than Veturina, middle thirties. Good-looking. He and Veturina are very close, more like mother and son.'

'Uh-huh. Eye for the girls?'

'What makes you ask that?'

'Just filling in the gaps. Besides, *young* and *good-looking* were the first choices you made.'

'Oh. I see.' Hyperion hesitated. 'Then . . . yes, he has, a little. But he's a conscientious worker, too, by all accounts, and by no means unintelligent. Quite a likeable man all round.'

'But he would've had access to the medicine bottle?'

'Naturally he would, in theory at least. As would any of the household. I told you, it wasn't locked away. Why would Castor want to kill his brother-in-law?'

I shrugged. 'I'm not saying he did. How could I? But if you and Marcia are right in your assessment of Veturina then she didn't, either. On the other hand, maybe one of them did, or both of them together, because they both had the opportunity. We're only playing empty possibilities at this stage, pal. Which brings me to the point. What do I do now?'

Hyperion frowned. 'But surely—'

'Find out who did it, of course,' Marilla said. 'I thought that was obvious.'

'Princess,' I said. 'Just think for a moment, will you? As far as everyone's concerned, including – overtly, at least – his doctor, the man's death was completely natural, end of story. I've no official standing, I can't even *ask* for official standing because the minute I raise the possibility of murder with the authorities they'll pull in his slaves. So I can't turn up on doorsteps asking embarrassing questions because the best I could hope for would be a raised eyebrow and the bum's rush. And unless I can do that we're stymied. Okay?'

'Ah,' Hyperion said.

'*Ah*, is exactly right.'

'Just a moment.' Marcia cleared her throat. 'I think you may perhaps be being a little over-pessimistic here.'

I turned to face her. 'Is that so, now?' I said.

She stiffened. 'Yes, it certainly *is* so,' she said. 'And, Marcus Valerius Corvinus, don't you *dare* use that tone with me.'

Oh, shit. I glanced at Perilla. She was grinning. Marilla sniggered. 'Uh . . . yeah. Well. I'm sorry, it's just that—'

'I'm glad to say I disagree with Hyperion on one important point. The Castrimoenian authorities are not ogres, and although I have little time normally for modern so-called morality it is sometimes superior to the variety which I was brought up with.' I kept my lips tightly shut. Jupiter! Coming from Marcia an admission like that was up there with the flying pigs! 'Besides, slaves are valuable commodities not to be wasted needlessly. You remember Quintus Libanius, of course?'

'Yeah.' Head of the Castrimoenian senate, and the only bearded town magistrate north of the Bay of Naples. 'Yeah, I remember Libanius.'

'He's not an unreasonable man, and you did impress him over that unfortunate business two years ago. I'm sure that if he were properly approached and talked to in advance he might be prepared to show a little flexibility.'

'Well, that's great. In that case maybe I could—'

She fixed me with a freezing stare, and I clammed up.

'I meant by me, naturally,' she said.

I winced. He wasn't a bad guy, Fuzz-face Libanius, as magistrates go, and I felt sorry for him in prospect: *properly approached and talked to* was three-line-whip standard in Aunt Marcia's lexicon. Knowing the old girl's powers of coercion, my bet was that by the time she'd finished with him the poor bugger would agree to anything short of selling Latium to the Parthians. Not that I was complaining, mind.

'Ah . . . fair enough,' I said.

'Good, I'm delighted that you agree. I'll send a slave. In the meantime' – she rearranged a fold of her impeccably draped mantle – 'I for one have had quite enough of murder for one afternoon, especially just before dinner. Change the subject. How *is* that little brat Gaius shaping up as emperor?'

Marcia's slave came back while we were halfway through the dessert with the news that Libanius would drop by mid- to late afternoon the next day.

We were in business. Maybe.

3

I was down to breakfast late next morning: at Marcia's, if the
weather's good, as it was that day, we always have it outside
on the terrace looking towards Mount Alba. Me, I'm not a
breakfast person normally, unlike Perilla, who can really shift
it, or the princess, who's been known to eat five two-egg
omelettes at a sitting, but the air in the Alban Hills gives you an
appetite, especially when the breakfast table's out of doors.
Marilla was ensconced already, shovelling in rolls and honey
like there was no tomorrow while Bathyllus hovered with the
fruit juice.

'Morning, Corvinus,' she said. 'Did you sleep well?'

'Like a brick,' I said. 'Or whatever. Bread and honey's fine,
Bathyllus, but wheel out a cup of the Caecuban, okay?'

'Very well, sir.' Impeccable butlerese: when we're at Aunt
Marcia's, the little guy is always on his best behaviour. Aunt
Marcia has *tone*, and Bathyllus is the snob's snob. 'I could ask
Meton to make you an omelette, if you'd prefer.'

'No, that's okay.' I reached for the rolls. Meton the chef
and Alexis, technically our gardener, were the other two
members of the Corvinus household we always brought with
us; Meton because Marcia's own chef, like Laertes the
major-domo, was well past his sell-by date and you took
your life in your hands with the canapés, and Alexis because
he was far and away the smartest cookie on our staff and a
good set of brains was never wasted. Oh, and Lysias the
coachman, but since his interests extended to horses and

chasing the local bits of skirt, total, we barely saw him. 'Got any plans for today, Princess?'

'Clarus should be over any minute. We were hoping that we might, ah—' She stopped dead.

'Might ah what?'

She grinned. 'I've never been involved in a murder enquiry. At least, not properly. Nor has Clarus.'

'And?'

'So we were hoping that we might tag along. Sort of. If that's okay.'

Hell. I set down the roll I'd taken from the basket. 'Now listen, Marilla—'

'Oh, good. That's marvellous. Here's Clarus now.' She waved. 'Clarus! Over here! We haven't finished breakfast.'

'Marilla, watch my lips,' I said. 'You are not going to—'

'Good morning, sir. Did you sleep well?'

'Morning, Clarus. I was just telling Marilla that there's no way that—'

'I thought before Quintus Libanius arrives we could show you where the Hostilius house is. Then we could—'

Gods! 'Clarus, pal,' I said. 'Shut up. Please.' He did. 'Now. I was just telling this fugitive from a maenad pediment that you're not getting involved in this. Neither of you, no way, never, nohow. Clear?'

'But Perilla said we could,' Marilla said.

I goggled. 'She did *what?*'

'Of course I did.' I whipped round. The lady was coming out through the portico in her dressing-gown, which considering I'd left her flat out and dead to the world upstairs practically put her in the Bathyllus bracket for omnipresence. 'After all, dear, it's only fair. They started it and they've got a vested interest. Besides' – she sat down and helped herself to a roll – 'the suggestion came from Aunt Marcia. If you've any objections then you can take them up with her. Yes, thank you, Bathyllus, I will have a cup of fruit juice.'

I stared. Bugger! Double bugger! It was a conspiracy! 'Now look here, lady—'

'You look, Marcus. How old were you when you forced the empress Livia to bring my stepfather's ashes back from Tomi?'

Shit. 'Uh . . .'

'You were twenty-one. Which is only a year more than Clarus is now, and Marilla is only thirteen months younger than him.' She broke the roll and reached for the honey. 'Oh, Bathyllus, ask Meton if he'd make me a cheese omelette, would you? Clarus, have you eaten?'

Clarus nodded. 'Yes, thanks,' he said, and turned back to me. 'We don't expect you to carry us with you everywhere like useless baggage, Corvinus. It wouldn't be practical, and it wouldn't be sensible. But my father feels responsible for Hostilius's death, and just staying out on the sidelines doing nothing doesn't seem right, somehow. Can you understand that?'

Hell's teeth; yeah, I could understand it easily, and what was more Perilla had a valid point about the Ovid business. Maybe I was just getting middle-aged and crotchety. Besides, like I said, I'd a lot of time for Clarus, more time than I'd've had for myself at his age. He might even be a steadying influence . . .

Ah, well. When you're beat, you're beat, and with Marcia and Perilla both slugging for the opposition I didn't have a hope in Hades anyway. All I could do was cut my losses.

'Invitation only?' I said.

He grinned. 'Invitation only.'

I held out my hand and we shook. 'In that case you've a deal, pal. Starting this afternoon, if and when Marcia fixes things with Libanius, and at points as and when I say thereafter. No beefing, no arguments and no comeback, especially from Penthesilea here. Agreed?'

'Agreed.' He gently removed the roll she'd just picked up from between Marilla's fingers and put it back in the basket. 'Okay, Marilla, plan B.'

'Plan B?' Marilla said.

'We keep out of Corvinus's hair pro tem. Go and fetch Corydon and we'll ride up to Caba.'

Perilla and I watched them go off in the direction of the stables. Perilla was smiling.

'We really will have to put our minds to a dowry,' she said.

'Yeah.' I'd just been thinking that myself. I picked up a roll, tore it in two and dunked it in the honey. 'Marcia'll miss her when she goes, mind.'

'Oh, I think Aunt Marcia's thought of that already. Marilla's always been far more hers than ours, she hasn't any living relatives now, and this villa's easily big enough for two households. I doubt if either Marilla or Clarus would think of moving from Castrimoenium. Besides . . . well, Hyperion's had a word with me. He's Aunt Marcia's doctor too, remember.' I glanced at her, but said nothing. 'She's eighty-four, Marcus. That's older than anyone expects to live to. And despite appearances she isn't well. Not well at all.'

Oh, hell. 'Does she know?' I said.

'Of course she does. She isn't a fool, and she's never been one to settle for half-truths. It isn't obvious yet, but it will be, soon.'

'How long?'

'Hyperion says six months. A year, at most, all told. So' – she took a sip of her fruit juice – 'we'd best get them married quickly. Aunt Marcia would like that.'

'Yeah.' Shit. Well, it came to us all, I supposed. And like Perilla said, the old girl had had a good innings. Still, she'd been one of life's fixtures, and I'd miss her when she went.

'She doesn't mind, if that's what you're thinking. And she doesn't want anyone else to, either.' Perilla was turning the cup in her fingers. 'Oh – Marilla doesn't know, though. Marcia's been very careful she shouldn't, and she'd like to keep it that way as long as possible. So please watch what you say.'

'Right. Right.'

'Now.' Perilla set the cup down. 'That's enough gloom and despondency for one morning. What are your plans?'

'I thought I might go into town, drop in at Pontius's, catch up on the local gossip. Maybe put out a few feelers in advance of meeting Libanius. That suit you, lady?'

'Fine. I wanted to have a quiet chat with Aunt Marcia in any case, and she won't be up and around for a few hours yet. Take your time, Marcus.'

Bathyllus reappeared with Perilla's omelette and my cup of wine – well watered, which was fair enough since there'd be more in the offing at Pontius's, especially if he'd got the local gang in. Like Perilla said, there was no hurry: the town was an easy half-hour's walk away, Libanius wasn't due until afternoon, and if Marcia wanted the time and space to soften the guy up without me breathing down her neck – which she did – then the longer I stayed away the better. Besides, the first-morning-of-the-holiday visit to Pontius's had become a tradition at Aunt Marcia's. Not, from what Perilla had just told me, mind, that that was going to continue much longer . . .

Well, there was no point in dwelling on it. Like the lady had said, eighty-four was a good age, better than I could expect to notch up, anyway, and there was no sense in grieving over something that hadn't happened yet. I finished my honeyed roll, took the last swallow from the cup and set off towards town.

4

Pontius's wineshop is in Castrimoenium's main square. Normally on a day like this I'd've sat on the terrace outside and watched the world go by, or as much of the world as you get in a town where a dogfight's an event, but there were no punters in evidence so I pushed the door open and went inside.

'Hey, Corvinus!' Gabba lifted his wine cup. Life has few near-certainties, but one of them is that whatever time of the day you push open Pontius's wineshop's door chances are you'll find Castrimoenium's most dedicated barfly on the other side of it. 'How's the boy? Holidays again?'

'Yeah, more or less.' I nodded to Pontius behind the bar. 'Can't keep me away. How's it going, Gabba?'

Pontius hefted a wine jar from the shelf. 'Nice to see you back, Corvinus. The usual?'

'Fine.' I put the money on the counter while he poured a half jug of the local wine and set it down with a cup in front of me. Not Latium's best, Castrimoenian, not by a long chalk, but it's not bad stuff for everyday drinking on its home ground, and Pontius's is as good as you'll get anywhere.

'More or less?' Gabba pushed his cup over for Pontius to refill. 'Not another murder, is it?'

'Uh-uh.' I poured and swallowed. 'No murders.'

'That chancer of a chef of yours trained any more sheep?'

'Not that he's mentioned.'

'He wouldn't, would he?' Gabba sniggered and took a sip of

his fresh cupful. 'Not to you, pal. You bring him up here with you?'

'Yeah, Meton's here.'

'Well, you tell him from me he did a good job and it's stuck. Last wine-tasting you couldn't get odds on Dassa for love nor money, and quite right too because she scooped the pot again hooves down. Even Lucky Maecilius was impressed, rest his bones, and that old bugger hadn't a good word to say about sheep.' Another sip. 'Especially ones that'd just crapped on his boots.'

'Maecilius is dead?' I said. Not that I was surprised, mind, because the last and only time I'd seen him was two years ago, and he'd looked like a pickled mummy even then.

'Sure. Hit by a lightning bolt just after the Winter Festival.' Gabba took a proper swallow. 'Right in the middle of a call of nature, too.'

'Lightning in *December*?'

'As ever was. From a clear blue sky, smack through the latrine roof. He had style, did old Lucky. One of nature's true incompetents to the end.'

'Left a tidy bit, too,' Pontius said. 'Fifty thousand, so they say. Plus the farm, and that's worth four times as much again.'

'Could be,' Gabba said. 'Could be, Pontius, boy. In the right quarter.'

I took another swig of the Castrimoenian and topped up my cup from the jug. 'So what else has been happening?'

'Not a lot, Consul.' Gabba emptied his own cup. 'Just the usual. Carrinatia's billygoat slipped his tether and ate his way through Titus Memmius's cabbage patch. Paetinius's youngest is pregnant again, father unknown – that's her third. Oh, and of course there was that killing in the street ten days back, but you wouldn't be interested in that.'

'*What?*'

'Tell a lie, it was twelve days. Or am I mixing it up with the day the wheel fell off Petrusius's cart and killed the chicken?'

'Gabba, you bastard!'

He was grinning. 'All in fun, just winding you up, boy. Twelve days it was.'

Gods! 'Never mind the exact fucking date! *What* killing?'

'Some mad bugger went for one of the local worthies with a knife, middle of the street, broad daylight, no reason. Could've saved himself the trouble, in the event, because the worthy pegged out himself not long after. No connection, natural causes.'

'Chap by the name of Lucius Hostilius.' Pontius was pouring a cup of wine for himself. He took a sip and put it down on the bar. 'The worthy, I mean. Local lawyer, or was.'

My brain had gone numb. 'You said a killing. So who was killed?'

'The man with the knife. You mind, Corvinus?' Gabba hooked my jug over and topped up his empty cup. 'Hostilius was lucky, he'd his partner with him, big strong bugger able to handle himself, and he did good and proper.' He clicked his tongue. 'Five seconds later and it was Goodnight Alexandria fair and proper.'

'Who was the knifeman?'

'I never heard a name myself.' Gabba took a long swig. 'Pontius?' Pontius shook his head. 'Don't think there was one, in the end. He wasn't a Castrimoenian, whatever, and whoever the bastard was he hadn't been living easy. Dressed like a tramp, stank to high heaven.'

'Why did he do it?'

'I told you, no reason, bugger was out of his tree. The pair of them were just crossing the street minding their own business when he runs up, draws a knife and goes for Hostilius.'

'He wasn't hurt? Hostilius, I mean?'

'Nah. The blade caught in his mantle-fold. That gave his

partner the chance to pile in, get the knife off of the bastard and skewer him.'

'This partner got a name?'

'Acceius. Quintus Acceius.'

'Many people see this?'

Gabba's eyes narrowed and he set his cup down. 'Ten or a dozen, maybe,' he said. 'I told you, it was broad daylight in the main street. What is this, Corvinus? You sure there hasn't been a murder?'

'Uh-uh. Just interested.'

'The hell with that, boy! I know interested, and that wasn't it, not by a long chalk.' He turned to Pontius. 'Know what I think? I think Lucius Hostilius got the heave after all and our Corvinus's been Sent For.'

Fuck! 'Gabba—'

'That true, Corvinus?' Pontius said.

Things were slipping fast here. He might look like a cow's backside and soak up more wine than a sponge, but Gabba could see through a brick wall with the best of them. And drop a juicy titbit like murder into the casual conversation at Pontius's and it'd be all over town before you could say 'oops!'.

Fuck was right.

'Yes, indeed.' Gabba emptied his cup again and reached for my jug. 'My belief, Pontius old mate, for what it's worth, is that someone slipped the legal gentleman a noxious foreign substance on the sly and someone else has rumbled the fact and called our lad down to finger the perp. What do you say yourself?'

'Gabba—'

'Of course I could be wrong. Put your head out the door and check for flying pigs.'

Jupiter! I tried again. 'Gabba, watch my lips. There has not been a murder. Okay?'

'You know your right eyebrow twitches when you lie?'

So must Sisyphus have felt when he saw his fucking rock roll back for the umpteenth-millionth time. I sighed and poured myself another shot of wine before the bastard finished the jug for me. 'Look, just get the hell off my back, will you?' I said. 'We're spending a few days with our adopted daughter and Perilla's aunt, right? No other reason, that is *it*. Finish, end of story.'

Gabba shrugged. 'Have it your own way, Consul,' he said. 'Not that it surprises me, mind. Word is the man was asking to be stiffed.'

'Is that so, now.'

'Could've been the wife did it. Could've been the partner.' He winked. 'Could've been the both of them together, wouldn't be the first time that'd happened. *Convenient*, that's what I call it.'

'Nah, I don't believe that one. Quintus Acceius isn't the philandering type.' Pontius picked up my jug and shook it. 'Looking a bit empty already, Corvinus. You want the other half?'

'Yeah, why not?' I said sourly. 'I might strike really, really lucky and have some of it to myself this time.' Shit. Well, I'd tried. And so long as I didn't actually *confirm* anything there was no comeback. 'I thought you said his partner saved this Hostilius's life. Why should he kill him six days later?'

'Did we mention exactly when the gentleman died, Pontius?' Gabba gave me a beatific smile. 'I suppose we must've done.' Bugger! 'Never mind. Well, Corvinus, the general consensus of local gossip is that relations between the two weren't exactly amicable. Chiefly because on separate occasions Hostilius had accused the man in public of screwing his wife and told Acceius's own wife to her face, ditto, that she was no better than a whore. Both loudly, at length, and with full appropriate embellishment. That do you for motive?' I said nothing. 'Me, I wouldn't blame either of them for getting rid of the bastard just on general principles. He was an embarrassment all round and getting worse.'

'Come on, Gabba!' Pontius grunted, setting down my fresh half jug. 'Have a bit of charity. Everyone knew he couldn't help it. Besides, the man's dead. "Nothing but good", remember?'

An easy-going lad, Pontius, but he was beginning to sound a little tetchy. Gabba in full flow tended to have that effect on people. Tactful and politically correct were two things the guy wasn't.

'Maybe so, maybe so.' Gabba took another careful sip of his wine. 'Of course, if Wonder Boy the great detective *isn't* looking for motives to murder Lucius Hostilius then he won't want to know about Fimus either. That right, Corvinus?'

'For the gods' sake!' Pontius had been leaning on the bar. Now he straightened and turned away. 'That's it, Gabba, enough's enough! You've had your fun, but the joke's over.'

'Fimus?' I said. The word means dung.

'Marcus Maecilius, Lucky's second son.' Gabba was grinning. Pontius still had his back to us.

'Yeah? So if he's got a handle already then why Fimus?'

'Ah, well, now, I'm glad you asked that. Nothing to do with non-existent murders, of course, but of marginal interest in itself. Would you happen to have any of that wine spare?' I sighed and slid the new half jug over. Gabba refilled his cup. 'Fimus is your solid agricultural type, you see, close to the earth and redolent of nature at her most basic, and he's also only got one eye.'

He waited, expectantly.

'Uh . . . so?' I said finally.

'One eye? Fimus as in *Poly*phemus? It's what we simple folk out here in the sticks call a bilingual pun, Consul, combined with a recherché literary illusion.'

Oh, *shit*!

'The word's *al*lusion, Gabba, boy,' Pontius murmured, turning round. 'Literary *al*lusion.'

'By gods, your wine must be getting better.' Gabba took a swallow. 'No, same old dishwater. Must've been just a slip of the tongue after all.'

Pontius snorted, and I grinned despite myself. 'Gabba, just tell me straight, okay?' I said. 'About how this Fimus fits into things.'

'No, I'll tell you.' That was Pontius. 'Fimus and Hostilius were talking together. Then Hostilius starts shouting, he calls Fimus a thief and a liar and smacks his face. That's all that happened, Corvinus. All there was to it.'

'Yeah? When was this?'

'Eight or nine days ago in the square outside.'

'You know why?'

'No, Fimus wouldn't say, nor Hostilius either. Fimus just walked off and left him standing. That's it. All there is.'

'Come on, Pontius!' Gabba took another swallow of wine. 'You know damn well what it was about, or you can guess!'

Pontius moved over to stand in front of him. He was looking serious as hell now, and he's a big lad. Their eyes locked, and Gabba edged back on his stool.

'Maybe I can at that,' Pontius said slowly. 'There again, maybe I'd be wrong. But in any case, boy, it's none of my business, and it's not yours or Corvinus's either. There's been no crime committed as far as we know' – he looked at me, and I stared back expressionlessly – 'and I won't hear the dead or the living slandered in my bar just for amusement. Now you've had your fun and it's over. Call it a day or drink up. The same goes for you, Corvinus.'

The silence lengthened. Finally, Gabba waved his hand like he'd burned the fingers.

'Ouch!' He shrugged. 'Very well, Pontius lad, point made

and taken on board. You care to choose a subject for conversation?'

Pontius sucked a tooth for a few seconds, frowning. Then
he grinned. 'Rome's always good for a laugh,' he said.

Confrontation over; a good lad, Pontius, and he can gauge
his clientele to a T. We shot the breeze about Rome, and the
new emperor, and finished the other half jug.

Hmm.

5

When I got home mid-afternoon Perilla was sitting reading in the atrium with the two youngsters head-to-head over a game of Robbers.

'Oh, hello, Marcus.' Perilla put down her book. 'Did you have a nice morning?'

'Yeah. Yeah, it was okay.' I planted the requisite smacker and pulled up a stool. 'Libanius arrived yet?'

'About fifteen minutes ago. He's with Aunt Marcia and Hyperion in the study.'

'Fine. Hey, Clarus!'

'Yes, Corvinus?' He looked up.

'You know of anyone by the name of Fimus?'

'Sure, he farms over by Six Cedars. Marcus Maecilius.'

'Hear of a connection between him and Lucius Hostilius at all?'

'Yes. Hostilius and Acceius are representing him in a court case against his brother.'

'Acceius?' Perilla said.

'Hostilius's partner.' I turned back to Clarus. 'You know what the case is about?'

Clarus grinned. 'If I didn't I'd be the only one in Castrimoenium.'

'They're wrangling over old Lucky Maecilius's will,' Marilla said.

'Happen to know the details?'

'Not as such,' Clarus said. 'But the gist of it is that although

his elder son got most of the cash, old Maecilius left all the land
to Fimus.'

'That so, now?' Well, as a valid reason for litigation you
wouldn't get better, not somewhere like Castrimoenium. In
farming districts like Latium they take land very, very seriously, and there isn't a surer way to split a family at a death
than a spat over how the acres are divided. Besides, Pontius
had said there was quite a bit of actual money involved, too,
which might well've complicated matters. But it raised a
question in its own right. If anything, barring a general
parcelling-out – and I could see that that'd cause problems
of its own – testamentary dispensations usually went the other
way, with the property *in toto* going to the eldest son and the
younger ones taking their share of the available cash. Maecilius
was a farmer to his boots, he must've known a cack-handed
arrangement like that would lead to trouble. 'He have a reason
for doing things that way, do you know? Old Lucky, I mean?'

'Certainly. Or at least, it makes good practical sense.
Fimus's worked Six Cedars with his father all his life. Bucca's
no farmer, never has been.'

'Bucca? That's the other son?' They did like their nick-
names, the Castrimoenians: the word means the mouth or
bragger.

'Yes. He's got a carting and saddlery business in town. His
name's really Gaius, but Bucca's what everyone calls him. It
fits, too.'

'Not a popular bunny, then?'

That got a grin. 'Oh, no. You won't find many locals who've
much time for Bucca Maecilius. Nor did his father, for that
matter. The general opinion is he was lucky to get as much as
he did, and as far as the court case is concerned he hasn't got a
hope in hell.'

'Why do you think Hostilius'd call—' I began, but I was
interrupted by the sight of Marcia and Hyperion coming from

the direction of the study with Quintus Libanius in tow. 'Never mind, we'll pick up on that one later.'

'Ah, Valerius Corvinus, you're here.' Libanius came across, hand outstretched, and I stood up. 'A pleasure to see you again.'

'Likewise. How are you, Libanius?' We shook.

'Hello, Marcus.' Marcia lowered herself carefully on to her usual stool and straightened a fold of her mantle. She looked old, even older than she usually did; but maybe that was just me noticing it more. 'Now. Hyperion and I have discussed the situation with Quintus and he fully understands the position.'

'Absolutely,' Libanius said. He had that glazed, punch-drunk look about him that being on the receiving end of one of Marcia's discussions leaves you with. 'Hyperion's quite right, Corvinus, the matter ought to be investigated. Consequently, I'd be grateful for any help you can give.' He paused. 'However, there is the major problem of a formal charge. I've told the Lady Marcia that as representative of the town authorities I'm more than willing to provide you with authorisation for an investigation, but—'

He stopped. The guy looked unhappy, and I didn't blame him. Yeah, that aspect of things had been worrying me too. Hell!

'But Hostilius's death wasn't obvious murder.' I filled in what he hadn't said. 'No obvious murder, no excuse for a public enquiry, certainly not without the family's permission. Meaning, in this case, the guy's wife. And if – what's her name; Veturina? – she doesn't give it, and why should she because she'd be a prime suspect if not the actual villain, then we're completely in shtook. Right?'

Libanius looked even more unhappy. 'Indeed,' he said. 'And that is exactly where we're likely to remain. As far as Veturina is concerned at present – assuming she wasn't responsible – her husband died a natural death. Nothing and no one has suggested otherwise. It would be unreasonable to expect her to approve an enquiry even if she were completely innocent, and if we did hold one she'd have a perfect right to refuse her co-operation.'

'I've told Quintus that, Hyperion being to all intents and purposes a client of mine, I would be prepared to bring a formal legal charge myself,' Marcia said. 'The drawback is that I would have to cite a specific person as the one responsible. Which of course in advance of a proper investigation would be a nonsense.'

'Yeah. Yeah, right,' I said. Bugger! This was *not* looking good.

'So you see, Corvinus' – Libanius spread his hands – 'we're caught. No proof of murder – or no formal accusation – no investigation; no investigation, no proof of murder. Oh, yes: if Hyperion were to report the business with the medicine bottle officially, even now, I could take unilateral action myself. Unfortunately, in law that would immediately entail, *ipso facto*, at least the torture of the household's slaves, and Hyperion will not accept this under any circumstances. Barring that, and given the Lady Marcia's understandable scruples, I see no course of action but to leave things as they are.'

Shit. 'So what you're saying,' I said, 'is that you need some piece of evidence – some *solid* piece of evidence – besides the medicine bottle, that points to a murder.'

'Yes. Until we have that then I'm afraid—'

'Excuse me, sir.' Bathyllus butlered in from the direction of the lobby. 'But there's a messenger arrived to speak to Quintus Libanius.'

'Ah.' Libanius frowned. 'I'm sorry, I left word with my major-domo that I'd be contactable here if I was needed for any reason. If you'll excuse me a moment?'

'Sure,' I said.

He left. For a moment, there was silence. Then: 'Corvinus, you *can't* give up!' Marilla snapped.

'Marilla's right,' Clarus said. 'Hostilius was murdered, you know he was. We can't just—'

'Princess. Clarus.' Jupiter, this was a real downer. 'You heard the guy. I told you, without some sort of official standing here my hands are tied.'

'That hasn't stopped you before,' Perilla said quietly.

'No, it hasn't.' Marcia glared at me. 'Nor should it be stopping you now. Marcus Valerius Corvinus, I'm surprised at you. If Libanius says we need additional proof then we will simply have to think how it is to be got. There's the Hostilius household for a start. One of the slaves might have seen something, or—'

'You heard Libanius, Marcia. I can't go questioning Hostilius's slaves without his wife's permission, and she isn't likely to give it.'

'Nonsense! Hyperion could arrange something easily. Couldn't you, Hyperion?'

'Certainly. Nothing easier,' Hyperion said. 'I'm sure under the circumstances Scopas – that's the major-domo, if you recall – would co-operate fully, and I'd stake my life that he's above suspicion himself.'

'There you are. It's a beginning. Also, Marcus' – Marcia's chin lifted – 'I may not get around as much as I used to, but I do have some influence not only locally but in Rome, which if necessary I am fully prepared to use.'

I was grinning despite myself. I didn't underestimate that last bit of unsolicited support, either. Given the choice of having the authority of the Castrimoenian senate behind me or a damn-your-eyes war-to-the-knife commitment from the widow of the Divine Augustus's friend and chief adviser, I'd take the second option any day. Like it or not, the steel-strong Old Boy and Old Girl network still runs the empire. A few carefully worded letters from Marcia to her blue-blood, henna-rinsed epistolary pals in Rome and we'd probably have the head Foreign Judge in person tanking down here with the authorisation ready signed.

'Yeah, well,' I said. 'Maybe—'

Which was as far as I got before Libanius reappeared. With that mass of facial hair getting in the way I couldn't read his expression exactly, but from the change in his manner whatever the message had been it hadn't come from his laundress.

'I don't know which particular god looks after the investigative proclivities of men like yourself, Corvinus,' he said, 'but I suggest that you owe him or her a whopping great sacrifice. That was one of the public slaves from the Town Watch office. Someone's found a body.'

I stared at him. Marilla whispered, 'Oh, *great*!'

'Whose body, Quintus?' Marcia said.

'A young slave belonging to Hostilius's household. His name was Cosmus.'

'Ah,' Hyperion said.

'You know him?' Libanius said.

'*Of* him, yes. Well, well. Now that's interesting.'

'He had certain articles in his belt-pouch that he could only have stolen, and stolen only from Hostilius's bedroom. They included, crucially, the dead man's signet ring. Taking that fact together with your suspicions over the medicine bottle, Hyperion, we now have a prima facie case for murder.'

'You think this slave murdered Hostilius for the sake of a ring and a few bedroom trifles?' Marcia said. 'It seems rather unlikely, doesn't it?'

'Of course it does.' Libanius frowned. 'That isn't the point. What's important is the existence of the technicality: that Hostilius died to someone's advantage under what can now be revealed as ambiguous circumstances. That's all I needed. You have your investigation.'

'And the slaves?' Hyperion said.

Libanius hesitated. 'There,' he said carefully, 'I think I'm entitled to use my discretion. Again technically, the murderer is already caught. If we don't push the letter of the law too far – and I'm trying very hard, at present, not to think too deeply about likelihoods and legalities here – then putting the rest of the household's slaves to the torture is neither strictly necessary nor – because it would seriously affect their value as commodities – would it be economically justified. You'd agree, Lady Marcia?'

'Oh, well done, Quintus!' Marcia murmured. 'Very neat!'

'It's *brilliant!*' Marilla was beaming. 'Isn't it, Corvinus?'

'Yeah.' It was, too: a beautiful piece of legal doublethink with a nice slice of good old-fashioned hard-headed business practice thrown in. I was beginning to have a lot of respect for Libanius. 'Uh . . . where was the body found?'

'In a well on the old Bavius property, not far from Hostilius's villa.'

'In a *well*?'

'It was sheer luck. The property's been empty since Bavius's widow died a year ago, and the new owner – he's a cousin, lives in Rome – hadn't shown much interest. Now, seemingly, he wants to sell it as a holiday home. He contacted two local builders to check the place over. One of the things they checked, of course, was the well, and – there you are.'

'So this Cosmus was murdered himself and dumped?'

'It's a possibility, Corvinus. That's for you to determine. However, it's also possible that his death was an accident. Seemingly the surrounding wall is very low, and broken completely in places.'

'Where's the body now?' Hyperion said.

'At the Town Watch-house.'

'Could I see it, do you think?'

Libanius's eyebrows rose. 'Of course. If you like. Though why you should bother to—'

'I may be able to tell things from it.'

'Indeed? Well, suit yourself, Hyperion, you know best, I suppose. One more thing I should tell you, though, Corvinus, although I'd rather stay out of your investigations altogether, if you don't mind.'

'Yeah?'

'The body was only identified as Cosmus's because one of the men who found it knew him by sight. As far as I know – and I *would* know – Veturina hasn't reported the boy missing, as would normally happen with a runaway slave. Nor had she reported any theft.'

Ah. 'Interesting,' I said.

'Isn't it? Well' – Libanius turned to Marcia – 'I think this has been quite a successful meeting after all. I'll be getting back now, if you'll excuse me. Hyperion? You wanted to inspect the corpse. And Corvinus, of course, if you'd care to join us. I can confirm officially, naturally, that from this moment on the investigation is yours and you have the full backing of the Castrimoenian senate.' He held out his hand, and I shook it. 'The best of luck to you.'

Clarus and Marilla stood up. 'I'll fetch Corydon,' Marilla said. 'Clarus, you brought Aster, didn't you?'

'Now just a minute, Princess—' I said.

'But of course we're coming,' Clarus said.

'Clarus, pal—'

'What?' He grinned. 'Look, Corvinus, I'll bet that I've seen more corpses than you've had hot dinners. Also, that thanks to Dad I can tell a lot more about them than you can. And Marilla – well, if I go then so does she.'

Gods! I glanced at Hyperion, but he shrugged. 'The boy's absolutely right,' he said. 'Besides, his eyesight's a lot better than mine.' Then, when I still hesitated, he said gently, 'Listen, my friend. You have your area of expertise; we – Clarus and myself – have ours. We may be able to use it to tell you something useful. Perhaps you should recognise that fact and accept help where it's offered.'

Yeah, well, that was fair enough. And if Marilla wanted to get in on the act then that was her business. 'Okay,' I said. 'Point taken. I'm sorry.'

We went off to view the body.

6

They'd got him in an outhouse, laid on a couple of boards raised on trestles: a kid of about fourteen or fifteen from his size, wearing a tunic that was upmarket for a slave but carefully darned in places. Fairish hair, plastered over his forehead, and a string of cheap glass beads round his neck. It wasn't obvious from first glance how he'd died, but his mouth was half open in an 'Oh' of surprise. He'd had good teeth. His eyes were open, too. Not that you could see the colour.

'Yes,' Hyperion said, 'that's Cosmus.'

Marilla was hanging back, wide-eyed but still in there. Which was more than could be said for Libanius. I'd seen him lose his breakfast under similar circumstances on a previous occasion, although then he'd had more reason. This time he might've been holding on to his lunch with more success, but from the look on his face it was a close-run thing. Well, we've all got our little foibles.

'Dad? Do you mind?' Clarus said.

'Not at all, son.' Hyperion stepped back. 'Go ahead.'

I watched – we all did – while Clarus made his examination, pulling at the skin, raising the eyelids, lifting the hands and examining the nails, all with a single-minded detachment that I found impressive as hell, and truth be told on the weather side of chilling. Finally he moved round to stand behind the head. He lifted it gently and moved it from side to side in a rolling motion.

'Well?' I said.

'Dead and in the water more than two days but not as long as five,' Clarus said. 'No broken neck, but there's a serious wound to the back of the head. You like to help me turn him over, Dad?'

Hyperion stepped forward and took the dead boy's legs. Together they manhandled the corpse on to its front. One arm flailed, settling itself round Clarus's shoulder, and he brushed it off absently. Beside me, Libanius gagged and left the room.

The back of the boy's head was a mess. No blood, of course, not after all that time in the water; but the skull was stove in like the shell of an egg.

'Anyone got a pen?' Clarus said.

A *pen*?

'I'll get one.' Marilla, heading for the door and the Watch office proper. Yeah, no doubt she'd be glad to take the break, but my bet was she wouldn't admit it, even to herself. She'd guts, the princess, and I was proud of her. She was back in a moment, handing the pen to Clarus.

They made a good pair, these two. Not that I'd go a bomb on this particular area of their shared interests, mind.

Clarus used the flattened end of the stylus to tease the hair away and expose the edges of the wound. 'Quite a narrow channel,' he said. 'But not a sword or an axe because the damage isn't clean enough for a blade. A very thin iron bar, maybe, used from above and behind, right-handed blow. Something like a length of railing. Force must've been con-siderable' – he reversed the pen and gently picked something out of the depths of the wound with the sharp point – 'to have driven skull fragments that deep into the brain. He was hit from behind very, very hard. Unless the wound was caused by some sort of cross-strut on the way down, which isn't likely, he was probably dead before he went into the water.'

'You tell fortunes on the side, pal?' I said.

Clarus grinned and looked up. 'No magic, just observation.

But if you need to be completely sure about that last bit then we'll have to clear it with Libanius first. Right, Dad?'

'Clear what?' I said.

'Corpses don't breathe,' Hyperion said. 'If he was dead already there'll be no water in the lungs.'

I stared at him. 'You mean you want to cut him open?'

'It would certainly confirm matters, one way or the other. If the boy was alive when he entered the water then as Clarus says it could still have been an accident; a freak accident, I grant you, but the possibility is there. However, if he was dead at the time then someone must have killed him first then dumped him. An examination of the lungs would tell us which it was for certain. Otherwise all you've got is a fair assumption.'

Gods! I was remembering a similar conversation with a doctor in Baiae not all that long ago. 'So before they burn the poor devil you'd happily open him up?' I said. 'Jupiter, that is *sick*!'

'There'd be little point in trying afterwards, now would there?' Hyperion smiled. 'And not "happily". Feelings don't enter into it.'

'But—'

He turned to face me. 'Corvinus, this is a corpse,' he said. 'A slab of dead meat of no more significance than a carcass in a butcher's shop. And the boy was a slave and a criminal, if that affects matters.'

'It doesn't.'

'I'm sorry, but in this case, in practical terms, it most certainly does, if we're to get Libanius's approval to take things further.'

'That wasn't what I meant, pal,' I said quietly. I looked at the dead kid's face, and at the string of cheap beads round his neck. A carcass in a butcher's shop, eh? Sweet gods, they were callous bastards, these medical types, and I'd never understand them, not if I lived to be ninety. 'You'd do it here and now?'

'Oh, no, I'd need my equipment and certain other facilities. The easiest thing would be to have the body transported to my surgery. In the meantime perhaps you and Clarus might go over to the Bavius farm and have a look at where it was found.'

'Yeah. Yeah.' Well, I'd grant that knowing for certain the kid had been murdered would be a big step forward. Even so, I still felt sick to my stomach. 'Uh, just to fill in the gaps before we go. You said you knew him?'

'Not to talk to, only by sight and reputation. Scopas can help you more there, and of course you'll be talking to him yourself now.'

'Right. Anything you can give me, though. Just to be going on with.'

'Very well.' Hyperion hesitated. 'He wasn't popular with his fellow slaves.'

'Any particular reason?'

'He . . . well, you can't tell now, of course, but he was a very . . . *pretty* boy. And he used his prettiness.'

Uh-huh: *pretty*, not *good-looking*. 'With the master, you mean?'

'Oh, no, Hostilius was not that way inclined. At least, not to my knowledge.'

'With the mistress, then?'

Pause. 'To a certain degree.' Then, quickly: 'Now don't misunderstand me here, Corvinus, I don't mean sexually, not at all. But Cosmus could project a sort of . . . vulnerable innocence when he wanted to, when he thought it would advance his interests. It was completely artificial, completely false. In fact, his true nature was quite the opposite.'

'That so?'

'The boy was rotten.'

'Ouch. 'Rotten's a strong word, pal,' I said. 'And you sound pretty definite for someone who didn't know him.'

'I'm being direct because it'll save you time, and it's relevant to the situation. Ask Scopas. Ask any of the household. Cosmus was an inveterate liar and thief, covering up his own misdemeanours by blaming them on his fellow slaves. Successfully, too, because as I said he had this air of innocent plausibility. Also' – he glanced at Marilla, who was still standing by the door, watching and listening – 'well, he had . . . liaisons . . . outwith the household. Quite openly. Again you can talk to Scopas on that subject.'

'Liaisons with men?'

'Yes.'

'You have any names?'

Again the hesitation. 'This is gossip, Corvinus, please remember that, but one name that is mentioned is Gaius Maecilius.'

'Lucky Maecilius's son? Bucca?'

'You've heard of him?'

I glanced at Clarus. 'Yeah. Yeah, I have,' I said. Shit; the case was complicating nicely here. 'Okay. Thanks, Hyperion. You've been a great help. You want to talk to Libanius or shall I?'

'Oh, I can do that if you like. There's nothing else I – *we* – can do here at present in any case.'

No. I looked down, again, at the dead, once-pretty face. No, there wasn't. Ah, well.

The Bavius place was less than half a mile outside town in the direction of Bovillae, but we took it easy because Marilla insisted on coming too and Corydon, her mule, wasn't a fast mover.

'Where did you learn all that stuff, Clarus?' I said as we cleared the town gate. 'About dead bodies, I mean?'

'Books.' He shrugged. 'And, like I said, observation. I've

helped my father out since I was eight. A doctor sees a lot of corpses, one way and another. Besides, since I've known Marilla and she first told me about you, examining bodies when I have the chance has become a sort of hobby.'

A hobby! Shit! When I was his age my hobbies had been simple, straightforward things like booze, girls and gambling. I just didn't understand kids these days. I didn't like the thought that I'd been partly responsible for getting him started, either.

'Clarus says doctors should be called in automatically when there's a murder, Corvinus,' Marilla said. 'It's silly that they aren't.'

'You mean they should be allowed to cut up the corpse as a matter of course?'

'Not just that, but why not?' Clarus glanced across at me. 'Like my father said, a body's only dead meat, not a person any more. And an internal examination could answer questions that can't be answered otherwise.'

Jupiter! I felt my gorge rise. 'You seriously believe that? That a corpse is nothing but dead meat?'

'What else? If I was murdered I'd want the murderer found, and if that meant having my body cut open when I was finished with it then fine. Wouldn't you?'

I shook my head. Doctors – however old they were – were a different species, and like I say they were one I didn't understand at all. 'Uh-uh. Not me.'

'Have you heard of Herophilus and Erasistratus?'

'Erasistratus the brain guy?'

'You *have* heard of him?' Clarus grinned. 'I'm impressed.'

'Only because another doctor I talked with recently mentioned the name. He was into vivisection, right? Condemned criminals. Opening them up, seeing what made them tick while they were still alive.' I jerked at my mare's rein. 'I'm sorry, pal, but you can keep that.'

'Agreed, but the principle's sound. And at least there was a point to it, a reason. Between them over fifty-odd years Herophilus and Erasistratus advanced our knowledge of how the body works more than anything or anyone in the three hundred years since. That was because in those days doctors were allowed to investigate a corpse scientifically at first hand. Corvinus, we could learn so *much*! Not just about how someone died, although there is that, but how we might prevent someone from dying. It's all such a bloody waste!'

I glanced at him. Yeah, well: I couldn't exactly sympathise with his opinion, let alone share it, but I could see where he was coming from. It still made the hairs on the back of my neck crawl, though. We finished the rest of the ride in silence.

'That's the Bavius farm up ahead,' Marilla said at last. 'And that' – she pointed further along the road to a set of gates on the left – 'is Hostilius's villa.'

Uh-huh: no more than a couple of hundred yards. If the kid had been hiding out – and my guess was that that's what he'd been doing there – then it couldn't've been more convenient. We rode up the short dirt track to the house and parked the horses by the watering-trough.

The front door was locked and barred, but there was an outhouse to the left.

'There's the well,' Clarus said.

We went over. Like Libanius had said, it was pretty basic: just a hole surrounded by a low wall no more than a foot high in places, with a wooden cover lying to one side and a bucket on a rope tied to a stake.

'Okay,' I said to Clarus. 'You're the expert. All yours.'

Clarus peered down the hole. 'Not much of a drop,' he said. 'And clear all the way down. He couldn't've got that head wound falling down there.'

I took a look for myself. 'Yeah, right,' I said. 'Good place to hide a body, though. The guys who found him must've had a hell of a job getting him out. Let's check the outhouse.'

There wasn't much to see there, either: a pen for a horse or a mule, or maybe a cow, with an empty manger and a pile of old bedding straw, plus a jumble of odds and ends in the corner next to the door. I scuffed through the straw and found a string bag with half a loaf of bread, a small empty wine flask, an onion and two or three dried figs inside. Well, apart from the goodies in his belt-pouch the guy hadn't taken all that much with him.

Clarus had been searching through the pile of junk in the corner. He pulled out a rusty gate-bolt, two feet long and the thickness of my little finger, and examined it carefully.

'Have a look at this, Corvinus,' he said, and held it out by the straight end.

'That what did the job?' I said.

'Yes.'

No *could have been*; a straight *yes*. Still, I was beginning to have a serious regard for his judgment. 'How do you know?' I said.

'Look at the part just short of the bend. Don't touch, just look closely. You see?'

Yeah, I did: there was a sticky crust half a hand's-breadth in length, with some fairish hairs embedded in it. I whistled. 'Well done, pal,' I said. 'I'm impressed.'

'It had to be something like that. So we don't actually need Dad to confirm that it was murder after all. Also, you see the way there's straw scattered between here and the door? Outside, too. And that bit' – he picked up a wadded scrap and held it out – 'has blood on it. He must've dragged the corpse to the well on its back.'

'You stiff the boy yourself?'

He grinned. 'I'm sorry, Corvinus, I'm just showing off. This is the first time I've had a chance to do this for real.'

'Don't apologise. There's nothing wrong with showing off, and for a beginner you're doing pretty well.' *Pretty well?* Shit; the kid just *had* to meet Decimus Lippillus of the Public Pond Watch! Lippillus would be as gobsmacked as I was. 'Uh . . . you said "he". You're sure the murderer was a man, then?'

'Not absolutely sure, no, but that's the likelihood. It would've taken real force to cause that much damage with this.' He held up the gate-bolt. 'She'd have to be a bloody strong woman. Also . . .' He thought for a moment. 'No. I'll show you. Marilla, you want to help?'

The princess had been standing in the doorway, watching and listening. 'What with?' she said.

'Just come over here. Stand in front of me.' She did. Clarus lifted the gate-bolt and brought it down gently until it rested against the top of her head. My balls shrank. 'You see, Corvinus?'

'Uh, Clarus—'

'Cosmus was about Marilla's height, more or less. I'm three or four inches taller. Unless he was holding his head back' – with his other hand, Clarus lifted Marilla's chin while keeping the gate-bolt where it was – 'someone my height or shorter would've caused a wound further down towards the neck. And if he was kneeling' – he pushed Marilla on to her knees – 'then the wound would almost certainly've been further up, on the top of the head itself, not down and to the side.'

Yeah; I saw what he was getting at now. Smart reasoning. Whoever had killed Cosmus must've been tall, certainly too tall for a woman, probably for most men. Tall as me, easy. Strong, too, which meant that they were in the prime of life, or at least kept themselves in decent shape. We were doing pretty well here. 'So,' I said. 'We've got a valid scenario. Cosmus poisons Hostilius on the instructions of AN Other, refills the medicine bottle to defer suspicion, again maybe as instructed, pockets what he can get his hands on – maybe that was his own

idea this time, but whatever – and lights out by prearrangement to his temporary bolthole. AN Other then – again by
prearrangement – meets him here, ostensibly to pay him off
and arrange his passage elsewhere but actually to get rid of a
potential embarrassment. He kills him and throws his body
down the well, where – he assumes – it won't be found for
quite some time, at least until things have a chance to blow
over. That work?'

'He can't have been very clever,' Marilla said. 'Cosmus, I
mean.'

'I don't think he was,' Clarus said. 'Not that I knew him
myself.'

'Well, at least the physical aspects of the murder let Veturina out. That's one thing.'

'Ah . . . no, Corvinus. No, I'm afraid that actually they
don't.'

'What?'

'You've never seen her before, have you? Veturina is . . . uh
. . . quite big.'

'Is she, indeed?' I said.

Bugger.

7

I found out what he meant the next day, when I went round to Hostilius's place and met the lady: Veturina looked like she could tie iron bars in knots, never mind use them to ventilate a kid's head. That said, there was nothing particularly masculine about her, quite the reverse. She might be well on the wrong side of fifty, but she was still no bad looker, even in zero make-up and a mourning mantle. And I'd just bet she was the kind to keep stuffed toys in the bedroom. She put me in mind of a fluffy Amazon.

'I'm sorry, Valerius Corvinus,' she said. 'This is . . . I'm going to find this very difficult. I knew Lucius was dying, he knew it himself, but first the suddenness of his death and now—' She stopped and took a deep breath. 'Forgive me. How can I help you? Where can I start?'

Well-spoken and articulate, but with a strong low-class Bovillan accent; yeah, Marcia had said she was a Bovillan innkeeper's daughter. Interesting, though, that after all the years she and Hostilius had been married – over thirty, hadn't it been? – and she'd been moving in, presumably, higher social circles than she could've been used to she hadn't gone to the bother of upgrading it. Maybe that said something about the woman.

'With the death itself would be logical,' I said. 'Unless you think there's a better point.'

'No.' She wasn't nearly as composed as she sounded, mind; I noticed she was gripping her fingers together, twining them hard, holding her hands close in her lap. They were big hands, but not mannish ones. The nails were bitten to the quick. 'Although I can't tell you very much about that, actually. Oh, I was with him when he died, but only because Scopas fetched me. We . . . Lucius and I lived separate lives for the most part. Not by my doing. You may have heard from Hyperion that he was . . . very difficult latterly.'

'Fetched you from where?'

'Only along the corridor. There're two rooms that I use, a bedroom and a sitting-room looking out through the portico over the garden. I spend most of my time there, just as Lucius spends – spent – most of his in a sitting-room of his own.' She hesitated. 'It's a big house, but I don't . . . didn't want to move too far away from him in case he thought I was . . . in case he suspected me of . . .' She stopped and took a deep breath. 'Forgive me. I'm trying to be frank and helpful, but being so is in itself embarrassing.' I said nothing, just waited. 'That was why I saw Cosmus coming out.'

I straightened. 'What?'

'I'm sorry, I'm not being very coherent. The fact that my day room overlooks the garden explains why I saw Cosmus come out through the portico. There's another door, you see, a little further along the corridor, between my rooms and Lucius's. He must've come through that.'

'Uh . . . what time are we talking about now?' I kept my voice neutral. 'The time when your husband died?'

'Oh, no. Much earlier, about an hour after dawn. I'm a late riser as a rule, unlike Lucius, but that morning for some reason . . . anyway, I was surprised because Cosmus had no business in that part of the house. And I'd just heard Lucius's footsteps in the corridor going towards the latrine. That's the other way, to the—'

I held up my hand. 'Hold on, lady. Let's get this clear. You're telling me that the morning of the day your husband died you saw Cosmus – the dead slave-boy – coming from the direction of your husband's room while your husband was out of it? Right?'

'Yes.'

'Don't you think that maybe you should've mentioned this earlier?'

I'd deliberately kept my voice neutral and unthreatening, but her chin went up.

'No, I don't,' she said. 'Why should I? Until this morning when Quintus Libanius brought you round I'd assumed that Lucius died a natural death, and that was several hours later. Why should I think anything particular of it, let alone think in terms of—' She stopped at the word, frowned and tried again. 'In terms of murder?'

Fair enough. 'Still, given that Cosmus had disappeared—'

'*I did not know that!*'

The sharpness of tone made me blink. I stared at her. 'Uh . . . fine, fine,' I said. 'No problem, lady, it was just a—'

'Why should I? I scarcely saw the boy. Not from one day to the next.'

Upset was one thing, but this was something else. Maybe Hostilius hadn't been the only one with a tile loose. 'So Scopas, your major-domo, didn't tell you?' I said, still keeping my voice carefully neutral. 'Or about the articles missing from your husband's room?'

She took another deep breath, and her hands twisted together in her lap. I could hear the finger-joints crack with the pressure. 'No. No, he didn't,' she said. 'Not at that point, anyway.'

Uh-huh; not like a conscientious major-domo, and I hadn't heard anything to suggest that Scopas was anything but. Quite the contrary. Well, that was something I could check with the guy himself later. 'So when did he?'

'I honestly can't remember. Perhaps it was the day after,

when we were clearing up, putting things in order. You'd have to ask him yourself.' She paused. 'Corvinus, I'm sorry, but my husband has died and I've just been told that he was murdered. The first shock was bad enough. The second . . . well, as you can understand I'm not thinking too clearly at present. You'll have to make allowances.'

Yeah. Right. Still, there was some pretence going on here, that I'd swear to. I was beginning to have my doubts about this lady. 'Even so,' I said, 'it's been – what? – seven days now since your husband died, and up to this morning there was no word of Cosmus being missing. Now, if there was the matter of a theft and as you say you saw the kid under suspicious circumstances leaving—'

' *"As I say"?*' She jerked round to face me. 'Are you accusing me of lying?'

'Uh, no. Not at all. It's just that—'

'Or perhaps of murdering Lucius myself?' She was on her feet now and glaring at me.

Shit. No sign of fluffiness now: what we'd got was pure Amazon – she must be six foot tall in her sandals, easy – and not friendly Amazon, either. 'Hang on, lady,' I said quietly. 'There's no need for this. No one's accusing you of anything.'

'No. But they will, won't they?' The big hands flexed at her sides in spasmodic jerks; if this wasn't hysteria it was the next thing to it. I wondered if I should call the slaves. 'As far as not reporting the fact that Cosmus had gone missing is concerned, I'm sorry, however important it may be it hasn't been up to now. Or not to me. But I'm not a fool, Corvinus, I know the boy wouldn't have murdered Lucius unprompted, he had no cause and he didn't have the wit. And when a man dies from poisoning his wife's the first to be suspected, isn't she, especially when she . . . when there were disagreements between them. So don't pretend that the possibility that I'm a murderess hasn't crossed your mind!'

'Veturina, I never—'

She held up a hand. 'Now I want you to listen to me very carefully, please,' she said. 'I loved and respected my husband for thirty-six years, since the day he took me from my father's wineshop in Bovillae. If he changed towards me – and that was only in the past year or so – then it was because he was ill. It wasn't *him* any longer, not Lucius, and in his right mind he would have despised himself for behaving as he did. I may have hated the way he treated me latterly, indeed I found it unbearably painful, but I did not stop loving him for what he had been for one single minute. Now under these circumstances if you or anyone else think that I could murder him then you're totally wrong.'

Well, if she'd been acting there then Roscius couldn't've managed it better. Not that the little speech didn't open up another intriguing avenue, mind, although in her present mood I wasn't going to bring that up with the lady. Not yet, anyway.

'Okay,' I said. 'Point taken. Then who do you think did?'

She held my eye for a good half minute. Then the anger and stiffness went out of her and she dropped her gaze. 'I'm sorry,' she said quietly. 'That was unfair, completely unfair. None of this is your fault, and you've been very kind. It's just that somehow I feel guilty for Lucius's death. Even although I've no reason to. Does that make sense?'

'Yeah,' I said. 'It makes perfect sense.'

She'd moved across to a pedestal with a marble bust on it crowned with cypress: Hostilius himself, presumably, when he was younger. The face was strong-featured and confident. If the artist hadn't lied, or exaggerated the way they sometimes do, he'd been a very good-looking guy who knew his own mind and took a pride in himself. Veturina rested her fingers on the bust's shoulder, like a caress. Then she turned back to me.

'The answer to your question is no,' she said. 'I can't even suspect. I'm sorry again, but there you are.'

'How about his partner in the firm?' I said.

'*Quintus?*' Her eyes widened. 'Why would Quintus want to kill Lucius?'

Quintus. Not Acceius. Interesting. 'Someone did. They didn't get on too well, I understand, and the situation was getting worse. Also' – I hesitated; we were on dangerous ground again here – 'there was your husband's, uh, personal accusation.'

Veturina coloured. 'You mean that we were committing adultery together.' I said nothing. 'Listen, Corvinus. Quintus and I were – are – friends, close friends and have been for years, ever since he and Hostilius became partners. I have the greatest respect for him, as he has for me, but I swear to you, and you can believe me or not as you please, that we are not and never have been lovers. Is that perfectly clear?'

'Yeah. Yeah, that's clear.'

'Good. I'm glad.' She turned her head away sharply and her voice tightened. 'Many of the things Lucius said to me – and about me, to other people – over the past year I found very, very hurtful. The charge that I was committing adultery with Quintus was among the worst. And, just to complete your education, if you're interested in other salacious details of a similar nature you might also like to know that he accused me, both in private and in public, of sleeping on a regular basis with a selection of our better-looking slaves.' She turned back to face me. Her cheeks were wet. 'If you should care to believe *that* unpleasant little squib then I'm sorry for you. You don't know me, and you didn't know Lucius in the final stages of his illness.'

'Right. Right,' I said. Then, gently: 'Veturina, I'm sorry, but I'm only doing my job, okay? The Castrimoenian senate have asked me to—'

'Then it's a filthy job, that's all I can say.' She wiped her eyes clear with a fold of her mantle. 'Whether it has to be done or not. As far as I'm concerned both you and the Castrimoenian senate can go to hell.'

'Yeah.' There was an awkward silence; then, abruptly, she turned her back on me again and lowered her forehead against the bust's. Well, it was time to leave – past time – and I'd got as much as I could reasonably expect at present. 'Ah . . . I wonder if I could talk to Scopas now?' I said. 'Oh, and maybe your brother, if he's around, and your adoptive daughter?'

She stood motionless for a second or two more. Then she turned round again and wiped her eyes. 'Scopas, of course,' she said, and from her voice you'd've thought we'd spent the last ten minutes discussing the weather. 'Castor's out at present, I think; he lives almost completely separately from Lucius and me in the other wing, so I can't be sure. Scopas will know for certain. Paulina, I'm afraid – there's been no formal adoption, by the way, she's simply our ward – has gone to Rome for a while to stay with Lucius's sister. She found the death very upsetting, and I thought it was for the best.'

Damn. Still, if she was little more than a kid she probably couldn't help much anyway. I really wanted to talk to this Castor, though. 'Fair enough,' I said. 'Thank you for your time, Veturina. And I'm deeply sorry if I—'

'You'll find Scopas in the servants' quarters, just across the courtyard from where you came in. He is expecting you. The door-slave will take you.'

'Yeah. Yeah, right.' I turned to go, and I'd got about halfway to the atrium's exit when she called.

'Valerius Corvinus!'

'Yeah?' I turned back. She was still standing by the plinth, her fingers against Hostilius's marble cheek.

'He was a lovely man,' she said. 'Before. A good, fair-minded man and a kind and faithful husband. We had thirty-five happy years together, and set against these that last horrible year was nothing, nothing at all. I want you to understand that, please, and remember it.'

I nodded, and left.

Hell. I could be wrong, sure, but I doubted it.

8

Scopas was a surprise: a big guy, broad-shouldered, with a boxer's face and close-cropped bristly grey hair, more like a prizefighter than a major-domo. Not that he was young: I'd put him at sixty, at least, which was probably – although I'd never asked – about Lucius Hostilius's age. He was sitting on a bench outside the servants' quarters, whittling a stick.

'Valerius Corvinus, sir?' He laid the stick and the knife to one side and stood up. Slow, broad-vowelled local-Latin voice, with nothing servile about it. This guy knew what he was worth. He was probably bang-on, too.

'Yeah. Sit down, Scopas.' He did, and I sat down on the bench beside him. 'Know why I'm here?'

'Of course. Because the master was murdered, sir. We're grateful.'

I frowned. 'Grateful for what?'

'A lawyer's slave knows a bit of the law. Should've meant the thumbscrews by rights, now, shouldn't it?'

'So long as you give me all the help you can, pal, you won't find me objecting.'

'All the same, like I say, we're grateful. And I'll help you as far as I'm able to, gladly. Lucius Hostilius was a good master in his day. The best.'

'You been his head slave long?'

'Since he and the mistress moved here from Bovillae, sir, fifteen years back.'

'That when Quintus Acceius became a partner?'

'No. He and the master'd been partners six or seven years by then.'

'Any particular reason for the move?'

'Lawyer in Castrimoenium died, Bovillae had a lawyer already. Still does, old Publius Novius.'

'Uh . . . what's this Acceius like, by the way? You see much of him around here?'

Long pause: Scopas gave me a level stare and sucked on a tooth. No fool, this guy.

'He's a good man,' he said at last. 'A good friend to the master, while he was himself, and a good friend to the mistress. A good *friend.*' He stressed the last word. 'And if you've been told anything more, Valerius Corvinus, sir, then you forget it, because it isn't true. That said, yes, he's in and out, on business and to dinner, him and his wife. Or they were, while the master was well.'

'He's married?'

'To Seia Lucinda, sir, lady from one of the biggest families in Bovillae. Father and grandfather were purple-stripers like yourself. Big poultry-breeding business, they had. Still have, the brother runs it now.'

'When was the last time Acceius was here?'

'Oh, that'd be about twelve or thirteen days ago, the day after that bit of trouble in town. You've heard about that?'

'When the guy attacked the pair of them in the street? Yeah; I've heard of that. You know anything about it?'

'No, sir. Nothing no one else doesn't. But it left the master very shaken. He stayed at home the next day and Quintus Acceius brought the business here.'

'What business was that? Do you know?'

'No, sir, I've nothing to do with that side of things; anything like that you'd have to ask the gentleman himself, or Fuscus in town. He's the master's clerk.'

'Not your mistress's brother?'

Was it my imagination, or did Scopas hesitate? If so, it was only for a split second. 'No, sir, Castor's just a messenger, a gopher, no disrespect intended. He wouldn't know either, no more than me. But it wasn't anything out of the usual, as far as I know. Acceius didn't stay long.'

'Does he usually?'

Pause; then, deliberately, eyes on mine: 'No longer than necessary, sir, this last year, anyway. And always with the master present. He was very careful about that, master being as he was.'

Yeah, well, that was me told. The adultery angle was looking less and less likely. 'So tell me about the day Hostilius died,' I said.

Scopas stood up. 'You'll want to see the room itself, sir. The mistress said you would.'

'Sure. If you don't mind.' I got up too.

'It's the other side of the house, overlooking the garden. If you'd like to follow me.'

We went through a narrow arched passageway and round the edge of the main building into a large garden with a portico. The garden had a wall, but I could see a gate at the far end. That must've been where Cosmus was heading for when Veturina had seen him. If she had seen him: I wasn't going to take all that lady had said quite on trust yet. Far from it.

'Just along here, sir.' Scopas led me along the portico and through a door back into the main building. 'Here we are. The master's suite is on your left.'

Where the corridor ended, in other words. Before going in, though, I looked to the right. There were several doors. 'Which are the rooms your mistress uses?' I said.

'Third door along, sir. The rooms're connected inside.'

Hardly more than half a dozen yards; yeah, Veturina had said that she didn't want to be too far away. 'And the latrine?'

'At the far end of the corridor, sir, next to the bath suite.'

Check. I opened the first door on the right after the exit to the portico. A small, anonymous bedroom, obviously unused. 'That other room empty as well, Scopas? The one between here and your mistress's?'

'Just a cupboard, sir. Linen press.'

'Fine.' Well, that was all pretty straightforward. It added up, too. I opened the door to Hostilius's bedroom and went in.

Like Scopas had said, it was a small suite; the same sort of thing, presumably, as Veturina's. The door led into a sitting-room that opened on to the portico outside and overlooked the garden beyond. It was a big room, light and airy, with frescos on the walls and a good mosaic on the floor, a couch and a table next to it, and a bookcase with most of the cubbies filled. There was a writing desk and a stool, too, and an alcove with a vase of fresh flowers.

'The master spent a lot of time in here, sir,' Scopas said. 'He preferred it to his study and to the atrium, specially in the summer.'

'This where he died?'

'That's right. On the couch here. He was taken bad while he was reading. Luckily – or it might've been luckily, if it'd done any good – Sestus the gardener was just outside, and he ran for me. I sent someone straight off for Doctor Hyperion.'

'When was this exactly?'

'Late morning, sir, an hour or so before noon.'

'Uh-huh. And you fetched the Lady Veturina at the same time, did you?'

Scopas hesitated. 'No. Only when I reckoned things was as bad as they could get. The master . . . well, you know the situation, Valerius Corvinus. They hardly met, hardly spoke at all, and he wouldn't have her in here at any price.'

'She was in her own room along the corridor?'

'That's right. Sitting-room like this one, with a bedroom beyond. It's where she spends most of the day.'

'So where was the medicine bottle kept?'

'On a tray in the bedroom. If you'd like to see, sir?'

We went through. It was almost the size of the sitting-room and just as well decorated: obviously the master bedroom of the villa, the one Hostilius and Veturina must've shared for most of their married life. There was a big double bed with a richly embroidered coverlet on it, several clothes chests, a shoe-rack and – next to the bed – a polished black marble table with a tray on it. On the tray were a stoppered silver wine flask and a matching cup.

'I put them back where they'd been, sir, on the mistress's orders,' Scopas said. 'The medicine bottle was there as well, of course, but—' He stopped.

'But Hyperion took that away with him. Yeah, that's okay, pal, understood,' I said. 'Fine. So how did it work?'

'The master had his routine, sir. Up about an hour after dawn, took a trip along to the latrine.' He glanced at me. 'Didn't hold with chamber pots, the master, always said that a bedroom was no place for . . . well, you understand. And he liked to sit and think in peace for a while before breakfast.'

'He had breakfast in here?'

'In the sitting-room. I brought it on a tray first thing when he woke and left it on the table for when he got back. And the . . . and the medicine, ready-mixed in the cup.'

'So the length of time between when you left the tray and the medicine ready and your master coming back would be what?'

'About fifteen minutes, give or take.'

Yeah, right. Plenty of time, in other words, for someone – Cosmus – to nip into the empty room, do the business with the bottle, and nip out again. And if he'd been hiding in the spare bedroom a few yards along the corridor, like Veturina he'd've heard the footsteps coming and going and known the coast was clear. Easy-peasy. 'The routine didn't change?' I said.

'No, sir.'

'And Cosmus would've known what it was?'

Scopas's face hardened. 'No reason why the—' He stopped, and I heard his teeth click as he pressed them together hard. 'No reason why he shouldn't've. It wasn't a secret.'

'Tell me about Cosmus. Had Hostilius had him long?'

'About a year. The master bought him from Tuscius over in Bovillae.'

'Tuscius?'

'Marcus Tuscius, the slave-dealer.'

'Where did he get him from?'

' 'Fraid I can't tell you that, sir. Cosmus' – Scopas looked like he wanted to spit when he said the name – 'never mentioned where he'd been before, and no one felt inclined to ask. He wasn't exactly popular with the other lads and lasses.'

'Yeah,' I said. 'Yeah, so I gathered. What about with the family?'

'He was a smarmy little bugger, sir, if you'll forgive the language, in with every chance he could get. He'd a way with him, Cosmus, I'll give him that, good-looking and well-spoken, and it was no secret he was angling for an above-stairs job. The master didn't like him for' – he hesitated – 'reasons that we won't go into but maybe you can imagine, having talked to the mistress, but he could get round the two youngsters easy enough. Especially Miss Paulina.'

Uh-huh. And I could guess what Hostilius's 'reasons' had been: *sleeping with the better-looking slaves*, didn't Veturina say? The fact that according to Hyperion Cosmus's natural proclivities lay in other directions was neither here nor there: it would've been business, not pleasure. 'Where did he work, usually?' I said.

'In the kitchen. He was one of the kitchen skivvies. He wasn't there more than he could help, though. Every chance he got he bunked off down to the stables where he could be on his own. Not that anyone cried on that account.'

'You, uh, reported him missing to the Lady Veturina the day your master died, didn't you?'

'Yes, sir, that's right. Before the master died, actually, because he should've been on duty to wash up the breakfast dishes and scour the pans. I didn't know nothing about the ring or so on then, mind, because the master kept them in the drawer of his desk and I didn't notice they were gone until the next day.'

Well, that settled that; not that I was surprised. Still: 'Uh, one last thing, Scopas. Castor. The mistress's brother.'

I couldn't've been mistaken this time. When I mentioned the name I could almost feel the guy tense. Interesting. 'Yes, sir?'

'He around at present?'

'No. No, I . . . don't think so.'

'Know when he'll be back?'

'That I couldn't say.'

Straight into the one-liners, and to anyone who's had anything to do with slaves that can only mean one thing.

'Look, pal,' I said wearily. 'You've been really, really helpful so far. Don't start giving me the run-around now, okay? Just tell me what you're carefully not saying and we'll call it a day. Bargain?'

He swallowed. 'Sir, I'd really rather not—'

Screw that. 'Listen, Scopas,' I said. 'I don't like to remind you of this, but if it wasn't for me you'd be answering any question anyone liked to put to you tied hand and foot to a couple of sliding boards. Answering it pretty damn quickly, too, because there'd be a set of sadistic bastards in attendance just waiting for the teensiest hesitation. So come on, let's have it.'

He rubbed the back of his neck nervously. 'All right, sir, but I'm sure there's a—'

'Scopas! Just give!'

Pause. 'The mistress's brother hasn't been home for eight days.'

Shit. I just stared at him. 'Since the day before your master died, in other words,' I said.

'Yes, sir.' He didn't look happy, and unhappy was an understatement.

'Any idea where he's gone?'

'No. No one does.'

'Know why he went?' He stared back. '*Scopas!*'

'He'd had a . . . quarrel with the master that afternoon, sir. At the office in town. I swear I don't know what it was about' – he must've seen my face, because that came out quickly – 'not the quarrel itself. But the master was furious and he . . . well, when he came back he took it out on the mistress. They've always been close, her and her brother.'

'Go on,' I said. 'Scopas, pal, you listened in. That's what slaves do.' I waited. Nothing. 'You want me to go back and ask the mistress herself?' No answer. I shrugged and moved towards the door. 'Fair enough, we'll just have to play it—'

'He accused Castor of being a spy, a traitor and a thief,' Scopas said woodenly. 'He accused him of adultery with Quintus Acceius's wife, he accused the mistress of aiding and abetting him, and he said that he wanted him out of the house for good. I'm omitting the filthy circumstantial details, Valerius Corvinus, because do what you like to me I won't put my mouth to them, and in his right mind the master wouldn't've either. Now does that satisfy you, sir?'

Gods. 'Yeah,' I said quietly. 'That satisfies me.'

'Then if you'll excuse me I'll get back to my duties. I'm sure you can find your own way out.'

'Right. Right. Uh, thanks, pal.'

He didn't answer, just walked past me and through the open door to the corridor beyond.

9

'She killed him.'

'Oh, *Marcus*!' Perilla put down her book on the small table beside her chair. 'You can't possibly be sure of that at this stage. Especially after what Marcia said.'

'I'm sure.' I took a morose swig of the wine Bathyllus had brought out when I'd got back as per standing instructions – Fundanan, not Caecuban, but none the worse for that – and stared out over the rolling Alban Hills towards Alba itself, smokily cloud-wreathed in the distance.

Bugger!

'But to murder someone after having lived with them for thirty years—'

'Thirty-six. And I didn't say that Veturina had murdered Hostilius. I said that she'd killed him.'

Perilla frowned. 'I don't understand, dear. They're the same, surely.'

'Uh-uh, not this time. That's the problem.' Still, thank the gods, the problem wasn't mine, and Libanius wasn't the sort to insist on the letter of the law. No doubt Marcia could weigh in as well where the praetor's rep was concerned, if things came to that.

'Marcus, you are not making sense. And Aunt Marcia gave the woman a glowing testimonial. Veturina was a good, loyal, faithful wife who loved her husband all their married life. To say categorically after only two days' acquaintance with the situation that she killed him or could even be remotely capable of killing him is—'

'That's the whole point. She was all of those things, and of course she loved him. That's why she did it.'

Perilla went very quiet. Then she said, 'Explain.'

'She practically told me herself. He wasn't the man she'd married any more. Lived with.' I took another swallow of wine. It didn't help. 'She'd watched him turning into someone he'd've hated. Hated and despised. If it was me, Perilla, if I went the way Hostilius went and didn't have the sense to recognise what I was becoming and manage to slit my own wrists before it got that far I hope you'd do the same. And if you did I'd bless you for it.'

Perilla said nothing.

'The poor sod was dying anyway. It was only a matter of when, and how, and whether he'd go with what dignity and self-respect he had left.' I lifted the wine cup, then set it down again without drinking. 'Me, I'd be grateful that someone had had the guts to make the decision for me.'

'What about the slave-boy?' Perilla said quietly. 'Cosmus.'

I frowned. 'Yeah, that's the only bit I can't get my head around. He wasn't necessary. And like I say Veturina's no murderer. Not in that sense.'

'Wasn't he? Necessary I mean?'

'No. Her room was only a few yards from her husband's, and she knew he wasn't in it at the time the business was done. She could even have got in round the front, through the portico. Why introduce a needless complication, especially since she'd know she'd have to get rid of the boy later?'

'Insurance? In case things went wrong, as they did. She'd have someone to blame.'

'The game wasn't worth the candle, Perilla. Not to someone like Veturina. After all, what were the chances of being found out? The death looked natural. The medicine bottle was in the other room, and to all intents and purposes it hadn't been tampered with. It was a pure fluke that Hyperion tested the contents, and he said himself they were no proof someone had actually consciously murdered the guy. The only conclusive proof of foul play was Cosmus's corpse. In effect, by using Cosmus as an accomplice the lady upped the odds on someone blowing the whistle and left herself a real murderer into the bargain.' I paused. 'And then if she didn't stiff the kid personally, which I grant she could've done, physically, she'd've needed an Accomplice Part Two. Shit. It doesn't work, does it?'

'No,' Perilla said quietly. 'No, I don't think it does. Not as things stand, anyway.'

'So where does that leave us?'

'Who else is there?'

I shrugged. 'With motive? The partner, for one. Quintus Acceius. He seems an okay guy, from what Scopas the major-domo said, but he'd have reason enough. Hostilius was a major embarrassment to him, professionally and socially, and the situation wasn't going to improve any. There needn't actually have been any outright hatred involved, either, quite the reverse. Veturina told me herself, and Scopas backed her up, that he'd been a close friend of the family for years. Hostilius's condition would've been as painful to him, personally, as to Veturina. There're different kinds of love. I can see this Acceius killing his partner for the same reasons that Veturina would've had, more or less: because he couldn't stand by and see a friend and colleague destroy himself.'

'There's still Cosmus.'

'Yeah. But at least he'd be necessary this time. If Acceius didn't want Veturina to know – and he wouldn't, for obvious reasons – then he'd need someone inside the house to do the job for him; also, if things went wrong, to avoid any chance of Veturina being blamed herself. As far as murdering the kid afterwards goes, well, we don't know the circumstances; the original intention might've been to smuggle him off somewhere alive. In any case, it may sound callous, but he was just a slave, and not a very nice person, at that.'

'It does sound callous.'

I sighed. 'Perilla, I'm not excusing the guy. I've never even met him. And it's only a theory. Besides, Acceius isn't the only fish in the pond. There's the brother, Castor. He hasn't been seen since he quarrelled with Hostilius the day before he died. Then there're the two Maecilii, Fimus and Bucca, for different reasons. Why either of them should've wanted Hostilius dead bad enough to actually kill him or have him killed I've no idea yet, but Fimus is on record as having had a spat with him recently and Bucca's a dubious character with links to Cosmus. Plus there's the business of that attack in the street.'

'The attacker died, didn't he?'

'Yeah, I know, but . . .' I frowned. 'Oh, hell, look, lady, all I'm saying is at present there're plenty of questions around with no answers. Let's not get bogged down in useless theorising, okay?'

Perilla smiled and ducked her head. 'Very well,' she said.

'Where's the princess, by the way?'

'Out with Placida. And Clarus, of course. They said they'd be back for lunch.'

'Fine.' We'd still got Placida, the hound from hell. Her erstwhile owner, Sestia Calvina, had decided she couldn't possibly deprive us of the brute's company and wouldn't take no for an answer, so she'd kept the puppies when they came and let us have the original. Placida had joined the Marilla Menagerie shortly afterwards, after she'd blotted her copybook irrevocably by nailing next door's cat and presenting it to its hysterical owner, who'd watched the whole gory business from the safety of her portico. Relations with the Petillius household were consequently at an all-time low and likely to stay that way until hell froze.

'That is,' Perilla said, 'if there is any lunch.'

'How do you mean?'

'We seem to be short one chef. Meton's disappeared.'

I sat up. '*What?*'

'I went along to the kitchen about an hour ago to talk to him about the dinner menu. The skivvy said he'd gone off after breakfast and hadn't been seen since.'

'Gone off where?'

'He didn't say. Meton didn't, I mean. The skivvy assumed he'd gone into town for the shopping, but he's usually back long before this.'

Yeah: Castrimoenium isn't Rome, and although Meton always liked to do his own shopping even he could get round all the places on offer in an hour. Besides, I didn't trust that bugger. This needed investigating.

'*Bathyllus!*' I yelled.

He shimmered out through the portico. 'Yes, sir.'

'You know where Meton is?'

'No, sir.' A sniff. Hell; at this particular point in the see-sawing relationship between our ultraconventional major-domo and our anarchistic chef we'd obviously hit a trough. What had caused it this time I didn't know – the last occasion had been a five-day-old fish nailed to the underside of a stool in the little guy's pantry as a jolly Winter Festival jape – but the result was that yet again they were Seriously Not Speaking. 'Not in the kitchen, as far as I'm aware, but that is all the help I can give you.'

Shit. 'So what happens about lunch?'

'No doubt the kitchen staff will rise to the occasion, sir. There is the remains of the pork from yesterday, and I'm sure the boy can heat up the leftover bean stew without burning it too badly.'

Oh, great. 'Listen, sunshine,' I said. 'When that bastard does deign to reappear you tell him I want to see him forthwith. Okay? First hand, no delegating, no little notes left on the kitchen table, all right?'

Another sniff. 'If you insist, sir.'

'I do.' Bloody hell! He'd probably use sign language. Still, that was his problem, and with Meton you didn't take chances. Give him an inch and he'd take the whole fucking Nilometer, then flog it to a pal in the trade down the Subura. I hadn't forgotten that sheep, either.

'Ah, here they are now,' Perilla said.

'Who's th—'

Which was as far as I got before I was hit in the chest by a ballistic Gallic boarhound.

'Oh, hello, Corvinus, you're back,' Marilla said, appearing round the corner with Clarus in tow. 'Down, Placida. Behave yourself.'

I fended off the brute while Clarus ran over and heaved back on her collar. Bathyllus had shot off like he was greased: Bathyllus and dogs don't mix, except on the most basic level. Where Placida's concerned I use the term 'dog' loosely, mind.

'Did you have a nice walk?' Perilla asked.

'Just the one bit of trouble with a pile of horse dung,' Clarus said. 'We're teaching her not to eat it.'

'Successfully?'

'Not quite. But we're almost there. She stopped halfway through.'

Placida got in a substantial lick across my mouth and nose before he manhandled her to the ground. I gagged and reached for a napkin. There wasn't one.

'How did your talk with Veturina go, Corvinus?' Marilla asked.

'Tie that foul brute to the railings and I'll tell you,' I said, wiping my face on my tunic sleeve.

She did, and I did.

'So you don't think she was responsible after all?' Marilla said when I'd finished.

'Let's say there's a strong possibility that she wasn't. As things go, anyway.'

'So who was?' Clarus said.

I gave him the suspect list that I'd just run past Perilla. Such as it was. 'You help me with any of these?' I said.

'Not much. Acceius has a good name locally. He's honest, he's well liked, and he's respectable. Also, he's a top-notch lawyer. The general opinion, far as I've heard, is that Castrimoenium's lucky to have him. He could've done a lot better for himself in Rome or somewhere else big like Naples or Capua.'

'That so, now?' I said. 'General opinion say why he hasn't?'

'No. But it doesn't suggest any reason why he couldn't've done, if that's what you're asking.'

I grinned. 'Well done, pal. Yeah, that was about it. What about his relations with Hostilius? Or lack of them?'

'Positive again. He's had a lot of sympathy locally, mostly for not dissolving the partnership, going it alone and landing the guy a sock on the jaw for good measure long ago.'

'Maybe he couldn't, for some reason. Financial or otherwise.'

'Pass.'

Well, that was fair enough. Clarus might be sharp, but he wasn't omniscient. 'What about his wife?' What was her name again? 'Uh . . . Seia Lucinda? Hostilius claimed she was having an affair with Castor, or so Scopas told me. Anything in that?'

'Pass. Look, Corvinus, Castrimoenium may be a small place but we don't live completely in one another's pockets. And me, I don't have either the time or inclination to listen to gossip. Ask your pal Gabba. He might be able to help more.'

Yeah, good idea; I probably would, at that, if I could find some way of keeping prim-and-proper Pontius from blowing the whistle and calling time. 'Okay. Leave Acceius. Castor.'

'Sorry again. At least, I've seen him, but—'

'I know Castor,' Marilla said. She was over by the railings, keeping Placida quiet and relatively civilised.

'*What?*' Clarus whipped round.

'Only slightly. We've talked in the street, once or twice. He likes animals. He's tall with brown eyes and brown curly hair, and he's very good-looking.'

'*Really?*'

'Clarus, he's ancient! Thirty-five, at least.'

I grinned. 'Actually, if you remember, we'd got the guy's physical description already from Hyperion, Princess,' I said. 'In essence, at any rate, barring the fine details you seem to have noticed. Anything you can add to it? If you can stop drooling long enough, that is.'

Clarus snorted.

'Marcus!' Perilla said.

'He's very serious,' Marilla said. 'When you speak to him, I mean. He actually *talks*. And he wants to be a lawyer himself.'

'Does he, indeed?' I said. 'Anything else about him?'

'He's very grateful to his sister. And to Quintus Acceius.'

'What for?'

'I don't know. I just got that impression from how he talked about them. When he did.'

'How about to Lucius Hostilius?'

'No, he didn't like him at all. And it was mutual.'

Well, that was understandable, given what I knew so far. 'You, uh, seem to've had quite a cosy chat with this guy, Princess,' I said. Beside me Clarus was grinding his teeth.

She coloured. 'Not all at once,' she said. 'We've bumped into each other maybe four or five times since last summer. And as I said, he talks.'

'Talks too bloody much, if you ask me,' Clarus muttered.

Fortunately he hadn't seemed to notice that *once or twice* had become *four or five times*; but Perilla had already put the kibosh on stirring things so I let that one pass unremarked. 'Anything else to throw into the pot while we're about it?' I said.

'No, I think that's—'

'You wanted to see me, Corvinus?'

I turned. Meton. 'Yeah, pal. Excuse us, Clarus, small domestic matter. Where the hell've you been?'

Meton sniffed. Meton's sniff is not like Bathyllus's: it's to the little bald-head's what Placida is to a pedigree toy poodle. He removed the result with a hairy finger and wiped it on his tunic.

'Shopping,' he said.

'Come on, Meton! You could've walked to Bovillae and back in the time you've been away. What about the lunch?'

' 'S in hand,' he grunted. 'I'm doing you a ragout of leftover pork an' a red cabbage an' walnut salad.'

'Okay.' Well, that sounded more like it, anyway. 'So what took you so long?'

'Checking out a new source of hares, wasn't I? Little farm out past the Caba Gate.'

Uh-huh. Yeah, I'd go for that: Meton's dedication to sussing out the best suppliers of meat, game, fish, vegetables or anything edible was absolute, and his exacting standards of quality control had put the wind up the wollocks of every market stall owner back home from Ostia to the fifth milestone. 'And?' I said.

'They're rubbish. Hutch-reared tat. And you know what they feed the buggers on? Bran. *Bran!*' He spat into the ornamental rosebush. 'I ask you!'

'Right. Right. Well, in that case I'm sorry I—'

'You know what a diet of bran does to the taste of a hare, Corvinus? I wouldn't boil the bugger up for fucking *soup*, let alone—'

'Yes, right, well, I think we've got the message. That's—'

'—stew it. And as for roasting, you can just fucking sod *that* for a game of soldiers completely, because—'

'*Meton!*' Perilla snapped. 'That is *enough!*'

He subsided, with another sniff. 'So. Lunch in half an hour, okay?'

'Okay,' I said.

He lumbered off.

'Small domestic matter?' Clarus said. Marilla grinned.

'Yeah. Yeah. Give or take.' I glanced at Perilla; the lady was simmering. 'You staying for lunch?'

'If you don't mind. Oh, and by the way, Dad says to tell you he's looked, just to make certain that Cosmus was dead before he went into the well, and there was no water in the lungs.'

'Oh, great.'

I'd really, *really* wanted to know that. Ah, well: at least he'd told me before we sat down to the pork ragout.

Doctors!

IO

I'd earmarked next morning for a talk with Partner Acceius: not before time, because despite Veturina's encomium squeaky-clean reputation or not as far as motive went he had to be up there with the prime suspects. Clarus had given me both of his addresses, the office and the house, though practically speaking there wasn't much difference: he might not actually live over the shop, but his house was just around the corner.

Office first, as being more likely. Also, Scopas had mentioned a clerk – what was his name? Fuscus – who might be able to fill in a few of the obvious blanks.

The office was on the main street leading off the town square, a smart-looking property with a plastered front, a marble-pillared porch and a smart-looking (but not plastered) young door-slave sitting on the steps outside. He stood up as I came over.

'Good morning, sir.'

'Morning.' I went up the steps and he opened the door for me. 'Quintus Acceius in?'

'I'm afraid not. His clerk's here, though. He'll look after you.'

'Fine. Thanks, pal.' I went inside. Impressive: the entrance lobby had a good abstract mosaic on the floor, pastel-blue walls with a bowl of fruit fresco and an alcove with a bronze Mercury. Tasteful without being showy; and if the quality of the decor went for anything the firm wasn't doing too badly.

The lobby opened on to a smallish room with a desk to one side and two doors leading off it. The decor wasn't cheap here, either, and just as tasteful: a painted and gilded plasterwork dado that ran all the way round the red-panelled walls, a big fresco of the Graces, all carefully draped, that could've been Greek work, and two or three very nice bronze candelabra.

The guy at the desk stood up. Like Scopas, he was in his sixties, but that's where the resemblance ended: five five max, thin as a rake and with a bright, quick eye like a bird's. He wore a neat beige tunic – tasteful again – and a freedman's cap.

'I'm—' I began.

'Yes, sir, I know. Valerius Corvinus. You're looking into the death of Lucius Hostilius.' Brisk and businesslike, but suitably grave. Yeah; we were dealing class here. 'I'm Fuscus, the practice's clerk. Quintus Acceius said you might drop in, and he told me to give you every assistance.'

'He's not in himself this morning?'

'No, he had to go up to Rome yesterday and he won't've got back until the early hours. But he did say if you weren't too prompt he'd be delighted to talk to you at his home. That's only a step or two away, just round the corner.'

'Yeah. Yeah, I know. Great, I might do that.'

'Fine. Do have a seat.' He indicated the chair my side of the desk: polished oak, with red leather upholstery. I sat, and so did he. 'Now. Please ask away, I'm at your service.'

'This, uh, attack on Lucius Hostilius fourteen days ago. Can you tell me anything about that?'

'Not personally, sir, as far as the attack itself went, but it happened just up the street and Sextus would be able to give you the full details.'

'Sextus?'

'The door-slave, sir. He saw the whole thing, although he wasn't quick enough to help. A very strange business altogether. The two gentlemen were quite shaken when they came in, understandably so.'

'Did they know the man at all?'

'No, sir. No one did, he was a complete stranger to the town, a vagrant. Deranged, obviously.'

'Obviously.' Well, I could check up on the finer points with the slave on the way out. It might not have anything directly to do with Hostilius's death, but I'd bet a gold piece to a sock in the jaw that there was more to that attempted knifing than met the eye. 'Okay; let's talk about Hostilius's brother-in-law instead. Castor. He works here, doesn't he?'

Fuscus hesitated. 'He . . . used to, yes, certainly. To tell the truth, at present I'm not sure myself of his position vis-à-vis the firm.'

'You mean after his spat with Hostilius the day before he died?'

Fuscus looked relieved. 'Oh, you know about that already? I'm glad. As I said, Quintus Acceius instructed me to give you every help possible, but Castor's not a bad young man by any means and I'd hate to prejudice you unduly against him. Especially since' – he hesitated again – 'appearances might be deceptive. Lucius Hostilius being the way he was, if you understand me.'

'Yeah. Yeah, I know all about that side of things, too,' I said. 'So tell me about the spat.'

'Castor came in just after lunch, sir. I was alone in the office: Quintus Acceius was out seeing a client and Lucius Hostilius had gone home mid-morning saying he wouldn't be back again that day. Castor said he'd just come from there and that Hostilius had forgotten to ask me to take a conveyancing deed round to Publius Decius; he has a potter's business, on the other side of the main square, and we were negotiating the sale to him of an adjacent property.'

I nodded. Jupiter, you could tell that the guy was used to legal work: every 'i' dotted and every 't' crossed.

'Normally Castor would have run the errand himself – that was his job, he was the firm's messenger – but the deed needed a little explanation which he couldn't give and I could. There was no problem: Decius's was only five minutes away and the explanation wouldn't take all that much longer, so I'd only be absent for half an hour, if that. I left Castor minding the office in case a client arrived unexpectedly and went off.

'As it happened Decius was out, so I came straight back. Lucius Hostilius was here, with Castor. I'd missed the . . . whatever the scene was about, but Hostilius was clearly very angry. He accused Castor of being an ingrate, a spy, a traitor and a thief, and virtually threw him out of the office.' He paused. 'There you are, sir. That's about all I can tell you. I haven't seen the young man since.'

'Did Castor say anything on his side?'

'No. He's quite a serious young man, for all his good looks, and he doesn't have much to say for himself at the best of times. When I came in he was just standing there while Hostilius shouted at him; very pale, with a sort of . . . tight expression on his face, if you understand me.'

'Hostilius give any explanation? After Castor was gone?'

'No, he didn't say a word. Just went into his office and slammed the door. He left a few minutes later, without a word again.' Fuscus hesitated. 'He was a . . . very difficult man, sir. Latterly. And as I say I wouldn't be in too much of a hurry, myself, to put all the blame for whatever had occurred on young Castor. If, indeed, anything *had* occurred, which wasn't necessarily so.'

Yeah; right. And there were bits there that needed serious thinking about, what was more. Not a clear-cut situation, by any means. 'Thanks, pal. Very lucid. The two, uh, didn't get on at the best of times, did they?'

'No, although . . .' Fuscus frowned. 'Valerius Corvinus, I must make something very clear, although you're probably well aware of it already. The Lucius Hostilius of the past twelve or eighteen months was a completely different man to what he'd been before. Increasingly so. If you'd asked me that question two years ago, when his brother-in-law joined the firm, my answer would have been quite different. The impetus may have come from Hostilius's wife – I believe that it did – but Hostilius certainly approved. Castor had no experience of legal work whatsoever – he was working with his father and elder brother in the family wineshop – but he was keen, intelligent and conscientious, desperate to do well. Professionally ambitious, too: he wanted to be a lawyer himself one day, or at least a lawyer's clerk, like myself.'

Yeah: Marilla had told me that, it was one of the things that the guy had mentioned in their streetside tête-à-têtes. 'So why didn't he get some in-house training?' I said. 'After all, he was a relative, and if like you say he had things going for him—'

'I'm afraid that was Lucius Hostilius's doing, sir. After he . . . fell ill he took a dislike to the young man, wouldn't have him as an apprentice at any price, to any degree. Quintus Acceius did what he could, tried to persuade him otherwise, but to have insisted or gone behind his partner's back would only have led to serious trouble, perhaps ending with Castor being dismissed altogether and packed off to Bovillae again. He was forced to leave the situation as it stood.'

Uh-huh. Well, that made sense; in effect, that was what had happened, finally. Or would've done, if Hostilius had lived. Interesting. 'Okay,' I said. 'Let's move on. I understand that Hostilius had another spat recently. With one of the Maecilius brothers.'

'Yes.' Fuscus nodded. 'Yes, that's correct, the elder of the two, Gaius. He—'

'Hold on, pal,' I said. 'That's Bucca, right?'

'Indeed it is.'

'I was told the quarrel was with the younger brother. Fimus. About ten days ago, in the square.'

Fuscus frowned. 'I'm sorry, Valerius Corvinus, I know nothing about any quarrel with Fimus; in fact, I'd be very surprised if you haven't made a mistake over the name, or that your informant has. After all, they are brothers.'

'Uh-uh. No mistake, pal.' There wasn't, I was absolutely sure of that. Bucca's name hadn't come up in the conversation at Pontius's at all.

'Then it's odd. Marcus Maecilius – Fimus – is the firm's client, and as far as I'm aware he has no complaints whatsoever about how his brief is being handled.'

'That's the disputed will business, right? Which of his sons gets old Lucky Maecilius's land?'

'Correct. We are defending the status quo, under which Marcus – Fimus – gets the property and a quarter of the monetary estate while his brother has the balance.'

'Who's on the other side, by the way? Just out of interest?'

'Bucca's lawyer? Publius Novius, in Bovillae.' Was it my imagination, or had there been just a touch of asperity in Fuscus's tone? 'The case is scheduled for next month.'

'Okay. So tell me about this quarrel between Hostilius and Bucca.'

'It wasn't only with Hostilius, sir, but I've nothing much to tell, actually. It happened the day before the knife attack. Bucca came into the office in the course of the morning and demanded to see both partners. Fortunately both Hostilius and Acceius were in and free. They took Bucca into Acceius's room – that's that one there' – Fuscus nodded towards the door on the right – 'and held the interview. It didn't last long, no more than ten minutes, all told, after which Bucca came out and left straight away. He was . . . not happy.'

'Uh-huh. You didn't bat an eyelid when I used the word

"spat", pal. So I assume this interview must've been pretty stormy?'

'Yes, sir. As you can see, the doors to both rooms are very solid. I would not, of course, ever think of listening in on one of the gentlemen's private conversations with a client, but normally it would be impossible in any case. In this instance I could hear the voices quite distinctly.'

'Uh . . . distinctly enough to make out what they were saying?'

Pause. 'Yes, sir. In part, at least, whether I wished to or not.'

'And?'

'I'm sorry, sir. You'll have to forgive me, but I really cannot take the responsibility for answering that question, not without consulting Quintus Acceius first. It's a matter of confidentiality, you understand. Acceius was present himself, as I say, and if you ask him I'm sure he'll tell you.'

Yeah, well; that was fair enough, and the guy was quite right. 'No problem, pal,' I said. I stood up. 'Thanks for your help. That's about it for the present, unless you've anything else you think is relevant.'

'No, sir. Or if it is then it's nothing I'm aware of.' He stood himself. 'Good luck with your investigations, Valerius Corvinus, and please feel free to return at any time. I'm sure, again, that you've heard this before, but Lucius Hostilius was an excellent man for most of his life, and a fine lawyer of great probity.'

I left.

Outside, the door-slave had gone back to sitting on the step kicking his heels. He was a young kid, no more than twelve or thirteen.

'Ah . . . Sextus?' I said.

He stood up. 'Yes, sir.'

'Fuscus said you might be able to tell me something about the knife attack on your master ten or so days back.'

'Yes indeed, sir.' He pointed up the street, towards the town square. 'Lucius Hostilius and Quintus Acceius were crossing the road just about the water trough. Coming in this direction.'

About a hundred yards away, in other words. 'Uh-huh. What happened then?'

'The man was behind them, following and getting closer. He shouted something – nothing important, just something like "Wait!" – and when they turned he drew a knife from his belt and went straight for Lucius Hostilius. Then . . . well, there was a struggle, I couldn't see exactly what was happening, but I started running over. Not just me, there were quite a few people. By the time I got there he was lying on the ground with his side all blood, stone dead, sir. I helped Acceius get Hostilius over here and he sat down on the steps a bit, just where I'm standing now, until he felt more up to things. They were both pretty shook, sir. Acceius as well.' He paused. 'That's about all there was to it, really.'

'The man didn't say anything when he attacked Hostilius? Besides shouting "Wait!"?'

The kid's brow furrowed. 'Actually, he could've done, sir, now you mention it. I saw his lips move, but I was too far away to hear anything. So was everyone else, except for the gentlemen themselves.'

Yeah. Yeah, right. Bugger! Well, whatever Acceius said, when I talked to him, I'd have to take his word for it. Or not, as the case might be. Still, we'd cross that bridge when we came to it.

'How about Hostilius himself? He say anything while you and Acceius were helping him over here, or when he was sitting on the steps?'

'No, sir. Not a word. I think he was too shocked, like. Fact is, I thought he'd peg out there and then, he was a terrible colour. Wouldn't have us fetch Doctor Hyperion, though, when we did get him inside, not at any price. Said he was fine, just wanted to be left alone. He went and sat in his room for a while, then got the litter-slaves to take him home.'

'What was Quintus Acceius doing while all this was happening?'

Sextus shrugged. 'Nothing in particular, sir. Nothing he could do, with Hostilius in the mood he was. Once he'd made sure he was all right he went home himself.'

'What happened to the corpse? You know?'

'They took it to Trophius the undertaker's. That's Trophius's over there.' The kid pointed again, this time the other way.

I reached into my belt-pouch and brought out a silver piece. 'Thanks, Sextus. You've been a great help.'

'You're very welcome, sir.'

I set off towards the corner of the block. Time to have a long-awaited word with Acceius.

The door-slave left me to admire the decor in the lobby while he checked that the master was receiving. If that was anything to go by, Acceius's private residence showed the same combination of expensive and tasteful as his office: top-of-the-range mosaic, artwork and statuary. Not short of a gold piece or two, then, Hostilius's partner.

'This way, sir.' The door-slave was back. 'If you'd like to come through.'

We went into the atrium. More marble and more bronzes including an absolute beaut of a satyr playing the double-flute. Oh, and one stunner of a lady sitting in a chair by the ornamental pool.

'Valerius Corvinus,' she said. 'I'm sorry, Quintus is just up and being shaved; he was in Rome on business yesterday and didn't get back until just before dawn. He does know you're here, though, and he sends his apologies and says he'll be as quick as possible. I'm Seia Lucinda. His wife.' She smiled. 'But you'd probably assumed that already.'

'Yeah.' I grinned back. 'I had, as a matter of fact. I'm pleased to meet you, Seia Lucinda. And any apologies due are mine. Your husband's clerk said he'd rather I wasn't too prompt.'

'No, your timing's perfect. *Almost* perfect; but that's not your fault. Sit down, please. Carillus, some wine.' The slave who'd been hanging around the entrance when I came in bowed and went out.

I pulled up a chair – they seemed to prefer chairs, in this house, although there were a couple of expensive-looking couches – and sat. Seia Lucinda was an absolute honey: mid- to late thirties, jet-black hair, an oval face, olive skin and big, almond-shaped eyes. Scopas had said she was from one of the old local families, but I wondered if there wasn't some African blood there; maybe even Carthaginian. It was possible, sure.

'You're staying with the Lady Marcia, I believe?' she said.

'Yeah. She's my wife's aunt. Courtesy aunt. We come up here quite a lot, really. Our adopted daughter Marilla's lived with Marcia more or less since . . . well, since we adopted her. It started off temporary, then became permanent because she prefers the countryside to Rome. Besides, Marcia'd be lost without her.'

'They are beautiful, the Alban Hills. But it must be nice to live in Rome. So much more going on. The countryside, I'm afraid' – she smiled again – 'oh, dear, can be very dull at times. I'm always telling Quintus that we should think of moving, but he's such a stick-in-the-mud I doubt if we ever will.'

'No argument there, lady. The country's fine for a visit, but with respect living here full-time would drive me up the wall.'

'Yes. Oh, yes.' She turned. 'Ah, the wine. Thank you, Carillus. That's all, you can go.' The slave set a full wine cup on the small table next to me and a second – equally full – on the marble pool surround next to Seia Lucinda's chair, then bowed and exited. 'I'll join you, if I may.'

'Sure.' I picked up the cup and sipped: Alban, and pure nectar.

'It's just unfortunate that your first visit here should be under such unpleasant circumstances.' Seia Lucinda picked up her own cup. 'I can't say I ever liked Quintus's partner, and of course in recent months he'd become completely impossible, but I'm sorry he's dead, particularly . . . well, you understand. I'm especially sorry for Veturina. She did love him very much, Valerius Corvinus, however badly he treated her, and in many ways she will miss him greatly.'

'Yeah. Yeah, I can see that.'

'It might have been better had there been any children, but of course there weren't. Not who lived, at least.'

'You have children yourself?'

'No.' She took a sip of the wine. 'No, no children. There's just me and Quintus.'

'Valerius Corvinus?' I turned round. A big guy, late forties and wearing a snazzy mantle, was coming from the direction of what was, presumably, the family rooms beyond the satyr bronze. He held out his hand. 'Quintus Acceius. Delighted to meet you.'

I stood up and we shook. Our eyes were on a level; if anything, he had a good inch on me. 'Same here,' I said.

'Lucinda looking after you?' I noticed his eyes had gone to the lady's wine cup, and that she'd set it down quickly by the side of the pool. 'Fine. We'll go into the study, if you don't mind. This is no subject for a woman. Bring your wine with you. I won't join you, if you'll forgive me. It's a little early for me, especially since I'm just up.'

'Fair enough. Seia Lucinda? A pleasure to meet you.'

She gave me another smile but said nothing.

'This way, Corvinus.' He moved towards the back of the atrium. 'How are things progressing? You've talked to Fuscus?'

'Yeah. He was really helpful.'

'I'm glad. I'd've had the old bugger's guts for garters if he wasn't.' We'd reached an oak-panelled door in the short corridor beyond. 'In you go. Make yourself comfortable.'

The study was large and obviously well-used: two couches with blue velvet upholstery, three or four bronze candelabra, a writing desk and more bookshelves and books than you could shake a stick at. Again, some very nice bronzes that looked like they might be originals and a couple of portrait busts in marble, one of a young woman who wasn't Seia Lucinda.

'That's the best couch there,' Acceius said, pointing. 'Stretch yourself out and I'll take the other one.' I did, and set the wine cup on the table next to it. 'Now. Straight in, whatever you like.'

'You and Hostilius had been partners for, what, twenty-odd years?'

'Twenty-two come August. When he took me on I'd just finished my training with old Simplicius in Capua.'

'So you weren't local?'

'No. Although I'd reckon myself a local man now, and so would everyone else around here. We're talking about Bovillae to begin with, mind, not Castrimoenium. Lucius and I didn't up sticks and move until seven years later.'

'He'd been in practice long himself?'

'Lucius had a good fifteen years on me; I'm forty-seven, he was sixty-three. He'd had an office in Bovillae for, oh, maybe twelve years when I joined him.'

'Why did you move here?'

'It seemed like a good idea at the time. Still seems so. The town was growing, with more people coming into the area, from Rome especially, buying holiday property. A lot of our business is conveyancing, acting as agents for one side or another.'

'But not all of it? I'm thinking of the Maecilius case.'

'Ah.' Acceius frowned. 'That, Corvinus, is an example of a legal dispute that should never have happened. Lawyers are often accused of encouraging litigation on the part of their clients, even of fomenting it, for their own gain. Some do – I could quote you examples, at no great distance from here – but most try to see the danger in advance on their clients' behalf and take steps to avoid it happening. In this case, Lucius and I

– we were old Maecilius's lawyers – warned him that there'd be trouble and bad blood over the will's execution, but the obstinate old so-and-so wouldn't be told.'

'You mind telling me exactly what the situation is? If it isn't confidential, I mean.'

Acceius laughed. 'Grief, no, it's not confidential! Ought to be, certainly, but thanks to Bucca and Fimus between them – they're the sons, as you're probably aware – plus old Lucky himself before the lightning got him the whole bloody town knows, and has done for years. So the answer to your question is no, I don't mind telling you at all. However, I don't quite see what it has to do with Lucius's death.'

'Nor do I, pal.' I took a sip of my wine. 'Maybe – probably – nothing. I'm just covering all the angles at present.'

'Fair enough.' Acceius settled on his couch. 'In that case . . . The terms of the will are quite simple. Fimus – Marcus Maecilius, the younger son – gets the Six Cedars property in its entirety, plus a quarter of the liquid assets, amounting to something just short of fifteen thousand sesterces, while his elder brother gets the cash remainder. Old Maecilius's point, valid, as far as it went, was that Fimus had put the work in over the past forty-odd years to build the place up and didn't deserve to have the farm sold out from under him – as it would have to be – just so that his worthless brother – Lucky's expression, not mine – could take an equal share without having earned it. Bucca, of course, is now trying to have the will overturned. Or rather' – he hesitated – 'that's not quite fair.'

'It isn't?'

'No. Bucca's quite willing to reach an out-of-court settlement. If his brother agrees to split both property and cash fifty-fifty – Bucca taking his half of the property in outlying lakeside land not at present under cultivation – then he'll immediately sell on to a Bovillan developer with whom he's already reached a prospective agreement and turn over a third of the sale price to Fimus. You understand?'

'Yeah. And presumably if it happened that way then Fimus would come out ahead on the deal?'

'Undoubtedly. He'd be left with what in effect is, at present, the entire working farm and – lakeside property prices being what they are – twenty times the amount he'd've had other-wise. While Bucca would net something just short of a million in hard cash.'

'So the farming son gets the land and the funds to put into it, the other guy serious loose change to do what he likes with. They're both winners, the thing's been settled amicably and they can go their separate ways. Seems a sensible deal to me.'

Acceius shrugged. 'Agreed. Absolutely, no argument. But then, with all respect, Corvinus, you're not a farmer and you're not a local. Most important, you are not Fimus Mae-cilius. Fimus won't have the deal at any price: he wants Six Cedars to stay intact even though the terms of the will don't leave him the money to develop it any further. Besides . . . well, Lucius and I have kept our charges down, under the circumstances, but we can't – couldn't – provide them gratis. Fighting a legal battle isn't cheap, and fifteen thousand ses-terces is certainly no fortune. Especially when Fimus can't expect to recoup his outlay even if he wins.'

'You've advised him to come to terms?'

'Of course we bloody have! Right from the start. The whole business is a nonsense and everyone is losing out. Except us, naturally, but we – I, now – would gladly see an end to it tomorrow. The firm's well enough off financially without the necessity of bleeding a client to death, and I take my profes-sional responsibilities very seriously indeed. If the bugger wasn't so completely pig-headed—'

'I understand he – Fimus – and your partner had a . . . well, a run-in shortly before Hostilius's death. Also that you both had a meeting with Bucca the day before the knife attack.'

Pause. 'Yes. Yes, that's right.'

'Care to tell me about them? Presumably they both had to do with the suit.'

Acceius took a deep breath. 'The first . . . well, I know the circumstances, of course: Lucius encountered Fimus in the street and slapped his face. Beyond that I'm afraid I can't go, although naturally Fimus would be able to tell you more. I wasn't there personally, I didn't see Lucius again subsequently and even if I had done there was no guarantee that he would've been forthcoming about his reasons, or even mentioned the matter to me at all. We didn't talk much, latterly, as I'm sure you're aware.'

'He called Fimus a thief and a liar.'

'Yes. So I was told.' Acceius looked uncomfortable. 'Corvinus, I wouldn't put too much store by that in itself, if I were you. My partner often made accusations that were completely unfounded. It was part and parcel of his illness.'

'You can't guess what reason he had?'

'I . . . wouldn't go that far, no. But a guess is what it would be.' He hesitated. 'I said that the circumstances surrounding the Maecilius case were common knowledge, and so not confidential as such. This is. I'm afraid that if I go on then I will have to insist on confidentiality because it affects the good name of the firm as a whole. Understood?'

'Yeah. No problem, pal.'

'Very well.' Another deep breath. 'The . . . interview with Bucca that you mentioned. Bucca accused us – Lucius and myself, as his father's lawyers – of suppressing a second will that, he said, old Maecilius had made very shortly before he died; a much more equable one which divided property and liquid assets fifty-fifty between the brothers. We'd done nothing of the kind, of course – I hope that goes without saying;

professional ethics aside, we'd have no reason whatsoever to do so, quite the reverse, as I told you – but he was insistent. Abusively so. The meeting ended acrimoniously on both sides.'

Shit. 'So what you're saying – guessing – is that Fimus suppressed the will himself and that Hostilius somehow found out and tackled him over it?'

Acceius was looking really unhappy now. 'There's a . . . strong likelihood, yes. Or at least, rather, a strong likelihood that Lucius believed he'd done so. Certainly it would be possible in practical terms. Old Maecilius and his son lived in the same house, and the fact that we knew of no second will doesn't preclude its existence, especially if he'd made it only days before he died. I wouldn't put suppression past Fimus, either, given his character and the circumstances. On the other hand, and I must stress this, Lucius being as he was . . .' He made a throwaway gesture. 'Oh, hell, you know what I'm saying. You can go round and round in circles forever and still not have an answer. The long and the short of it is that I don't *know*, one way or the other. Certainly not enough to venture a worthwhile opinion. The best I can do is to assure you, in the strongest possible terms, that if a second will existed then we knew absolutely nothing of it, and would certainly have welcomed its appearance if it had because it would've solved the whole ridiculous problem. Fair enough?'

'Fair enough.' Gods! Food for thought there, and no mistake. Also, it gave Fimus a potential motive in spades for wanting the guy dead. Definitely an angle to chase. 'Uh . . . you mind if we move on?'

'Not at all.'

'The attack in the street. What can you tell me about that?'

Acceius frowned. 'Very little, I'm afraid, barring an account of the event itself, which you've no doubt already heard.'

'You didn't recognise the man? Neither you nor Hostilius?'

'No. At least I didn't, and Lucius gave no indication then or later of having done so. It was . . . most odd. However—' He stopped.

' "However"?'

'I'll leave that for the moment, Corvinus, if you don't mind. Don't worry, I'm not prevaricating, and I won't forget. No, as far as I'm aware the man was a complete stranger. Mind you, to be honest I can't swear even to that categorically: he was in a filthy condition, beard and long matted hair, ragged clothes, and he wasn't young or well-preserved, either. A complete tramp. I have wondered if he couldn't've been a . . . well, someone who had a past grudge against one or both of us, real or imagined. Someone either Lucius himself before we became partners or we together, subsequently, had prosecuted.' Another shrug. 'As I say, it would've had to've been a long time ago, because if not then one of us would have been sure to recognise him, but it's not outwith the bounds of possibility by any means. Memory does fade. And the fact that, whoever he was, he wasn't a local man makes it even more likely any connection can't've been at all recent.'

Yeah, well: I'm not stupid, and I'd been thinking along those lines myself. 'Did he say anything? When he attacked you?'

'He shouted "Wait!", I remember. Then when he was going for Lucius he said . . . well, I think the words were, "Take that, you bastard." Certainly something like that, nothing very significant or original. But then again it happened so quickly that I can't be sure.'

' "Bastard" singular? And a singular verb?'

Acceius smiled. 'Really, Corvinus,' he said. 'I hardly think—' He stopped. 'No. Oh, no, my apologies. I see, and you're quite right, it does matter a great deal. You'd make a fair lawyer yourself. Still, my answer is yes, definitely singular: he was speaking only to Lucius.'

'Did you have to kill him?'

'No, that was a complete accident. The knife caught in Lucius's mantle and I grabbed the man's wrist and forced it back. At least, that was all I meant to do, but as I said he was old and in poor condition. The result was that I overestimated his strength in comparison with my own, his hand went further than I intended, and the knife took him full in the side. I won't lose any sleep over his death, I admit, but the killing was not a deliberate act.' He hesitated. 'In fact, and this brings us back to the *however* I mentioned earlier, I wish now that I *had* disarmed him.'

'Yeah? Why's that, pal?'

'This is . . . I'm sorry, but this will sound . . . the only word is "silly".' Another hesitation. 'You know . . . have you ever felt, Corvinus, that you're being watched? Followed, even? I mean, had the feeling completely irrationally, with no objective proof whatsoever?'

I straightened. 'You think someone's watching you?'

'Yes. I have done since the day of the attack. Which' – he grinned – 'I'm perfectly ready to admit need have no sinister implications at all. This is not Rome. In Castrimoenium we don't expect to be attacked in the street, in broad daylight, by knife-wielding thugs, and the incident shook me, perhaps to the extent that it's made me imagine things. As I say, I have no proof, none at all, and just talking about it embarrasses me. *But* . . . if you put me on oath then I'd have to say yes, I do think someone is watching me. And although it is probably sheer imagination, because I haven't the slightest idea who would bother or why, I thought I should at least mention it. Now. That's said, and we can both forget that I spoke. Is there anything else I can help you with?'

'Uh . . . yeah.' My brain was buzzing. 'Castor. Your part-ner's brother-in-law. I understand he and Hostilius had a . . . call it a quarrel at your office, again the day before Hostilius's death. You know what that could've been about?'

'You've talked to Fuscus?'

'Yeah. Yes, of course.'

'Then you'll have all the information that I have myself, since Fuscus was my only source. No, Corvinus; apart from saying that Lucius had taken an irrational dislike to Castor and wanted him dismissed – again I'm sure you knew this – I can't provide any *specific* reason for the quarrel at all, nor even guarantee that there was one. Castor, of course, I haven't seen since, and nor has anyone else to my knowledge.'

'You've no idea where he might have gone?'

'None.'

Well, that about covered things for the present. I got up. 'Thanks for talking to me, pal. It's been very useful.'

He stood too. 'My pleasure, Corvinus. Any time.'

'Ah . . . one last question, before I go. Quite a personal one, if you don't mind.'

'Carry on.'

'Were either of you thinking of terminating the partnership at all? Would it have been possible, uh, financially, I mean?'

He nodded. 'Yes. I was. Or rather, I was sorely tempted to, although I doubt very much if I'd've carried the intention through in practice. As for your second question, the answer is also yes, as far as I was concerned. Lucius was the senior partner in terms of age and the history of the firm, certainly, but . . . well, the balance had shifted completely over the years, even before he fell ill. Had the partnership been dissolved – by him or by me – he would have suffered financially and in every other way far more than I would.' A smile. 'I can give you a note for my banker, if you like, and you can discuss the matter in confidence with him.'

'Uh-uh. That won't be necessary,' I said. 'And I'm sorry I asked the question.'

'Oh, don't be sorry, no umbrage taken. I'd be a poor excuse for a lawyer myself if I didn't recognise my own value as a suspect, and a financial motive for murder would be one of the more obvious ones.' I said nothing. 'Let me just add one thing, though, Corvinus, in my own defence. Lucius and I were not only partners but close friends for over twenty years, and I still regard his wife as such. Very much so. Dissolving the partnership – especially since . . . well, in the natural course of things it would end of itself in two or three years at most – would have been a poor return for these years of friendship and a terrible blow to Veturina. I could not and would not have done it, whatever the provocation. You understand me?'

'Yeah. Yeah, I understand.'

'Then I wish you good luck in your investigations. Don't hesitate to call again if you have further questions, or I can help in any way.' He held out his hand.

We shook, and I left.

12

Okay; it was past noon and I reckoned I'd earned myself a cup of wine and some cheese and olives at Pontius's. Especially if I could manage to combine them with a little gossip from Gabba. First, though, I went in the other direction from the town square, to the undertaker's shop where Sextus the door-slave had said they'd taken the corpse of the guy who'd attacked Hostilius.

It was the usual set-up you'd get in any small town: a frontage with a tasteful urn tastefully draped and, inside, a sombre-looking guy in a sharp mantle hovering attentively without seeming to be touting for custom. Not that funeral establishments get all that many browsers, mind.

'You Trophius, pal?' I said.

I could see him give me the quick once-over: no mourning mantle, reasonably freshly shaven, fringe unclipped. The sombreness slackened off a distinct notch. 'Yes, sir,' he said.

'Marcus Valerius Corvinus. I'm, ah—'

'Looking into the death of Lucius Hostilius on behalf of the senate,' he said. 'Yes, I know.'

Well, that saved us a bit of time. And no doubt most of Castrimoenium did, by now. 'The corpse from that incident up the street fourteen days back. It was brought here, I understand.'

'That's right.'

'Care to describe the guy to me? Is that possible?'

'I never forget a face, sir, although in this instance, ha ha, there was no question of taking a death mask.' He looked at me. 'I'm sorry. Just my little joke.'

Yeah. Right. 'The description, pal?'

'Looked in his sixties, at least, but that could just've been the condition he was in, he could've been years younger. Hair long, completely grey, matted with grease and worse. Beard ditto, fingernails like talons. Most of his teeth missing, nothing to him, skin and bone practically. No belt-pouch, no rings, necklets or bangles, nothing but the knife. Oh, and he'd shackle marks on his wrists and ankles.'

'*Shackle marks?*'

'That's right. Not recent, the abrasions'd healed, but he'd worn them for a long time in my opinion. A very long time, years, certainly. His wrists and ankles were one big scar.'

Shit; well, that fitted with Acceius's theory that the guy had been involved with the firm, anyway, on the receiving end. Chained wrists and ankles meant the galleys; or the mines, maybe, although it came to the same thing. Whichever it was, he'd have to be tough: if you lived longer than a few months in either you could count yourself lucky, and as for escaping . . . well, it was possible, sure, but the chances were in the flying pigs league. Certainly it'd explain his condition, his state of mind and his attempt on Hostilius: with obvious shackle marks on his wrists and ankles most people would think a lot more than twice before they gave him a job or a handout because sheltering a runaway slave or an escaped criminal is a serious offence, and who'd take the risk? And if Hostilius – or he and his partner – had been responsible for putting the marks there then it was no surprise he'd want to get even. The question was, had the meeting been accidental or had it been deliberate? And who the hell was the guy himself? Not that I'd much hope of finding the answer to that last one, mind.

The undertaker was looking at me. 'That all I can help you with?' he said.

'Uh, yeah. Yeah, thanks, friend.' I turned away. 'Oh what happened to the body? No one claimed it, I assume.'

He laughed. 'Oh, no. We kept him a couple of days, just on the off-chance, but no such luck. The lads took him to the cemetery out beyond the gates and burned him with some scrap timber we had lying in the yard. Got most of him, too, before the wood ran out.'

Uh-huh. Not a bad man, this Trophius. At least he'd given the guy a funeral of sorts where he could've just dumped him with the token sprinkling of earth for the local wildlife to dispose of. Considering that he had no hope of any return, and the man had been practically a murderer, that was pretty generous. 'Well, thanks again,' I said. 'I'll be—'

'Funny thing, though. While they were burning him the lads thought they were being watched.'

I whipped round. '*What?*'

'Probably just a gawper, of course, you get them at every funeral. Morbid so-and-so's. Strange thing is, gawpers usually come out into the open and stand as close to the mourning party as they decently can so's to get a good view. This one didn't. In fact, the lads weren't sure he was there at all after they first spotted him.'

'They manage a description?'

'Nah, too far away, and they only glimpsed him among the tombs. Also, why should they be interested? He was just a gawper.' He frowned; then, as the penny finally dropped, he glanced at me sharply. 'Wasn't he?'

I didn't answer. Brain buzzing, I left and made my way to Pontius's.

Gabba was there, propping up the bar with a couple of the other regulars. They gave me a funny look when I came in, then went back to their wine.

'Oh, it's you, Corvinus.' Pontius hefted a wine flask from the rack. 'Usual?'

'Yeah. Plus some cheese and olives to soak it up, pal.'

He filled half a jug and set a wine cup beside it then went off to the back room for the edibles.

'So much for watch-my-lips-no-murders, Consul,' Gabba said sourly. 'Fibber.'

Word certainly got around fast. Mind you, Gabba kept his ear so close to the ground they could've used him for a drain cover; which was exactly the reason I was there. I shrugged, half filled the cup and drained it.

'Yeah, well,' I said.

'Me, I'd bet it was the wife,' one of the other loungers grunted. 'Bloody women, you can't trust any of them. Not that I blame her, the bugger was out of his tree.'

'No reason to go killing a man, though, is it?' The other lounger emptied his cup and refilled it. 'Just gives the rest ideas. Wives get the idea they can poison their husbands whenever they feel like it and it's the end of fucking civilised society as we know it.'

The first lounger chuckled. 'My wife's been trying it for years, boy. And it's going to get worse now she's—'

Gabba, next to him, shifted sideways and trod hard on his foot. 'Oops,' he said. 'Sorry, sunshine, total accident.'

Pontius came back with the cheese and olives. 'There you go, Corvinus. That do you?'

'Fine.' I reached into my belt-pouch, took out some coins and put them on the counter. 'Uh . . . Gabba? You mind a quick word in private? Outside?'

He beamed. 'No problem, Consul. Except that my jug seems to be unaccountably almost empty at present.'

I sighed and put a few more coins down. Pontius gave me a suspicious look, reached for a flask and half filled Gabba's jug. 'Okay now?' I said.

'You're a true gentleman, Corvinus. One of the truly greats.'

Lounger B sniggered. I ignored him, picked up the plate of cheese and olives in one hand and my jug and empty wine cup with the other and led the way outside.

We settled at one of the tables overlooking the square. I topped up the cup and drank. Gabba did the same and filched a slice of cheese.

'Now,' he said. 'What can I do you for?'

'Quintus Acceius's wife. Seia Lucinda. She got anything going with Hostilius's brother-in-law that you know of?'

He took a long swallow before answering. 'Could have. Could have, Consul. There've been stories. Mind you, if she has then they've been discreet. Of course, there was that incident at the party about half a month back, but you'll know about that already.'

'Come on, Gabba, you bastard! You're drinking my wine, remember?'

'True.' He filled his cup. 'It was Seia Lucinda's birthday. Acceius puts on a bash for it every year, lots of guests, all the local nobs, no expense spared. You know the sort of thing.'

'Yeah. And?'

'Hostilius and Veturina turn up – invited, of course – and they're in the line to wish the lady many happy returns. So when he gets face to face with the birthday girl Hostilius brings out a bottle of perfume and hands it to her. "Happy birthday, Lucinda," he says, "this'll suit you perfectly. It's a real whore's scent." Then he just walks off back to his carriage leaving everyone standing, his wife included.' He chuckled. 'Course, he never mentioned Castor by name as such, but you get the general idea.'

I sat back. Shit; talk about provocation! Well, if Acceius hadn't stiffed the bastard after that he had a lot more for-bearance than me, that was all I could say. And as far as 'ill' went, in Rome he'd've been locked up. Even so . . . 'You think it's likely, pal?' I said.

'That Seia Lucinda is having a bit on the side? Why not? She's still a fine-looking woman. You've seen her?' I nodded. 'Right. Too fond of the juice, by some accounts' – he held up his wine cup – 'and bored out of her skull. Still, that's her own fault, isn't it?'

'How do you mean?'

'She was the one did the chasing in the first place, or so they say. She was quick enough to hook up with Acceius after his first wife died.'

The hairs stirred on the back of my neck. 'His, uh, first wife? He was married before?'

'Sure. Years back, before he came here from Bovillae. And don't look at me like that, Corvinus, there was nothing funny about it, or not that I know of. She died in childbirth; it was their first kid, and it went wrong the way they do, sometimes. Seia Lucinda was from a big local family, couldn't've been much more than half through her teens, but a real tearaway. She set her cap at Acceius and nailed him a couple of years later. At least' – he emptied his cup and refilled it – 'that's what the gossip said when they moved to Castrimoenium.'

'So what went wrong?'

'With the marriage?' Gabba reached for another slice of cheese. 'Oh, that's okay, far as I know, in general terms. I could name you shakier ones. But the lady's no happy bunny. You want my opinion, she thought that when she bagged Acceius the next stop would be Rome. He's a top-notch lawyer, Corvinus, a sturgeon in a carp-pond, but he's content with where he is and what he is. He could've ditched Hostilius years ago, long before all this shit started, but he didn't. Hasn't since, either.' He took a swallow of wine. 'Ask me, he's just too nice for his own good. You get these stupid buggers now and again. Like I say, the result's that his wife drinks too much and she's bored. Take all that with the fact that she's a stunner and you've got a lethal combination.'

Yeah, I'd agree with that. I took some of the cheese before the scrounging bastard wolfed the rest of it. 'How about the brother-in-law? Castor? He got form?'

'He's good-looking, certainly. And he likes the girls. There've been two or three irate daddies knocking on the Hostilius door since he moved here.'

'Connections with Seia Lucinda in particular?'

'He's the firm's gopher. He's bound to see something of her in the natural course of events. But like I say if there is anything then they've been discreet.'

Bugger; I'd heard enough. 'Gabba, pal, you do realise that all this amounts to zilch, don't you?' I said. 'My bet is that there isn't a scrap of actual evidence linking Castor and Acceius's wife. All you've given me is assumptions and generalities, plus a reported insult at a party where the guy who delivered it ought to've been smacked in the mouth on the spot. Right?'

'I aim to please, Consul. Not an unreasonable return for half a jug of wine.' Gabba refilled his cup. 'Anyway, that's what gossip is. Substantiated gossip is what you might call a contradiction in terms, and for that you pay extra. Not that it's my field of expertise, mind.'

I stood up and retrieved the plate of cheese and olives – mostly olives now: Gabba wasn't too keen on these – plus the wine jug and cup. If that was all I was going to get then I might as well go back inside. Just as I moved to the door, the door up above at the top of the staircase leading to Pontius's second storey opened.

'Come on, Corvinus.' Gabba was suddenly right behind me with his own jug and cup. 'If you're going in then go.' He pushed me through and closed the door behind us.

'What the hell!' I said.

'Sorry, Consul, tripped over my own feet.'

'Gabba—'

'Concatenation of circumstances, boy. Purely fortuitous, and you have my abject apologies.'

'You want a top-up, Corvinus?' Pontius said.

'No. No, I'm fine.' Jupiter! I carried the jug, cup and plate, minus a couple of the olives that hadn't made it across the threshold, back over to the bar. 'What's going on?'

'Beg your pardon?'

'You branching out, Pontius? Running an illegal gambling den or something upstairs that you don't want the authorities to know about?' He looked at me blankly. The other two punters set down their wine cups and stared at me too, like I'd sprouted an extra pair of purple ears. I sighed. 'Never mind; it doesn't matter.'

'What doesn't matter?'

That was Gabba. I turned to look at him: blank stare number four on full power. Bugger. Whatever it was, it was obviously private Castrimoenian business, the locals had closed ranks and Roman purple-stripers could just put up the blinds and go home.

'*It*,' I said. 'Whatever the hell *it* is it is not . . . fucking . . . important. Just leave it. Okay?'

'You feeling all right?' Pontius said, frowning.

I poured a cup of wine and sank half of it at a gulp. 'Bugger off, sunshine.'

'You want to watch that stuff, Corvinus,' Lounger B said. 'It rots the brain.'

13

Well, there was a fair slice of the afternoon left before the dinner gong; plenty of time to pick up one of the case's loose ends. Clarus had said that Bucca Maecilius had a carter's business near the Caba Gate. Since I was in Castrimoenium anyway I might as well pay the guy a visit, see what he had going for himself.

I found the place easy: a patch of waste ground that stood out like a rotten tooth in what was otherwise a respectable edge of town street. There was a wall fronting it, sure, but it hadn't been replastered for years and the iron gates that should've closed the entrance looked rusted open on their hinges. 'Business' was dignifying it. Not a profitable concern, obviously.

I went through the gates past a couple of tarpaulined carts parked next to tumbledown stables.

'Anyone around?' I called.

A guy came out of the stables holding a hay-rake; a big guy, fat as lard, bald as a coot and no youngster: I'd put him sixty, easy, and not a well-preserved sixty, either. He was wearing a tunic that might've had a colour at one time but hadn't seen the inside of a wash-tub for months. The same might be said for the guy himself.

'Yes?'

'Bucca Maecilius?'

'That's me.' He squinted; short-sighted, too, to add to his charms. 'You want to hire a cart?'

'Uh-uh. Name's Valerius Corvinus. I was wondering if I could have a word with you.'

'What about?'

'Quintus Libanius of the senate has asked me to look into Lucius Hostilius's death. The lawyer.'

'Is that so, now?' He leaned the hay-rake against the stable wall and came over. He didn't look too friendly. 'What's it got to do with me?'

'I understand you had a . . . talk with Hostilius and his partner fifteen days ago at their office.'

'Yeah. And?'

'Care to tell me about it?'

'Why should I?'

'Oh, because from what I heard it ended in a shouting match and seven days later your little friend Cosmus interfered with Hostilius's medication and stiffed the guy. Nothing particularly crucial.'

He was glaring at me. 'You accusing me of being mixed up in that? Because if so—'

'You knew Cosmus, then?'

'Yeah, I knew Cosmus.' There was a trace of uncertainty in his voice now. 'So did a lot of other people.'

'You have any names, maybe?'

He shook his head. 'Look, Corvinus, if that's who you said you were,' he said. 'Let's start again, okay? I've got nothing to hide. You want to ask me about that day I went round to Hostilius's office, you go ahead.' He jerked his chin towards a bench beside the stable door. 'Take a seat. We might as well be comfortable.'

I followed him over and we sat down. 'It was about a second will you say your father made, wasn't it?' I said.

'He made it, sure enough. Four days before he died. Told me so himself, the next day.'

'He give a reason?'

'He didn't need a reason! I was his elder son, he owed me!' I looked at him. 'Yeah, well. He said his conscience was troubling him. We'd never got on, sure, but blood's blood and he didn't want to cause trouble after he was dead.'

'Did you see it?'

'No. But he told me what was in it. A fifty-fifty split between me and Fimus, everything right down the middle. That was fair, I'd've had no quarrel with that. He said he had to have it witnessed first, then he'd take it round to his lawyers and make it official.'

Uh-huh. Well, Lucky had been cutting it fine, if this had happened three days before the lightning got him. Not that he was to know that, mind, but it'd be all of a piece with the rest of the old bugger's sense of timing. One of nature's true incompetents, Gabba had called him, and he'd been spot on. 'And did he? Give it to his lawyers, I mean?'

'Dad never broke a promise in his life.' He glanced sideways at me. 'Look, I don't *know*, right? Not for sure. But he said he would, okay? That's enough for me.' For all his sixty-odd years his voice had the petulance of a child's. In fact, half close your eyes and you might just believe that Bucca Maecilius was a great hairless whining baby.

'What about the witnesses? If he'd had it witnessed I'd've expected that they'd've come forward.'

'Don't you believe it, Corvinus! They're bastards in this town, they've got it in for me, the lot of them.'

'So you went to Hostilius and Acceius and accused them of suppressing the will.'

'I'd reason. Dad said he'd give them it. Besides, they're no shining lights, that pair. Hostilius was straight enough before he lost his roof-tiles but for all Quintus Acceius sets himself up as a model of virtue these days he's cut a neat few corners in his time.'

I blinked. 'Uh . . . has he, indeed? Such as?'

'You talk to Novius. He'll tell you.'

'Novius?'

'Publius Novius, in Bovillae. My lawyer.' He said the word with pride, stressing it.

Right: Fuscus had mentioned him, I remembered. Not with a great deal of underlying respect, mind, or that was the impression I'd got. And I wouldn't be surprised if Novius turned out to be the guy Acceius had been alluding to when he'd said that he could name certain lawyers not too far away who encouraged their clients in litigation. A certain amount of professional rivalry there, I'd imagine, if not outright antagonism, which might, lawyers being lawyers, explain things. Still: Acceius cutting corners, eh? Interesting . . .

'Why should Hostilius and Acceius suppress a second will?' I said. 'What's in it for them?'

'Acceius. Not Hostilius, I'd got nothing against him. You ever heard of a guy called Aulus Decidius? Little guy, dwarf, but one of the richest bastards in Latium.'

I'd really sat up now, and something with a lot of legs was working its way up my spine. 'Uh . . . yeah,' I said carefully. 'Yeah, I've heard of Decidius.' Met him, too: like Bucca said, he was one of the richest men in the region, if not the whole of Italy, and though he was strictly legit – as far as I knew – he owed a large slice of his income to buying property anonymously through agents, then developing it and selling on to the Roman luxury holiday home market. Especially lakeland property. Like Maecilius's Six Cedars was.

'He's a friend of Acceius's. A good friend.'

'Ah . . . how do you know this, pal?'

'I know a thing or two,' Bucca said smugly. 'I told you. I've got a lawyer.'

Publius Novius. In Bovillae. Shit! Professional antagonism or not, Novius was someone I had to talk to. 'So how would it work?'

'You know I've offered Fimus a deal? To settle out of court?'

'Yeah. Yeah, I knew that. Split the land and the money half and half, then you'll sell your share of the property and give your brother a third of the proceeds gratis, right?'

'Right. I'd do it, too, Corvinus. I'm not greedy. The guy I'm dealing with is offering a fair price, I've got no one to follow me, and what I'd make out of the sale would take me out of this' – he nodded at the carts in the yard – 'for the time I've got left. I'd be happy with that. Understand?'

'Yeah. Yeah, I understand.'

'Now if Fimus gets the land it'll go, all of it, to Decidius, and – this is the point – that bastard Acceius'll earn a whacking commission on the deal.'

'Hang on, pal.' I was frowning. 'I'm sorry. You know your brother far better than me, sure, but I was told in no uncertain terms that he'd never sell, under any circumstances. No way, nohow, never.'

'Maybe he wouldn't, left to himself. But you haven't heard the price yet. And you've never met Faenia.'

'Who's Faenia?'

'Fimus's wife. She's got her head screwed on and she leads him by the nose. Six Cedars is one of the biggest stretches of land in the area, been in the family for two centuries. If it was sold entire to Decidius, as a package, then he could afford to pay the premium price, because it'd be a major estate, top of the market: three million, plus ten per cent to Acceius as a finder's fee. And Decidius'd still make a clear profit of over five times that when the property's developed. Or so Novius tells me.'

I whistled. Three million sesterces was serious, serious gravy by anyone's reckoning, and three hundred thousand just for suppressing a will wasn't a bad return for the risk, either. As a motive for murder, taking everything else into consideration –

and there was a hell of a lot of *that* – it might well tip the balance.

'You're beginning to convince me, pal,' I said. 'Uh . . . does Acceius know you know this?'

'You think I didn't tell the bastard to his face I knew what he was up to, right there in the office?'

'Fine. Fine.' I stood up. So did Bucca. 'Well, thanks for your time, friend. It's been . . . informative.'

'You're welcome. It was nice to have a friendly ear for once.' I turned to go. Then he said, 'Corvinus!'

'Yeah?'

'One last thing. Cosmus. How did he die?'

I paused. The big eyes were watching me. 'He was slugged from behind with an iron gate-bolt,' I said. 'At least, that's the expert view.'

'The poor, silly little bitch,' Bucca murmured. 'He never did have much sense.'

'No,' I said. 'No, I don't think he did.'

I left. Home, and dinner.

14

When I got back home Alexis was in the front garden doing something horticultural with a trowel to one of Aunt Marcia's flower-beds; Alexis, if you remember, is the brightest button on our household staff who we'd brought along as an intellectual counterweight to Meton. I went over.

'Hey, pal,' I said. 'You got a moment?'

'Of course, sir.' He shoved the trowel in, stood up and wiped his hands on his tunic.

'I've a job for you. A bit of digging.'

'Ah . . .' He glanced around.

'Metaphorical digging. You know the public records office in Bovillae?'

'I could find it, sir, yes.'

'I need a name. Guy who came off second best in a prosecution, almost certainly criminal and top-of-the-range, and who got himself sent to the mines or the galleys. Something along those lines, anyway.'

'No problem, sir. I think I can handle that. Would you like me to—'

'Hold on, sunshine, I haven't finished. Prosecuting counsel was either Lucius Hostilius or Quintus Acceius or both. That's the good news, easy-peasy so far. Now we get to the difficult bit. The date could be anything between fifteen and thirty-four years ago. Best to add on a couple of years either side to be safe.'

He looked at me and his lips framed a word that Alexis just

didn't use. I grinned. 'Sir, do you have any idea how long that will *take*?' he said carefully.

'Uh-huh. Probably the best part of a month unless you strike lucky or find a shortcut, in which case we're screwed. The trouble is, it's important and I can't think of another way to do it. We'll just have to keep our fingers crossed.'

'Couldn't you ask Quintus Acceius himself, sir? He might just—'

'No. I don't want to do that. If Acceius does know then the question might jog his memory if it needed jogging, sure, but . . . well, in that case he might not want to tell me the answer. And then he'd know I was looking. You follow?'

Alexis nodded: like I say, our Alexis is a smart cookie. 'What happens if there's more than one possibility, sir?'

'I'll settle for a list, pal. At present I'd settle for anything. But give me them as you turn them up, fine?'

'You want me to start right away?'

I looked up at the sun. 'Uh-uh, no point: it'd take you a good hour to get to Bovillae on horseback and the office'd be closing anyway. First thing in the morning, okay? And every day thereafter. Or – better – I'll give you a note for Quintus Libanius asking if he can arrange to put you up somewhere local and you can take it round to him yourself before dinner. That do?'

'Yes, sir. Perfect.'

'Great. Thanks, Alexis. Stay away from wineshops and loose women while you're in Bovillae, okay? Except in the line of duty.' Then, when he blushed – Alexis is a sensitive soul: 'Joke, pal.'

I left him to his trowelling and carried on into the house. Bathyllus shimmied up with the obligatory wine tray.

'Mistress around, sunshine?' I said.

'In the back garden, sir.'

'Thanks.' I picked up the cup and wine jug and went

through the atrium towards the peristyle. She was sitting in the rose arbour with the usual book in her lap.

'Profitable day, dear?' She lifted her head for the welcome-home kiss.

'Not bad.' I sat down in the wicker chair opposite. 'Things seem to be moving. Quintus Acceius might not be the squeaky-clean paragon he sets himself up for.'

'Really?' She set the book aside.

'You remember Aulus Decidius? From a couple of years back?'

'The entrepreneur? I remember you talking about him, yes.'

'Turns out that Acceius is a friend of his and there's a possibility that he might've sat on a second will of old Maecilius's to further the chances of a deal happening with Decidius. Also, the guy may not be as straight-down-the-line ethically in general as he pretends to be.'

'Ah.' Perilla hesitated. 'It all sounds a little woolly, dear, lots of mights and maybes. Have you any actual proof?'

'Uh . . . no. Not yet.'

'Very well. Where did you get the information?'

'From Bucca Maecilius. You know, Lucky Maecilius's elder son? He, uh, got it from his lawyer in Bovillae.'

'Who is, presumably, the one on the other side from Acceius in the court case.'

'Yeah. Yeah, that's right. Guy called Publius Novius.'

'And who might therefore have a vested interest in blackening the opposition.'

I was beginning to feel definitely irritated here. 'Jupiter, Perilla, I'd already thought of that, okay? I'm not swallowing this hook, line and sinker but it merits chasing up, right?'

She smiled and ducked her head. 'Yes, Marcus. I'm sorry. You talked to Quintus Acceius himself this morning, didn't you? How did he strike you? Gut feeling?'

I could see what she was getting at. Bugger. I took a morose gulp of the wine. 'He was *nice*,' I said defensively. 'The bastard was *nice*, okay? In Gabba's words, slightly modified and upgraded, far too fucking nice and reasonable for his own good.'

'Don't swear, dear. It's not my fault.'

'Yeah, well.' I took another swig and topped up the cup from the jug. 'He was. And I liked him.' The irritation boiled over into frustration. 'Perilla, this case is turning out a total and absolute bugger, you know that? I've talked to two of the main suspects now, the wife and the partner. Both of them have motive coming out of their fucking ears—'

'*Marcus!*'

'And after the amount of gratuitous provocation they've had to put up with, separately and together, if it'd been me I'd've stiffed the bastard myself, months ago. By any sort of logic one of them should've killed him, or both, and he'd've deserved it a dozen times over. The only problem is that I'd bet a gold piece to a poke in the eye that neither of them did. Or if they did then they are bloody good actors, that's all I can say.' I slammed the wine cup down on the marble table between us and the wine spilled. 'Hell!'

'Marcus, stop it.'

I frowned, then grinned and reached down for the jug beside my chair. 'Okay. Sorry, lady. Tantrum over. But it's frustrating.'

'Yes, so I see. Tell me about your day, in detail.'

I took a deep breath and did.

'So what we've got at present,' she said when I'd finished, 'barring the will business and the question of who the man who attacked Hostilius was, is the missing brother-in-law Castor as prime suspect. Yes?'

'Yeah. Obviously whatever happened that last day between him and Hostilius is crucial, but even without it the guy has form. One' – I held down a finger – 'he's got ambitions to be a lawyer himself, he has his sister's and Acceius's support, but he's been stymied because his brother-in-law's taken a violent dislike to him. Two' – I held down the second finger – 'Hostilius has just blown the final whistle; he's out of the firm and out of the family home. Three' – the third finger – 'he and Veturina are very close, and if he's got anything going for him at all he won't've taken too kindly to the shit that both of them have been putting up with and unlike her he might well've been prepared to do something drastic about it.' I paused. 'Sound reasonable so far?'

'What about opportunity? From what you told me Castor would've had none. He disappeared the morning of the day before Hostilius's death and hasn't been seen since.'

'Yeah.' Bugger. I'd been trying to avoid thinking of that one.

'Unless of course he didn't disappear. At least, not immediately.'

I looked at her. 'You're saying he went back home when he left Hostilius's?'

'It would be the natural thing to do, wouldn't it? In fact, I'd be surprised if he didn't, certainly if he intended to go away for any length of time. After all, he'd left Hostilius in town, he knew where he was. He'd need clothes, money, that sort of thing. And if he was as close to his sister as he's supposed to be then he wouldn't leave her without a word of explanation, would he? He might even tell her where he was going.'

Shit. She was right, of course, and when you thought about it it was obvious. The only reason I hadn't done was it meant that sweet-as-pie Veturina was lying through her teeth; not to mention straight-down-the-line-honest Scopas, because no major-domo worth his salt could *not* know what was going on in his own manor. And *that* meant . . .

'Veturina knows or suspects that Castor was responsible for her husband's death,' I said. 'Or thinks he could be.'

'Yes. Or, of course, she and Castor engineered the thing

together, or at least she knew beforehand that her brother was planning it and did nothing to stop him,' Perilla said calmly. 'Remember, we don't know what Castor's quarrel with Hostilius was about, only the result. And even that might have been sufficient to tip the balance. Veturina might've been prepared to put up with Hostilius's ill-treatment when it harmed only herself, but if she saw he was on the point of ruining her brother's life as well that would've been another matter.'

Yeah; right. Everyone has their breaking point; it was just a question of where, and, love him as she undoubtedly did, like I'd said the lady had been pushed well to the edge already. I took a swallow of wine. Shit. Whatever the explanation, one thing was clear: Veturina still had serious beans to spill. And the sooner she spilled them the better.

'Okay,' I said. 'I'll go and see her again tomorrow. Meantime, lady' – I refilled my cup – 'I've had enough. I'm giving sleuthing a break for the evening. What's for dinner?'

'Ah, now that was something I was going to tell you, dear,' Perilla said nervously. 'I don't know if Meton's back yet. He served us an early lunch and disappeared again immediately afterwards. I saw him heading down the drive myself.' She paused. 'He was wearing . . . well, he was wearing a new tunic.'

'A *what*?' I stared at her open-mouthed. Gods! Meton never, never *ever* wore a new tunic! Oh, sure, he must've had one, in fact I know he did because Perilla kitted out the whole household fresh, me included, every Spring Festival, and we'd had that not long ago. But he never wore it, not *new*. How the slovenly bugger managed things, I don't know – probably the way those narcissistic young prats-about-town manage to keep their designer stubble just the fashionable length – but he was a three-day-old tunic man to his grimy fingernails. Meton without grease stains and a distinct whiff of underarm sweat just wouldn't be Meton.

'Also,' Perilla continued in a small voice, in the tone you'd use if you were telling someone their granny had just been run over by a stonemason's cart, 'he passed Alexis on the way to the gate, and Alexis thought he could smell perfume.'

'Perfume? *Meton?*'

'Now don't overreact, dear. I'm sure there's a perfectly rational explanation somewhere or other. And after all Alexis could've been mistaken.'

Mistaken, hell: empires could rise and fall in the space between Meton's normal body odour and the scent of perfume. I'd heard enough. I turned round and yelled, '*Bathyllus!*'

The little bald-head came running up like there was a fire in the hypocaust. 'Yes, sir.'

'Meton. Here. Now.'

'I . . . ah . . . don't know if he's . . .'

'Ascertain, sunshine. And when you've fucking ascertained and if he is around then tell him I want to see him as of yesterday. If he isn't then let me know and when the bugger does get back I will personally detach his testicles using the bluntest knife I can find in his knife box. Clear?'

He started a sniff, then caught my eye and thought better of it. 'Clear, sir. Yes, sir.'

He left. I fumed quietly while Perilla sat in silence, giving me occasional nervous looks.

'Yeah? What is it now, Corvinus?'

I turned round. Well, he'd changed back into his familiar gravy-stained togs, anyway. Alexis had been right, though: sweat there undoubtedly was, but it was laced with a distinct odour of violets.

'Okay, Meton,' I said. 'What's going on?'

'About what?'

I sighed. 'Look, pal, I'm not an idiot.' He sniggered. 'You've got something cooking, and I don't mean pork with cumin and onion seeds, either. So give.'

'Don't know what you mean.'

'Meton. When was the last time you put on a new tunic to go out and sprinkled yourself with essence of fucking violets?'

'This afternoon.'

Bugger. 'Yeah, I *know* it was this afternoon, sunshine! That's the whole point! What I want to know is why?'

'No law against it, is there? Lookin' and smellin' nice? If I want to look an' smell nice there's no law that says I shouldn't look and smell—'

Gods! Enough! 'Meton, you are grounded as of now, okay? I don't know what you're up to, but it's something, and I am not taking the risk. Not after that sheep caused the biggest sodding damage to Roman prestige in Latium since the First Fucking Samnite War.' He sniggered again. 'Is that perfectly clear?'

'Fine.' He inserted a finger into his left nostril, waggled it about, withdrew it and inspected the result. 'So I won't be able to do the shopping in town from now on, then?'

'Gods, Meton, we have a whole household of fucking bought help here—'

'Marcus,' Perilla said quietly.

'—most of whom have the requisite nous to be able to negotiate the intricacies of a shopping list and bring home the bacon, the cabbage, the lentils, the what-fucking-ever—'

'*Marcus!*'

'—that you need perfectly well without your personal in-volvement. Which is what will happen from now on.'

He drew himself up like Scaevola getting ready to spit in Porsenna's eye. 'Suit yourself, Corvinus, you're the boss. It's your right to decide. Executive decision, like.' He sniffed and inserted the finger again. 'An' if you're fully prepared to take the responsibility an' the consequences then . . .'

Pause. Long, long, *ominous* pause. What is known, in the trade, as a hanging minatory apodosis. Shit. I knew what the bugger was saying, we all did. It was the culinary equivalent of moving up the heavy artillery to point-blank range, cranking the winches and saying, 'Right, then, lads, on a count of three . . .'

Maybe I'd been just a little hasty here.

'Ah . . . hold on, there,' I said. 'Maybe if we just agreed that you didn't sort of loiter over the shopping, pal. Straight in, straight out, no messing, sort of thing. How would that be?'

'Never fucking loitered or messed in my life. My shopping is *constructive*, Corvinus.'

'Yeah. Yeah.' I shot an anxious glance at Perilla, but apart from a slight tightening of the lips and two red spots on the cheeks the lady was keeping shtum. 'Well, that's *very* good, Meton, but—'

'And what's wrong with wanting to look smart? 'S an inalienable human right, is that. Just because I'm a slave doesn't mean I have to—'

'Yeah, right, Meton, okay, pal.' I was beginning to sweat myself. 'Got it. Understood, no problem. Let's just—'

'I had that scent off Lysias since two Winter Festivals ago. It needed using.'

'Yeah, that stuff does, or it rots the bottle. Ah . . . let's just forget it, sunshine, okay? Perfume under the bridge. Water. Whatever. What's for dinner?'

His eyes lit up. 'Actually, you're lucky there, Corvinus. I've got this marinade I've been working on for braised kidneys. Pepper, aniseed, mint and ginger in wine must and vinegar, although I have my doubts about the ginger. The original recipe says dates, but I thought if I replaced them with figs—'

'Great. Great. That sounds great, pal.' Whew! He was talking food again. Crisis over. I stood up, clapped him on the shoulder, turned him round and gave him a gentle shove kitchenwards. 'Look forward to it.'

He ambled off. Perilla and I looked at each other.

'Oh, well done, dear,' she said. 'Nicely handled again. Two nil to Meton, I would say.'

'You want to live off gristle meatballs and mushy beets for the next month, lady? Because I don't.'

'You don't think it's a woman, do you? Remember all that trouble with Bathyllus?'

'A woman? *Meton?*' I considered the possibility. For about a tenth of a second. 'Nah. No chance.'

'That's all right, then,' Perilla said. 'So long as you're sure.'

We were having breakfast the next morning when a messenger arrived from Hyperion to say that Quintus Acceius had been knifed.

15

'So what happened exactly?'

Acceius was sitting on a stool in his study, naked to the waist, while Clarus changed the dressing and bandages his father had put on the evening before. The guy still looked pale.

'I was coming home from a late visit to a client,' he said. 'Near the old shrine of Juturna. You know it?'

'Yeah.' On the outskirts of town, in the direction of the Bovillae Gate. Not the most densely populated part of Castrimoenium because of the smell from the tannery and slaughterhouse nearby.

'He came out of an alleyway behind me after I'd passed.' Acceius winced as Clarus carefully removed the blood-soaked pad of linen from the wound. 'He must've got ahead of me and been waiting. No warning, he had the knife drawn already. I was lucky, I managed to turn as he struck, and the fact that I was wearing a full mantle helped.'

I looked while Clarus sponged the stitched-up wound clean. Yeah, he'd been lucky, all right: not a puncture wound but a long, deep cut running across his lower back all the way from side to spine. If it'd been the point of the knife that'd caught him, rather than the edge, he'd've had Trophius the undertaker in attendance this morning rather than Clarus.

'You get a look at him?'

He grinned. 'Are you kidding, Corvinus? I had more important things to worry about at the time than taking notes on the bugger's physiognomy for future reference. Such as staying alive. I have never, ever been so bloody petrified in my life! Besides, it was dark.'

'Yeah, well . . .'

'He was about three-quarters my height, perhaps a fraction more. Short, thick, wiry hair, no cap, fairly heavily built. Breath smelled of raw onions. Oh, and he wasn't young.'

'About the age of the guy who attacked you and Hostilius?'

Acceius considered. 'No. I can't be sure, of course, but . . . no, a bit younger. Middle-aged, and, as I say, in much better physical condition. Unfortunately.'

'What happened then? After he stabbed you?'

'I caught him a good sock in the face.' He held up his right hand: the knuckles were bruised and cut. 'Sheer bloody luck again that I connected, but I must've loosened a tooth or two at least. Then he . . . well, I think he'd've tried a second time but just then there was a noise from one of the houses nearby, someone opening a window and calling a cat in. That must've panicked him because he turned and ran.'

'You didn't follow him?'

He laughed, then winced. 'Corvinus, don't do that, please! It hurts even to breathe at present. No, I bloody well did not! I never even thought of it. I just stood there with my back against the wall feeling grateful that I was still alive and would be allowed to stay that way. Besides, I was beginning to hurt. I didn't, at first, but now I was.'

'So what did you do then?'

'Went straight round to Hyperion's. There was no point doing anything else. I knew I was bleeding like a stuck pig but so long as I kept moving the actual pain wasn't too bad, and it wasn't all that far, closer than home and much more sensible. I hammered on his door and fainted on the bloody doorstep.' He grinned. 'Bloody being the operative word. He patched me up, sent round to my house for slaves and a litter, and here I am.'

'You hadn't thought of taking a litter originally? To the client's house, I mean? Or slaves, at least?'

He shook his head. 'This is Castrimoenium, not Rome. As far as distance goes you can walk from one side of it to the other, Bovillan to Caban Gates, in fifteen minutes, and where street crime's concerned it's more likely to take the form of a straying mule than a footpad. Besides, I prefer walking about on my own, without dragging a pack of slaves along. Even after dark. I always have.'

Yeah, well, I could appreciate that. I was the same, and walking around town after dark without protective muscle in Rome was a whole lot riskier than out here in the sticks. Even so . . . 'You were the one who said you were being watched, pal,' I said. 'And you'd been attacked once already. Or your partner had.'

'Yes, I know.' He drew his breath in sharply as Clarus pressed the new dressing over the wound while he made a start to the bandaging. 'Corvinus, I *know*! It was stupid, I fully admit that, it almost got me killed, and I won't make the mistake again. But you don't think, do you? You imagine yourself immortal.'

True: Perilla was always complaining that that was how I looked at things.

'A couple of questions,' I said. 'Since I'm here.'

'Of course. Ask away.'

'When was the last time you actually saw Lucius Hostilius?'

'To talk to, you mean?'

'Does it make that much difference?'

Acceius smiled. 'Oh, yes. We . . . tended to avoid one another, as a rule, even when we were both in the office. Unless there was a reason not to, and then I was careful to be formal, polite, unconfrontational and brief. So I suppose it would be the day after we were attacked, five days before his death, when I went round to see him at his villa. He hadn't felt strong enough to come into town and there were two or three relatively urgent bits of documentation I knew he'd want to look at and discuss, so I took them up myself. Not that it was a long meeting, naturally, no more than half an hour if that. As I say, all our dealings latterly were wholly confined to business.'

'You said the documents were urgent?'

'Relatively urgent, yes.'

'Mind telling me what they were about?'

'In detail? Oh, they were a ragbag, Corvinus, and relatively urgent doesn't preclude trivial. The only really important one was a letter from Publius Novius over in Bovillae – he's the arch-enemy, in case you didn't know, the rival firm – saying that a client of his who was selling property, hopefully to a client of *ours*, had decided to up his asking price by ten thousand.' He grinned. 'Which made Lucius absolutely livid, because our client had written to him originally quoting what was now the take-it-or-leave-it price as the maximum he was prepared to pay. Still, these things happen, and the locals around here are far more aware of what their property will fetch than they were twenty years ago.'

'Yeah. Yeah, right.' I was frowning. 'You discuss anything else? Like the Maecilius case, maybe?'

'No. Not at all. There isn't a lot to discuss about the Maecilius case, barring how to get Fimus out the other side of it with as much of his patrimony intact as possible. When it comes to court next month it'll be a straightforward head-to-head, and I'm afraid that any exchange between me and Lucius on that subject latterly took the form mostly of mutual commiseration. It was one of the few topics we still saw eye to eye on.'

'Right. Right.' I'd been standing next to one of the pedestals with a portrait bust on top, the one of the young woman. Now I half turned and caught it gently with the edge of my arm. The bust rocked a little and I put out a hand to steady it. 'Sorry, pal. I'm getting clumsy in my old age.'

'No harm done,' Acceius said.

'That, uh, your first wife?'

Clarus had finished winding the bandage and was slitting the end and tying it in place. He hadn't said a word all the way through, although I'd've betted he was listening hard, but our eyes met and he half grinned at me over Acceius's shoulder. A smart cookie, Clarus.

Acceius hesitated, just for a moment. Then he said, 'Yes, that's Tascia. How did you know I'd been married before?'

I shrugged. 'Someone mentioned it to me. Maybe it was Aunt Marcia. She's a devil for family histories, especially when they don't concern her.'

Acceius was reaching for his tunic. 'Thank you, Clarus. That's very comfortable.' He pulled it over his head and said, 'She died a long time ago, Corvinus. More than twenty years, now, before I moved here. It was . . . she died in childbirth; something went wrong, she wouldn't stop bleeding. She was only eighteen.' His head reappeared; there was a trace of tears in his eyes.

'I'm sorry,' I said.

He stood up. 'Nonsense. I told you, it's twenty years ago and more. Water under the bridge, long forgotten. Now; is there anything else I can tell you?'

'Uh-uh.' I shook my head. 'That's it for the present, pal. Glad to see you're not too much the worse for wear. Clarus? Walk you back?'

'Fine.' Clarus took a box of pills from his belt-pouch and set them on the table. 'To help if the pain gets bad, sir,' he said. 'And to help you sleep. They're quite strong, so only one in four hours.'

'Thank you. And thank your father, too.'

'He'll call in ten days to remove the stitches. One of your own slaves can change the dressing for you – daily, please – but if there's any inflammation of the wound you're to contact us at once.'

'Understood. Thank you again. Goodbye, Valerius Corvinus.'

We left. There was no sign of Seia Lucinda – hadn't been, when I'd arrived – but it was early, so presumably she was in the family rooms having her hair done and her make-up applied. I wondered if Tascia had been anything like her replacement; probably not, from the fresh, girlish look of her portrait.

Clarus didn't speak until we were well clear of the door. Finally, he said, 'Is Acceius still on the suspect list, Corvinus?'

I grinned. 'Pal, at this stage of the game I am not ruling *anyone* out.'

'Well, he most certainly didn't stab himself. Or have himself stabbed to get himself off the hook. Dad says if the knife had gone in he'd've died for sure. He almost did, anyway, the amount of blood he lost.'

'What about that description of the attack? It work out?'

'Sure.' Clarus frowned. 'Upward-slanting wound, left lower back, deeper nearer the spine than at the side. If the man came from behind and held the knife low, underarm stab upwards from the right, and Acceius had twisted to his left then that's how it would've happened. The description of the man'd work too: tall, but not as tall as Acceius, capable of a fair degree of force.'

'Also no amateur,' I said. 'Real knifeman's punch, no overarm shit.'

He nodded. 'You noticed that.'

'Uh-huh.'

'Perhaps you should forward the description to Quintus Libanius. Not many strangers in Castrimoenium, and if Acceius belted him in the mouth it'll make him even easier to recognise.'

I looked at him sideways. 'Fancy going and telling your granny to suck eggs, son?' I said.

Clarus laughed. 'I'm sorry.'

'That's okay. No offence.' We walked on for a bit in silence: Hyperion's house – and his surgery – were near the temple of Juno; south of the market square, in other words, and as Acceius had said not all that far from the Bovillan Gate. 'You noticed the business with the bust.'

'Yes. I didn't know he'd been married before. How did you find out?'

'Gabba. He said there'd been nothing funny about the death that he'd heard of, and childbirth deaths are common enough, but a sudden widower getting hitched again practically before his wife's bones've cooled is bound to be suspicious. Especially to a stunner – a *rich* stunner – like Seia Lucinda.'

'And did he? I mean, that quickly?'

I shrugged. 'Maybe I'm exaggerating. It was two years. But from what Gabba said they took up together fast enough.'

'You've got a nasty mind, Corvinus.'

'Yeah. Still, what kind of wife-murderer keeps a bust of the victim in his private study? And those tears weren't fake.'

We were almost at Hyperion's door now. Clarus stopped. 'Any idea who attacked him?' he said.

'Uh-uh. My best guess is the obvious one: a friend or relative of the guy who attacked Hostilius. Of course, then we've got the question of why. Was it because originally both partners were targets or out of revenge because Acceius had killed the man's pal?'

'Could it have been Castor?'

I looked at him sharply. 'Why the hell should Castor want Acceius dead? It was Hostilius he had the trouble with. Besides, if it'd been Castor Acceius would've said so.'

'Yes. I suppose that's true.' Clarus hesitated. 'It was just an idea, and he is missing, after all.'

'Jealousy's a terrible thing, pal,' I said, grinning. 'Don't let it warp your judgment.'

He grinned back and ducked his head. 'Fair point. You coming in?'

'No, I think I'll get on. I wanted to have another word with Veturina. Oh, one thing more, before I go.'

'Yes?'

'Publius Novius, the lawyer over in Bovillae. He got any sort of reputation locally?'

'Not really, in the sense that you mean, at least that I've heard of. He's been in the business for years, of course, and you don't get to be a successful lawyer without knowing when to take the main chance. You have any particular reason for asking?'

'No. Or rather, maybe, but it's just an idea at present. Thanks, Clarus. You coming round for dinner this evening?'

'I might be.'

'Fine. See you then.'

I set off for Veturina's.

16

She was in her private sitting-room this time. The room was practically identical to the one further along the corridor, that Hostilius had used – big, light and airy, opening on to the portico and the garden – except that instead of bookcases stuffed with law books the place was full of plants, growing plants as well as vases of cut flowers. No couches, either, just the well-padded high-back chair where Veturina was sitting, a low table and a couple of stools.

'Valerius Corvinus. Welcome. Do sit down.' The lady was still wearing her mourning mantle. 'That's all,' she said to the slave who'd brought me. He bowed and exited.

I pulled up one of the stools and sat. 'Veturina, I—' I began.

She held up a hand. 'First let me apologise for the . . . well, the scene I made two days ago when you were last here. I was overwrought, yes, but that's no excuse. I behaved dreadfully.'

'No problem.' I cleared my throat. 'Ah . . . I was just wondering about your brother. Whether he—'

'Whether he's at home this time? Yes, he is, actually.'

I stared at her. '*Castor's back?*'

'I've just said so.' She was looking at me coolly. 'He came back an hour or so ago. I'm sure he'd be glad to speak to you if you have the time.'

'Where's he been?'

'Staying with a friend in Bovillae. But that's something you can ask him about yourself.'

Jupiter! 'You knew, last time I was here, that he'd been

missing for eight days, didn't you, lady?' She said nothing, but her lips tightened. 'Did you know where he was then?'

'No. I might have guessed, but I didn't think—'

'He didn't call back that evening? The day he had the quarrel with your husband in town? He wasn't here when you had your own row with Hostilius and he told you he wanted him out of the house?'

Two red spots had formed on her cheeks. '*Valerius Corvinus!*'

Oh, hell; here we went again. None the less . . . 'I'm sorry, Veturina,' I said, 'but this is too important for pussyfooting. I just can't believe that Castor disappeared into the blue without telling you where he was going, or at the very least that you knew he'd gone and why. And *that* raises the question of why you tried to cover for him.'

She was glaring at me now. 'If Scopas has told you—' she began.

'It isn't Scopas's fault,' I said quietly. 'He started by lying to me too, only I twisted his arm and threatened to ask you yourself. He was just saving you pain, or thought he was.'

'Then I've nothing further to say on the matter.' Her lips clamped shut.

I sighed. 'Very well, lady. You're being really, really foolish, but have it your way. I'll just have to ask the guy himself.' I stood up. 'This is where you saw Cosmus from?'

'Yes,' she said stiffly. 'He came out of the portico to the right and went down the garden towards the gate at the far end.'

I stepped out on to the portico and looked along it. Yeah; there was the door Scopas had brought me in by on the previous occasion, with the opening to Hostilius's sitting-room beyond it. Not all that far, only a few yards. 'Incidentally,' I said, 'the, uh, day that Quintus Acceius came to see your husband, the day after he was attacked, did they meet in his room?'

'Yes.' The ice was still in Veturina's voice, but I had the impression that – again – she was beginning to regret the way she'd behaved. Not changed her mind, just begun to be sorry she hadn't been a little less abrasive. Definitely not a looker before she leaped, Hostilius's widow. 'That's right.'

'And you were here?'

'I was.'

'You hear anything? Of the conversation?'

'Valerius Corvinus, I am not in the habit of eavesdropping!'

'Right. Right.' She'd hesitated for a split second, though, before she'd answered, and that was interesting, especially since what I'd got wasn't a simple denial. Grieving widow though she might genuinely be, I had very serious doubts about Veturina. I didn't trust her much above half, for a start. 'Just checking. Quintus Acceius told me it was bread-and-butter legal business, nothing very important.'

'Oh, you've asked him already?' She looked relieved. 'Yes, that's right. Or the occasional words and phrases that I did hear when the breeze was in the right direction would suggest it, anyway.'

Uh-huh; too quick, lady, too quick! And much too eager. 'Such as?' I kept the tone flat.

'I . . . can't recall anything specific.'

And I was Cleopatra's granny. 'Come on, Veturina!' I said. 'There has to be something you remember.'

She was looking flustered. 'I . . . did hear Lucius mention a Julian inheritance tax law. Or so Castor—' She stopped dead.

I gave it a couple of seconds, then I said neutrally, 'You, uh, passed on what you'd heard to your brother.'

Veturina coloured. 'I may have said something to him later, yes. Just in conversation.'

Just in conversation. Yeah, right. Me, I'd bet a flask of Caecuban to a rotten fig that whatever juicy snippet she'd chosen to pass on *just in conversation* had had nothing to do with inheritance tax; and a second flask that – because she *had* passed it on – I already knew what it must've been, at least in broad outline. 'You heard something that affected Castor, didn't you?' I said.

I caught a quick flash of . . . yeah, it had to be fear; no other word would cover it. Then her face shut down like a door slamming.

'Why on earth should you think that?'

'Acceius mentioned bringing a letter from Publius Novius, the lawyer in Bovillae, informing them that the asking price of a property one of his clients was selling had gone up.'

'So?'

Now *that* was curious. I wasn't wrong – I'd swear on all the sacred shields of Mars I wasn't wrong – but some of the tightness had gone out of her, as if she'd been steeling herself for me to say something different. 'The price went up to just the amount your husband's client was prepared to pay. Me, I'd wonder if that was coincidence. I'd bet that Hostilius had the same thought.'

She was on her feet now. 'How dare you!' she snapped. 'How *dare* you!'

'You want to tell me what the quarrel between your brother and your husband was about?' Silence; she was glaring at me. I stood myself. Our eyes were on a level. 'Fair enough, lady,' I said. 'I'll take it up with Castor himself. Still, I'll give you one piece of advice before I go. Your brother's a grown man now, he should be taking responsibility for his own actions. He doesn't need you to protect him.' *Unless it's the other way round, of course*, I added mentally; but I wasn't going to say it aloud, not to this devious bitch.

'Talk to Castor if you must,' she said. 'Any of the slaves will take you to him. But, Corvinus, I'd be grateful if from now on you left me strictly alone.'

Yeah, well, we'd see about that. I nodded a curt acknowl-edgment and walked out.

He'd got his own suite of rooms, over in the east wing. The slave I'd buttonholed took me there, bowed me into a study and left.

Castor was lying on the reading couch with an open book-roll in his hands: a tall, big-boned, well-built, strong-featured guy, the male equivalent of his older sister. He glanced up and set the book aside.

'Valerius Corvinus?' he said.

I could see why he'd be attractive to women, and why – like Marilla – they wouldn't be too critical. Good-looking, sure, but he also had a deep, serious, *brown* voice and a way of looking straight at you that suggested he meant what he said. There was something in the eyes, though, that I didn't like at all. Hasty first impression or not, when push came to shove I wouldn't trust this bugger an inch. No more than I would his sister.

'Yeah, that's me.' We shook.

'Have a seat.' I pulled up a stool while he got up off the couch and crossed over to a small table with a wine jug and some cups. 'Would you like some wine?'

'Sure.'

He poured for both of us, brought me my cup over then settled back on the couch with his own. 'Right,' he said. 'I assume I'm in for some kind of interrogation.'

'Spot on, pal,' I said.

He'd been smiling: a sort of conspiratorial, all-mates-to-gether smile that faded now that he saw it wasn't getting a return. 'Want to tell me why I should put up with that?' he said.

'Because the day before your brother-in-law died he'd finally got the proof that you were passing on privileged information to a rival firm.' I sipped my wine. 'Because I think you came back here and may not actually have gone wherever the hell you went until the next day, the day of the death, giving you motive *and* opportunity. Because for some reason your sister is lying herself black in the face to protect you. Because you *did* disappear for almost ten days, and that isn't the action of an innocent man. And finally because I can't be bothered to pretend it's anything but an interrogation, because otherwise you'd just give me the fucking run-around.'

He leaned back. The colour – and what little was left of the friendliness – had left his face. 'You can't—' he began.

'Can't what? Talk to you like that? Prove anything? Yes, I can, sunshine. I can do both. As far as the second goes it's just a question of putting the idea into Quintus Acceius's mind and then going over to Bovillae to have a quiet, official word with Publius Novius.'

He stared at me for a good ten seconds, turning the wine cup round and round in his hands. Finally, he set it down.

'All right,' he said. 'Yes, I was giving Novius the occasional scrap of information. But nothing very important, and not for money.'

'For what, then?'

He picked up the book-roll and handed it to me. I looked at the title: a commentary on the praetorian edicts for the last ten years of Augustus's principate. 'This belongs to Novius. He lent it to me a few days ago. I want to be a lawyer, Corvinus; I've wanted it as long as I can remember. If my brother-in-law wouldn't help, wouldn't treat me as an apprentice, then I had to go elsewhere.'

'Come on, pal! You're a free agent! If Novius was willing to take you on then—'

'It wasn't that simple. You know how my brother-in-law was. How do you think he'd've reacted – what do you think the result would've been where Veturina was concerned – if he'd found out I'd joined the rival firm? Besides, the set-up suited Novius already. He wasn't going to change it.'

Yeah, fair points, both of them. Still . . . 'But that's what happened, isn't it? Hostilius did find out. Care to tell me how?'

'I don't suppose it matters, now. Or not much.' Castor took a deep breath and a long swallow of his wine. 'He'd suspected for some time. Months. Then came the business of the letter, that Novius sent and Acceius brought round the last time he was here, raising the price of the Lutatius property. You know about that?'

'Yeah, I know. Go on.'

'That . . . confirmed it for Hostilius. He set a trap. He sent me to the office with some documents that I was to tell Fuscus to take round to one of our clients. He'd left the door to his room open when he'd gone home earlier, and the key in the lock of his deed box. I . . . well, he'd obviously followed me into town and just waited until Fuscus had left and I'd had time to find the open box and look through the contents before sneaking back in. He caught me red-handed.'

'The papers in the box. Any of them unexpected?'

'What do you mean?'

'There wasn't a will in there, by any chance?'

His eyes shifted. 'No. No will. Why should there be?'

Uh-huh. 'No reason. It was just an idea. So then you had the shouting match, Hostilius called you names, Fuscus came in, and you left.'

'Yes. There wasn't anything else I could do.'

'You went home first? Came back here?'

'Not for long. Just long enough to pack some clothes, borrow some money from my sister.'

Liar! I thought, but that I couldn't prove; not yet, anyway. And Veturina would back him to the hilt, I'd bet on that. Probably Scopas, too. 'So where did you go?' I said.

'To a girlfriend of mine. In Bovillae. Her name's Stratyllis.'

'You've been there all this time?'

'Yes.' He must've noticed the look on my face. '*Yes!* She's a dancer, she's got an attic flat in a three-storey building near the town granaries. You can check if you don't believe me. It's the one with the oil shop on the ground floor.'

'You missed the scene between your sister and your brother-in-law?'

'*Yes!* I told you, I wasn't here when he got back. Do you think I'd wait around?' He looked sullen. 'If you don't trust Veturina to confirm it you can ask Paulina. She would've been there, I expect.'

'Paulina? The ward? She's gone to stay with her aunt in Rome.'

Castor frowned. 'She hasn't got—' he began. Then he clammed up, so suddenly that I could almost hear his teeth click.

Everything went very quiet. 'Hasn't got what?' I said finally.

'Nothing.' He took a sip of his wine. 'I'm just back, Corvinus, I didn't know. Veturina didn't mention it.'

'Paulina hasn't got an aunt in Rome to go to, has she?' I kept my voice very soft. 'So where the hell has she gone?'

'I don't *know!* I told you, I'm just back myself! All I know is, she was here when I left. Ask Veturina.'

'Yeah,' I said, getting up. 'Yeah, I'll just do that now.'

It took me the best part of half an hour and the threat of a full-scale torture of the household slaves to drag the information out of Veturina that her ward had disappeared the morning of Hostilius's death with what she could pack into a carpet-bag. Or so Veturina said. Veturina had no idea where the girl had gone or why she had gone at all. Or so Veturina said. Some clothing had disappeared at the same time from the slaves' washing line, boy's clothing that, when worn with a freedman's cap and roughspun cloak which had also disappeared, would guarantee that no one would look twice at the wearer, let alone see a fifteen-year-old girl on the run from her upper-class family. Or so Veturina said. Not that I believed the bitch for two consecutive seconds, no more than I believed that shifty brother of hers. They were both lying through their teeth and covering like mad, I'd bet my last copper coin on that. It was only a question of why.

I was simmering nicely as I collected the mare from her mooring-ring by the horse trough; certainly in no mood to give the big red-haired guy in a slave's tunic crossing the courtyard in the direction of the east wing more than a passing glance.

Which, as it turned out later, was one of the biggest mistakes I'd ever made.

17

I was feeling pretty sick when I got back home later that afternoon and reported to Perilla on the terrace. Sick and frustrated and very, very angry.

'I've sent word to Libanius that he's got a missing kid on his hands and that she's been missing for nine days without a fucking dicky-bird from her guardian,' I said. 'That's all we can do. Unfortunately.' I downed a good half of the wine in my cup at a swallow. It tasted sour. 'Me, for two pins, Roman citizen or not, if I were Libanius I'd take the bitch in and sweat her. Her and her sodding brother both.'

'Gently, dear,' Perilla said. 'You don't know the girl's come to any harm. And if Veturina's telling the truth then she genuinely—'

'That woman wouldn't know truth if it sodding jumped up and bit her. And where genuinely's concerned—'

'Marcus, that is *enough*!' Perilla adjusted a fold in her mantle. 'Veturina may be guilty of the sin of omission but there is no evidence that she has actually committed a crime.'

'Gods, lady, they're working a double act, those two! Whether Castor's covering for her or she's covering for him or they're each covering for the other I don't know, but it's happening, and the result is that all I'm getting from both of them is a mixture of stalling, lies and half-truths. It's like wading through fucking glue!' I gulped down the rest of the wine and reached for the jug. 'And if there isn't something rotten behind it all then I'll eat my mantle.'

'Very well,' Perilla said. 'Let's have your case. Against Veturina first, omitting her personal motives for killing her husband, which I'm perfectly willing to concede.'

'Okay.' I took a deep breath. 'Three members of the household went missing either the day before Hostilius died or on the day of the death itself: Cosmus the slave, her brother and her ward. She didn't mention any of them until – this is the point – she was faced with hard outside evidence. Cosmus, fair enough, I'll accept that as far as not reporting him over the wall immediately is concerned she may've had other things on her mind. But she lied to me about when Scopas actually told her that he'd gone, and she certainly lied deliberately first to last about Castor and Paulina.'

'Her reasons?'

'Assuming she's guilty as hell? Or at least knows more about Hostilius's death than she's saying?'

'Yes. Go on.'

'Cosmus because he was supposed to disappear altogether and his body turning up so soon was an embarrassment. Castor . . . well, we'll leave Castor for the moment, because he's the biggie. Paulina . . .' I hesitated.

'Paulina?'

'Because she heard something, or knew something, or suspected something. Maybe as a result of that last scene between Veturina and Hostilius, the day before he died. Something that was too dangerous to let her pass on.'

'Such as what?'

'Perilla, I don't *know*, right? I can't even make a decent guess. But whatever it was she couldn't be allowed to repeat it.'

Perilla was quiet for a moment. 'You think she might be dead, then?' she said.

I nodded. I felt empty. 'Yeah. Yeah, I do. There's a good chance of it, anyway.'

She laid aside the book resting in her lap, that she'd been

reading when I arrived. 'Marcus, this is sheer supposition, and nonsense at that! Veturina's no murderer, you said that yourself! To kill her husband out of kindness, yes, but—'

'Castor's not Veturina.'

'You think he's capable of murder? Of killing not only the slave-boy but his own niece?'

'Foster-niece. If that.'

'Don't split hairs. You know what I mean.'

I sighed. 'Yeah, I know; valid point. Search me, Perilla, I've only met the guy once. He's crooked to the core, sure, absolutely, no question; but a murderer? It's possible; I think he might commit murder if it'd get him something he really wanted, or he was desperate enough, but I could be wrong. Where Paulina's concerned I hope I am.'

'All right. Let's have Castor. Again, I'll concede the motive, because we've been through that.'

'Not quite. Oh, I know the details now of his spat with Hostilius, or at least what he told me they were, which isn't the same thing, and that's fine as far as it goes. But we've got another strand.'

'Namely?'

'The business of the will. The gods know what it has to do with Hostilius's death, if anything, but I'll bet you a gold piece to a poke in the eye that Castor knows more about it than he's saying. That's an avenue to chase. As far as the actual murder goes . . . you want the scenario with Castor as the killer?'

'Yes.'

'Okay. General motive as we said: Hostilius is blocking his career and treating him and his sister like dirt. Add to that, now, that he's been nailed for unprofessional conduct, possibly criminal, and – again possibly – some underhand jiggery pokery involving Maecilius's will. Fair?'

'Fair.'

'So he decides, there and then, to kill Hostilius. Only he's got a major problem because if he *does* kill him it has to be more or less straight away, to stop him blowing the whistle. Unfortunately the quarrel's been witnessed, and if Hostilius is too obviously stiffed then he's the prime suspect. Unless—'

'Unless he disappears from the scene forthwith and Hostilius's death seems due to natural causes.' Perilla was frowning. 'You know, dear, this is quite clever.'

'Then he has his stroke of genius involving the medicine bottle, which gets round the obvious murder snag. The only problem *now* is that he can't manage things without help, witting or unwitting, because ostensibly from now on he's shacked up with his girlfriend in Bovillae, with whom ten gets you fifty he's since arranged an alibi.'

'The help being Veturina.'

'Right. How much the lady knew or guessed about what was going on beforehand I don't know, but let's be charitable and say she only made the connection much later, when Libanius told her about the medicine. Anyway, Castor rides back to the villa, explains the situation – that he's had an almighty row with Hostilius and has to leave first thing in the morning – and clears off out of the way—'

'Hold on, Marcus. What about Scopas? Wouldn't he have known, if Castor was in the house?'

'Scopas could be squared, lady; after all, Veturina and Castor are family, and if push came to shove, given the circumstances, he might well support them over Hostilius. Besides, as far as he was concerned the actual murderer was Cosmus.'

'Yes, what *about* Cosmus?'

'I reckon you can play him two ways, depending on how much of a cold, calculating bastard you think Castor is. Not that it matters all that much, because it comes to the same thing in the end. Scenario one is that Cosmus's involvement wasn't deliberate on Castor's part. Maybe the boy suspected something for some reason and kept his eyes open, maybe it was a total accident, but he finds out what's going on and Castor has to take him into account. Scenario two is that Castor set him up from the start so as to have an insurance policy in case things went wrong.'

'The first seems much more likely.' Perilla was twisting a strand of her hair. 'It's the same argument we used for Veturina: recruiting Cosmus would've been more of a risk than a benefit.'

'Yeah.' I took a sip of wine. 'Fair enough. Besides, the impression I'm getting of Castor is that he's someone who can improvise and think on his feet. The same goes for Veturina. Remember, the subject of Cosmus didn't come up until his body was found, and like I say I don't think that was supposed to happen, not until all this had blown over anyway. My bet is that Castor thought that if he had to kill him – which he did, for safety – he might as well turn a profit on the deal, make him an insurance policy after all. When he did his trick with the medicine bottle, he stole the ring and so on out of the desk drawer and gave them to Cosmus. Then if things went pear-shaped in future—'

'Marcus. Wait. Are you saying that Cosmus wasn't in Hostilius's room at all?'

I nodded. 'It was Castor, the whole thing. If Veturina saw anyone at all from her room coming out through the portico – and I'd bet good money that she didn't – it was her brother. Like I said, they've been covering for each other: Castor makes sure that, if a murder *is* suspected, there's a ready-made murderer provided with a ready-made motive of simple theft; while Veturina conveniently remembers seeing said murderer leaving the scene of the crime. It fits. It's perfect.'

'Then Castor gives Cosmus the stolen articles and tells him to run off to the Bavius farm where he—' Perilla stopped. 'I'm sorry, but that doesn't make sense.'

'What doesn't?'

'If Cosmus hadn't been directly involved in the murder, then why should he run? Especially with stolen goods from the dead man's room in his possession. The boy may've been stupid, but he can't've been that stupid. He would have suspected he was being used, surely.'

'Fine. So what's to stop Castor from having planted the stuff on the body after he killed the kid but before he pitched him down the well?'

'That's . . . more viable.' Perilla was looking thoughtful. 'You'd still have to explain how he persuaded Cosmus to go to the Bavius place and stay there, mind. And if he did manage to invent a plausible reason for sending him to an empty property, one that didn't involve the element of subterfuge where the boy was concerned, how would he know that Cosmus wouldn't tell someone where he was going, or keep his presence there a secret? I'm sorry, Marcus, but it still raises serious questions of practicality.'

'Yeah.' I frowned. Bugger: she was right. In any case, it was pure theorising. What we needed now were hard facts. 'Okay, never mind. That's as far as we can go at present. Leave it.'

'Very well. So what's the next step?'

That was the biggie; worse, it was a question I really, *really* didn't have an answer to. 'The gods know. Follow up the business with the will, at least; that's a loose end that needs tying. Apart from that' – I took a morose swallow of wine – 'just hope like hell that somewhere there isn't another body.'

The problem with the last one was that the cold feeling in my gut told me that there was. It was only a matter of time before we found it.

18

I was over at Six Cedars fairly prompt the following morning. It was an old-fashioned working farm, which meant the farmhouse itself was part of a rambling complex of stables, workshops and storage rooms centred round a rough-cobbled courtyard that was definitely seriously bucolic in parts. I made my way carefully past the worst spots and knocked on the door. A slave opened it, a house-slave, sure, but not the neatly tunic'd variety; strictly functional, like the rest of the place.

'Yes, sir?' he said.

'Is the master in?' I said.

'Master's up in the top field harvesting beets, sir. Mistress is in the solar, if you want to see her instead.'

'Yeah, that'd be fine.' What was her name? Bucca had told me. 'Uh . . . Faenia, isn't it?'

'That's right, sir. Oh, no need to wait, I'll take you straight through. Follow me, and mind your head. The lintel is a bit low.'

I went in. He wasn't kidding: the place must've been built when Cato was in rompers, and not by anyone who'd much time for spacious rooms and high ceilings. Dark, too. He led me through a maze of stone-flagged corridors to a room at the end of a passage with a door that was six inches of solid oak.

'Here we are, sir.'

He opened the door for me, and light spilled through: a big room full of old-fashioned, heavy furniture and with a big south-facing window. The woman sitting by an easel at the far end of it turned as I went in.

I'd never met Fimus, but as old Maecilius's son he had to be in his late fifties at the very least. If so then his wife was a good fifteen or twenty years younger; no spring chicken, sure, but not much more than halfway through her forties. She wasn't a bad looker, either: her figure might be what you'd charitably call 'comfortable', but she'd a pretty enough face and a nice smile.

'Yes?' she said.

'Valerius Corvinus,' I said. 'I'm—'

'Oh. Lucius Hostilius's death.' The smile had set. She put down the paintbrush she'd been using, and it rolled unnoticed off the table and on to the floor. 'A dreadful business. Shocking.'

I looked at the picture on the easel: one of these standard still lifes you get, with a dead hare and assorted vegetables. The actual bits and pieces were arranged on a small table in front of her, and there wasn't much resemblance between them and the painting. Forget the hare: even the carrot looked suspect.

'Unusual hobby,' I said.

'Yes. I've painted since I was a girl. One of our slaves taught me.' She glanced towards a settle against the white-plastered wall, but then her eyes came back to me and she said, 'What can I do for you, Valerius Corvinus?'

I was having to revise my ideas about Faenia pretty drastically. I'd expected a fairly typical Latin farmer's wife, stolid, grey-haired and country-spoken, and this lady wasn't her. Oh, sure, she had the rural Latin burr, but it'd been smoothed out so much as to be practically unnoticeable; and an *artist?* Not a very good one, granted, but all the same I reckoned you could count the number of artistic Latin farmers' wives on the fingers of one hand and still have three or four left over. Not that there'd be all that many more Roman matrons ditto, mind you. 'Uh . . . it's a bit embarrassing,' I said. 'Your husband had a . . . call it a disagreement with Hostilius the day before he died. No hassle, lady, I'm just filling in the corners, but I was wondering if he'd care to tell me about it.'

Was it my imagination, or did the eyes shift? 'Marcus is out in the fields at the moment,' she said. 'I can get one of the slaves to take you to him if—'

'Unless you can tell me about it yourself, of course. I understand it could've had something to do with a missing will.'

She stood up quickly; no smile now, there was a definite tremor in her voice and a redness in her cheeks. 'No, I'm afraid you'd really have to speak to Marcus himself,' she said. 'It's no problem, I'll get Venustus to take you.' She walked past me to the door, opened it and shouted, 'Venustus!'

I hadn't moved. 'Your father-in-law stayed with you here?' I said. 'In this house?'

'The . . . the other way round. We lived with him.' She was sounding nervous as hell now, and her eyes were fixed on the corridor outside. '*Venustus!*'

'Only your brother-in-law said that he'd made a new will just before he died, and that he thought your husband's father had delivered it to his lawyers.' I kept the conversational tone. 'Maybe it didn't get that far. Maybe it did.' I shrugged. 'Maybe it never existed in the first place. It'd be nice to know for sure.'

I might as well have been talking to the wall for all the attention she was paying me. 'I'm sorry about this,' she said, and there was a definite tremor in her voice. 'He must've gone back to the kitchen, and he'll be out of earshot. I'll show you to the front door myself and there'll be someone outside who can take you to Marcus. Follow me, please.'

And she was off, without a backward glance. I went after her, but she didn't slow her pace or turn her head until we reached the entrance lobby, and even then she checked only long enough to open the door.

There was a slave wheeling a barrowload of manure across the yard.

'Onesimus!'

He stopped and tugged his forelock. 'Yes, madam?'

'Take Valerius Corvinus here to the master straight away, please. He's in the top field. A pleasure to have met you, Valerius Corvinus. I hope Marcus can help you more than I can.'

She stepped back to let me past, her hand on the door to close it behind me. I turned and rested my own hand on the door-jamb.

'Incidentally,' I said. 'You don't happen to know a guy by the name of Castor, do you? Hostilius's—'

But that was as far as I got before I had to whip my hand away and the door was closed quickly and firmly on a pair of very frightened eyes.

I stared at the woodwork, brain racing. Shit!

Fimus – Marcus Maecilius – was a big guy, huge-limbed and shaggy as a bear, in heavy countryman's boots and a rough, homespun tunic that looked like it'd started out in life as a sack for turnips and might be that again some day. He and his slaves – and a kid of about ten who was his spitting image in miniature – were topping beets and throwing them into a wagon. He looked up as I trudged across the remainder of the crop towards him. Right: I'd forgotten about Gabba's Fimus/Polyphemus gag, but the second name fitted him as well. His single eye glared at me through a mass of tangled black hair.

'Yeah?' he said.

'Valerius Corvinus.' I waved my thanks to the yard-slave who'd brought me and was turning to go back. 'Looking into—'

'Lucius Hostilius's death. I know. What's it to do with me?'

Not exactly brimming over with cheerful welcome and bonhomie, this guy. Ah, well. 'I, uh, was wondering if you could help me out over a couple of things,' I said.

The stare rested a moment longer. Then he spat to one side, shoved his beet-topping knife into his belt and lumbered over. Close to, he had the same bucolic smell as his courtyard: score another one for the Castrimoenian nicknamers. 'Carry on, lads,' he growled over his shoulder to the slaves. 'This won't take long.'

I nodded towards the kid. 'Your grandchild?' I said.

'Yeah.' Then, maybe because he thought he was overdoing the unfriendly bit: 'He belonged to my only son and daughter-in-law. They died of a fever eight years ago come August.'

'I'm sorry,' I said.

He shrugged. 'These things happen. So what d'you want?'

'I understand you had a run-in with Hostilius the afternoon of the day before he died,' I said, keeping my voice as unthreatening as possible: Fimus Maecilius had as much chance of winning the All Comers' Friendliness Stakes as he did the Mr Charisma title or the Perfumiers' Customer of the Year award, and his hand was resting casually on the knife hilt.

'That's right.'

I waited. Nothing more. 'Uh . . . care to tell me what it was about?' I said.

'He accused me of keeping back a second will that Dad was supposed to've made in favour of that poncy brother of mine.'

'And did you?'

That got me a long, hard stare. Finally, he said, 'No. I didn't.' He turned away, cleared his throat and spat to one side. 'Now if that's all you wanted to know I've got work to do.'

'So why did Hostilius think you had?' I said.

He turned back, slowly. 'Listen,' he said. 'Dad had no more time for that chancer than I have, never did. He wouldn't't've left him a penny if he hadn't been kin. And what Lucius Hostilius might've thought was his own business. I don't bear the man a grudge, mind, least of all now he's dead, but he'd some queer ideas these last few months, did Hostilius. He wasn't responsible for half what he said. You had to make allowances.'

'So where do you think your brother got the idea from?' I said.

'Of Dad making the will? Or of me hiding it?'

'Either. Both.'

He spat again. 'Out of his own head, probably. Bucca was always full of piss and wind. Or it could've been that fancy lawyer of his over in Bovillae put him up to it.'

'What about your brother's offer? To split the cash with you and give you a third of what he got for his half of the property?'

I thought I'd gone too far. His head went down like a bull's and his shoulders hunched. 'Look, Corvinus,' he said. 'This is my land, all of it, every inch, and it stays that way. I've farmed it all my life, my father farmed it all his, so did his father and his grandfather, right the way back to when you fucking Romans were still sitting on your fucking seven hills minding your own fucking business. And when I go young Aulus over there' – he nodded towards his grandson – 'will farm it after me. Bucca can take his offer and stuff it. That answer you?'

'Yeah,' I said quietly. 'Yeah, it'll do.' I'd been afraid he'd say that because it made things really, really nasty, but, well, that was life. You had to take it as it was. 'Thanks for your help, pal. Sorry to've troubled you. Much obliged.'

He didn't answer. I could feel his single eye boring into my back all the way across the field to the road.

★   ★   ★

The news was waiting for me when I got back home. A messenger had arrived from Libanius to say that a hunter and his dog had found a woman's body in the woods near Caba, and if I was in before lunch would I ride up there asap.

Hell!

19

It wasn't an easy place to find, even with Libanius's detailed instructions: two or three hundred yards up a heavily wooded cart track off the main drag about a mile before the village, with no other houses or farms anywhere in sight. The back of beyond, in other words.

Libanius and Hyperion were waiting for me, together with a couple of the town's public slaves and a mule-cart plus – presumably – the guy who'd found her, minus his dog.

'We've only just got here ourselves, Corvinus, no more than ten minutes ago.' Libanius was looking green. Shit: however the kid had died, it must've been nasty. 'She's over there, by the rock wall. Whoever killed her covered the body with brushwood, but the dog . . . well.' He stopped. 'Of course, it might have nothing to do with the Hostilius business at all, but contrary to current showing we don't actually have all that many murders around here, so I thought you'd like to know.'

I was feeling sick, and depressed as hell; had been since I'd got the news. 'Sure it's connected,' I said. 'It has to be. Paulina was his ward.'

'Paulina?' Libanius was looking puzzled. 'Why on earth should it be Paulina?'

I stared at him like he'd grown an extra head. 'You mean it isn't?'

'Certainly not! I've known the girl for years! Besides, I distinctly told the messenger to say it was a woman's body.

She must've been forty-five if she was a day, and I've never seen her before in my life.'

Shit. I turned to Hyperion. 'Uh . . . how did she die?'

'Strangled with her own necklace. Do you want to see, Corvinus?'

'Yeah.' My brain still felt numb. 'Yeah, sure.'

'I'll just wait here, if you don't mind,' Libanius said faintly.

We went over to view the corpse. Uh-huh. I could see Libanius's point: not pretty, not pretty at all. 'How long has she been dead?' I said, looking down at her. Forty-five was probably about right; maybe a little older, but it was difficult to tell under the circumstances. Tall for a woman, chunkily built. 'Any idea?'

'More than a day. Probably not longer than three.'

'What was she doing out here?'

'I'm sorry.' He smiled. 'That's your department, Corvinus, not mine.'

Fair enough. 'Anything else you can tell me, pal?'

'Not a lot. She wasn't a gentlewoman, as you can tell from her clothes' – she was wearing a rough ankle-length tunic, belted at the waist with a knotted rope, and cheap sandals of undressed hide – 'but more importantly from the state of her hands.' He held one up, back, then palm. 'You see? Short chipped nails, trimmed with a knife, not scissors. Rough skin. She's been used to manual work. Her teeth aren't bad, though, and there's no obvious slave mark, so probably freeborn. No jewellery, apart from the necklace, and that's just a cord with an evil-eye stone.'

'You've no idea who she was?'

'No. Nor had the man who found her – you can ask him for yourself – and he's local, so she probably isn't from Caba or anywhere around here.'

Uh-huh. Like the guy who'd attacked Hostilius, in other words. And the guy who'd knifed Acceius. Interesting. Still, there were differences. I hadn't seen the other corpse, of course, but from what the undertaker Trophius had said that guy had been a good step down from this lady, socially. She may not have been a gentlewoman, sure, but she was no tramp: she hadn't been starving, and she'd kept herself in reasonable trim. Also, although her clothes were cheap they were no worse than you'd see on, say, a vegetable-seller in the market.

'I'll be taking her home with me, if Libanius doesn't mind, for Clarus to have a closer look at.' Hyperion dropped the woman's hand and stood up. 'He has sharper eyes than I have, and to be frank a sharper mind for extrapolating detail. External details, at any rate.'

I swallowed. Jupiter! Yeah, well, like I say, doctors are a different species, but the matter-of-fact way Hyperion talked about the dead woman, like she was some sort of parcel to be carted back and unwrapped, gave me a cold feeling in my stomach. And I'd bet that Clarus would be the same as his dad. 'You're not going to . . . ah . . . open her up, then? Like Cosmus?'

'Good gracious, no!' Hyperion smiled again. 'Much though I'd like to on general principles I doubt if Libanius would allow the law to be stretched that far. Besides, it's obvious how she died.' He indicated the bulging eyes, protruding tongue and purple face, plus the necklace cord twisted tightly round the throat, as if they were botanical specimens. I swallowed again. 'He must've been strong, whoever did it, though. She was quite a powerful woman.'

'Yeah.' I turned away and walked over to the guy without the dog. 'Hi, friend.'

He nodded cautiously. 'Afternoon, sir.'

'Anything you can tell me at all?'

'Not a lot, that you don't know already.' He had the slow, Latin burr in spades. 'I was hunting, just after sunrise. Blackie

– that's the dog – she started rooting around over there and barking. I went to look and there she was.'

'Covered up?'

'Yes, sir. Dead branches, some green stuff. Just where she is now. I went back home – I've a farm this side of Caba, sir – and the wife says get the hell down to the authorities in Castri-moenium, tell them. So I did.'

'You're sure she's not local?'

'She's not from Caba or anywhere five miles around, that I'll swear, and I'm not mistaken, even though it's difficult to—' He stopped. 'No, sir, she isn't local. Certainly not.'

'So what could she've been doing here?'

He shrugged. 'No idea, sir. Nothing around here, you can see for yourself. Mine's the closest farm, and that's on its own and half a mile off. It's rough country, this bit, only good for hunting.'

'There's a cart track, though. Where does that lead?'

'Nowhere. Leastways, it stops a few hundred yards further on. Charcoal burners use it, but not all that often.'

'So nobody would be up this way? In the normal course of events?'

'Oh, you'd get passing traffic on the main road, sure, plenty of that, what with the quarry and all.' Yeah; I remembered the Caba quarry. So that was still a going concern? 'Not up here, though.'

'Right. Thanks, pal.'

'You're welcome.'

I turned back to Libanius, who was taking the air well away from where the corpse was lying.

'Finished, Corvinus?' he said.

'Yeah. Nothing more I can do,' I said.

'Good.' Obvious relief; I grinned to myself. He signalled to the slaves. 'You can load her on to the cart now, boys.'

As the lads went over – I noticed that one of them had a

stretcher and a blanket – I moved back across to Hyperion and took his arm. 'Quick word, pal?' I said. 'Before I go?'

'Certainly.'

'It's . . . ah . . . nothing to do with the body. Or the case. I was just thinking we'd best, uh, think about fixing things up between Clarus and Marilla. If you're agreeable, that is.'

Hyperion smiled. 'Oh, I'm agreeable, Valerius Corvinus,' he said. 'Very much so. And I can certainly answer for Clarus.'

He held out his hand, and we shook. Well, that was that arranged, anyway. I collected my mare from where I'd parked her tied to a tree and rode back to Castrimoenium. Maybe under the circumstances a half jug in Pontius's wouldn't go amiss.

I'd left the mare fraternising with a couple of her cronies at the town square watering-trough and was heading towards the wineshop's veranda when I saw Meton. He was standing on the corner of one of the side streets, dressed to the nines in a snazzy blue tunic, and he was talking to a woman. Not just any woman either: mid-twenties max, and with a face and figure that would've made Praxiteles bite his chisel.

The woman laughed. So did Meton . . .

I gaped. Meton never laughed, never-fucking-ever. Sneered, yeah; Meton could do sneer with the best of them, it was his natural default expression. The bugger could even chuckle, if something happened to tickle his warped, sadistic sense of humour. But *laugh*? And with a *woman*? A woman who would've knocked the eyes out of a septuagenarian priest at fifty yards?

Forget the wine; we'd got serious problems here. And I'd caught the bastard slap bang in flagrante. I changed direction, fast.

I'd got to within ten yards, just close enough to hear her say:

'Make it tomorrow, then,' and Meton to answer: 'Yeah, right.'
Then she turned and walked off up the street.

'Oh, hi, Corvinus.' Meton did a double-take when he saw
me coming and gave me his best scowl. 'Didn't see you there.'

'Yeah, I'd sort of assumed that, pal,' I said. 'Who the hell
was that?'

'Her name's Renia.'

'That so, now?' I took another glance at the retreating
figure. Gods! Make that an octogenarian priest at sixty yards.
'What were you talking about?'

'This an' that.'

'Meton . . .'

' 'S my own business, innit?' He inserted a finger in his ear,
screwed out a bit of wax and flicked it away. Then he leered.
'Good-looker, though, isn't she?'

'Meton, you bastard . . .'

' 'S okay. She's married.'

'*She is what?*'

'Yeah. Husband's a locksmith.' He sniggered. 'Not a very
good locksmith, from what I hear.'

Oh, gods! This was the stuff of nightmare. And *Meton?* To
my certain knowledge the closest that single-minded bugger
ever got to having designs on a woman was lusting after her
recipe books. 'Ah . . . listen, pal,' I said. 'I'm being serious
here. Do you have any – *any* – idea what the penalty is for a
slave who . . . devalues a freeborn wife?'

'Uh-huh.' Another leer. 'Might be worth it, though, in
Renia's case.'

I gaped afresh.

'Joke, Corvinus. 'S all under control, nothing to worry
about. Just forget it, okay?' He removed another flake of
wax. 'Now I don't know about you, but I've got better things
to do at present than stand an' chat.'

He ambled off.

I shook my head to clear it. Forget about problems; what we'd got here was a full-blown domestic crisis in spades. Home, and Perilla. Fast.

I made it as far as the lobby. There was a woman there, talking to Marcia's door-slave. She turned as I came in.

'Valerius Corvinus, sir?' she said. Small, middle-aged and mousy, and obviously nervous as hell.

'Yeah,' I said. 'Yeah, that's me.'

'I'm Tyche, sir. The mistress Paulina's maid. She wants to speak to you, sir.'

I stared at her. '*What?*'

She ducked her head. 'The mistress Paulina sent me to say she wants to speak to you, sir. Straight away, if you can manage it.'

Holy gods! 'You know where she is?'

'Course, sir. She's at my cousin's, that's Mika, sir, she's a freedwoman, lives above the baker's near the shrine of Latinus. I . . . well, I arranged it, sir, when the mistress said she wanted somewhere to go.' She hesitated. 'I wouldn't 've come, sir, only the mistress insisted. Don't you believe her, Valerius Corvinus, when you do see her. She don't know what she's saying.'

'Yeah? And what's that?'

Tyche swallowed. 'That she did it, sir. Killed the master.' Shit!

20

Paulina was a wisp of a girl, mid-teens, with a long face, big teeth and mousy hair like her maid's; no looker, certainly, and from the self-effacing way she was sitting on the chair opposite me in what was obviously Mika and her husband's bedroom she was probably more conscious of it than I was. She'd a nice voice, though: low-pitched, quiet and serious.

'I didn't actually kill him myself, Valerius Corvinus,' she said. 'That was Cosmus, I know, because I saw him come out of Uncle Lucius's rooms that morning. Not that I knew at the time what he was doing there, although—'

'Hang on,' I said. 'You *saw* him? You're sure?'

'Oh, yes. Absolutely. At about an hour after dawn. I've been . . . getting up very early these last few months.' She lowered her head, and unaccountably blushed. I noticed that Tyche, who'd come in uninvited and was sitting on a stool by the door, shot her a quick glance.

There was something odd there, but I left it alone for the moment. We'd come back later. 'So where were you?' I said. 'In your room?'

'No. In the garden. He didn't see me, at least I don't think he did, because I was sitting in the little arbour by the rose-bed. You can see out from there, but it's difficult to see in.'

The *garden*? An hour after *dawn*? Odd was right. Still, we'd better sort out the most important point first. 'Paulina,' I said carefully. 'If you saw Cosmus leaving your uncle's rooms and you know – at least now – that he was the killer, then where do you come into things?'

She looked at me wide-eyed. 'Because I was responsible, of course. My uncle wouldn't have died at all if it hadn't been for . . . well, the way he treated me.'

Yeah; I could imagine life hadn't been too pleasant for the kid. After all, if Veturina had been going through hell these last twelve months for no reason then Paulina had probably been doing the same. Even so, for her to suggest that as Cosmus's motive for murder was complete nonsense. From all I'd heard of him he didn't exactly seem the altruistic type; certainly not to the extent of risking his own neck by bumping off his master as a favour to Paulina.

'Uh . . . you sure about that?' I said gently. 'I mean, that that was Cosmus's only reason?'

She was scowling. 'You're down on him like everyone else, Valerius Corvinus, and you never even met him!' she said. 'Do you think that's fair?'

I caught Tyche's eye. Her lips were set in a tight line and she nodded imperceptibly. Yeah, well: whatever the mistress's opinion of Cosmus was, her maid certainly didn't share it. I remembered what Scopas had said, about Cosmus being able to use his charm to get round the youngest members of the family, especially Paulina. Now that I'd seen her for myself, that made complete sense; it certainly explained her view of the boy and the large slice of wishful thinking involved where his motives were concerned. No surprises there, quite the reverse: he'd been good-looking, about her own age, attentive and probably good fun, and even if he was a slave that combination would've weighed a lot with someone like her. She'd never have let things go beyond mild flirting, sure, or if she had done then she was a bigger fool than I thought she was, but I'd bet she hadn't had much experience even of that. Yeah, I could see how Paulina would easily get starry-eyed over Cosmus.

'Maybe it isn't fair, at that.' I temporised. 'And if your uncle was being cruel—'

'I never said he was being cruel.'

Said very quietly. The head was down again, and Tyche was looking at her hard, with pursed lips.

Uh-oh.

I let a few seconds go by. Then I said gently; 'You want to tell me, Paulina?'

'No. But I will.' Her chin came up. 'It . . . never got beyond touching, and that was when Aunt Veturina found out and put a stop to it. Besides, I kept my bedroom door locked so even if he tried to get in he couldn't.'

'That's why you'd been getting up so early, isn't it?' I kept the conversational tone. 'Because he did try.'

'Sometimes, yes. First thing in the morning. Most mornings, by that stage.' She frowned. 'Valerius Corvinus, my uncle was a good man! He was! Before he was ill he'd never, ever have done anything like that, he'd have died first, believe me!' There were tears in her eyes. 'And now he is dead, and I'm glad. And that's terrible.'

Gods!

'No, it isn't,' I said quietly. 'It's not terrible at all. And maybe it's for the best, that part of it. Whoever killed him, and whatever their motives were.'

'Yes.' She nodded. 'Yes, that's what I'm hoping. That they did it for the best of motives.'

There was something in her voice that made the hairs rise on the back of my neck. Besides, that wasn't exactly what I'd said. In fact—

The penny dropped. Oh, shit!

'You think your aunt killed your uncle, don't you?' I said.

'Cosmus killed him.' She wasn't looking at me. 'And I was responsible.'

We needed to take this slowly. I drew a deep breath. 'Look,

Paulina,' I said. 'You may've liked Cosmus – he may've liked you – but you have to admit he wasn't the greatest brain in the world. He'd never have thought of doctoring that medicine bottle on his own, however much he wanted to help you. And if you didn't give him the idea then somebody else must have.'

'I was responsible. My uncle wouldn't have died if—'

'No. Listen. You didn't know, that morning when you ran, that your uncle had been murdered, did you? No one knew, except Cosmus and whoever told him to do what he did, and that wasn't you, was it?' She shook her head. 'Fine. Your uncle was dead, sure, but to all intents and purposes his death was natural. So why did you run? You must've had some reason.' Silence. Bugger! 'Paulina, I'm sorry, but you really have to tell me.' Silence: she'd dropped her eyes again and she was staring at her hands. 'Something'd changed, hadn't it? Something important, so important that when your uncle died right after it happened you linked the two events and you panicked. Maybe it was something you heard, or saw, the evening before when your uncle and aunt—'

'*Stop it!*' Her head came up. She was glaring at me. Over by the door, Tyche shifted on her stool, but she didn't say anything.

'All right,' I said. I leaned back, away from her, and waited.

Paulina's gaze didn't shift. 'My uncle accused Aunt Veturina of sleeping with Uncle Castor,' she snapped. 'He said that as far as he was concerned she was nothing but an incestuous whore, that he wanted her out of his house and that he'd see to the formal divorce and prosecution as soon as they could be arranged. Is that what you want to know?'

Sweet gods!

'Yeah,' I said softly. 'Yeah, that's it. Thank you, Paulina.'

Well, that explained things. Scopas had known, of course, he had to have, and when I'd grilled the poor bastard he'd twisted the truth as far as he dared, given me a sanitised version. For Castor's adultery with Seia Lucinda read incest with his sister with the result that Veturina was under threat of divorce and the two of them, not just Castor alone, were out in the street. Still, I didn't blame the guy for lying, no way: he'd only been protecting his mistress as best he could, for the best of reasons; and, in a way, protecting his master as well. If it'd been me instead of Hostilius, I'd hope that Bathyllus would have the sense to do the same.

Paulina had burst into tears, and Tyche shot over like she was greased. The girl pushed her away and wiped her nose on the sleeve of her tunic. She was still glaring at me. 'If Aunt Veturina did kill him the next morning, Valerius Corvinus,' she said, 'or have him killed, then she had every reason to, and my uncle – my *real* uncle – would've blessed her for it.' I closed my eyes, briefly. 'But she wouldn't have done, not just for herself, I know she wouldn't. She did it for me. If you'd been me what would you have done, when my uncle died? I couldn't stay and face her, every day, not saying anything; not knowing what I knew. I had to leave. I *had* to.'

'Right. Right.' Shit, what a mess!

'Are you going to tell her? Where I am?'

I'd been asking myself the same question. Legally, the answer had to be yes: the girl was Veturina's ward, and no one had formally accused Veturina of any crime. Even so, there were good reasons why I shouldn't, not the least being that the lady herself had tried to cover up the fact that the girl was missing.

'Not if you don't want me to,' I said. 'But I'll have to tell Libanius. Have you got any other relatives anywhere?'

She shook her head. 'No. Not close ones, anyway. That was why Uncle Lucius and Aunt Veturina took me in.'

'Maybe Libanius can arrange something, then.' I stood up; I felt sick to my stomach. 'We'll leave it to him.'

'All right.' Paulina lowered her eyes. 'Thank you for coming, Valerius Corvinus. I'm glad I talked to you. And . . . if you do see my aunt, and it's possible, could you say thank you to her as well, from me? Don't say why, just say I said it.'

'Yeah,' I said. 'Yeah, I'll do that.'

'Veturina killed him, or got her brother to,' I said to Perilla when I finally got home a couple of hours later after a long talk with Libanius. 'And the gods know I don't blame her for it. Him, either.'

'You're absolutely sure?' Perilla was looking grave. We were sitting on the terrace with a pre-dinner drink. I hadn't told her about Meton yet: there was no point in worrying the lady unduly, and anyway I hadn't decided how to handle that particular problem.

'Yeah.' I put my head back and closed my eyes. 'What Paulina said clinches it. The situation had just got impossible, and all three of the family members were involved. If Hostilius had lived another day, Veturina would've been divorced and out of the house, she and Castor would've been formally accused of incest, and unless Paulina went with her aunt she'd've been left alone with her uncle and raped within the month. Veturina'd have to be less than a step down from one of the Graces *not* to kill him.'

'What about Cosmus?'

I opened my eyes and shrugged. 'Under the circumstances, lady, he's a detail, and if it was Castor set things up then he's explicable. Not excusable, but explicable.'

She was quiet for a long time. Then she said, 'What happens now?'

'That's up to Libanius. I've made my report, and he can arrange for Veturina to be prosecuted, with or without her brother, or he can just let the whole business drop. Me, I'd say that'd be by far the best course for all concerned, Hostilius included. Veturina might go through a hard time with the locals, sure, but she can always sell up and move if things get too bad; the same goes for Castor. Case over, close the book.' I slammed my wine cup down. 'Fuck!'

'Gently, Marcus!'

'Yeah, well.'

'What I don't understand is how it was allowed to get this far. The man was clearly certifiable, he wasn't responsible for his actions. Under any reasonable circumstances he would have been locked up months ago.'

'That would've needed the impetus to come from his next of kin,' I said. 'Veturina herself. And it would've been an admission that the situation was hopeless. Where would you have drawn the line yourself, Perilla, if it'd been you who had to decide?' She didn't answer. 'Besides, when push came to absolute shove she made the kindest decision. Oh, Hostilius would've brought the charges, of adultery and incest, like he threatened, I don't doubt that; but no judge in the country who knew the background would've given them a moment's credence. She was safe enough there. Only—'

'Only she'd have to defend herself on the grounds that her husband was insane, with the inevitable result. Then watch him getting worse, more unlike himself, day after day until he died in any case. Hating her for what she'd done.' Perilla shivered. 'The poor woman. The poor *man*. You're right, Marcus, it was the kindest decision she could make.'

'Yeah.' I took a morose swig of my wine.

'What about the rest of it? The dead woman up in Caba and the will? Are you dropping those too?'

I shook my head. 'Uh-uh, or not unless Libanius objects. They may not be pieces of the same puzzle, lady, but they're puzzles that need solving in themselves. Besides, Alexis has been beavering away in the public records office over in Bovillae for the last two days trying to fit a name to the man who attacked Hostilius. If I pulled the plug on him now the guy'd never forgive me. Clarus and Marilla wouldn't be too happy about it either.' I grinned. 'Which reminds me. You want the good news or the bad? Nothing to do with wills or murders. I'd recommend the good, because the bad is pretty horrific, but it's your choice.'

'All right then.' I told her about my short conversation with Hyperion, and she beamed. 'Oh, that is *excellent*! Aunt Marcia will be so pleased!'

Yeah; that was partly why I'd hurried things. Marcia had been taken bad the evening of Libanius's visit, and although Hyperion had said it was nothing really serious, so long as she kept to her bed for a few days, it was a sign of things to come.

'I'm quite pleased myself,' I said. 'Clarus is a nice guy.'

'When did he ask you?'

'For what?'

'Permission to marry Marilla, of course.'

'Ah . . .'

Perilla stared at me open-mouthed. 'You mean he *hasn't*? Not at all?' She started to laugh. 'For Juno's sake, Marcus, you can't just assume that!'

'It'll be okay, lady. Trust me.'

'Oh, I do. I do. It's only that I sort of imagined that the original idea might come from Clarus and Marilla themselves, that's all.'

'Yeah, well . . .'

'So what was the bad news?'

'Meton's having an affair with a married woman.'

Pause. 'I'm sorry, dear? Say that again?'

'Meton's having an affair with a married woman.'

'He's *what*?' Perilla doesn't do gobsmacked, normally. On this occasion she did, in spades.

'Yeah. Her name's Renia, she's married to a locksmith, and she is *hot*.'

'Marcus, this is dreadful! You're absolutely sure?'

'I saw them myself.'

'Oh, *bugger*!'

'Ah . . . Perilla . .?'

She ignored me. 'So what do we do?'

'We could ground him after all and take the consequences. I mean, we're not here forever. Once we go back to Rome—'

'It won't make a blind bit of difference, in fact it'll make things worse. He'll sulk for months. He might even break into the cooking wine.'

I shuddered. The last time Meton had hit the booze it'd taken Decimus Lippillus of the City Watch and an incendiary device to get him out of the kitchen. I wasn't going through that again. 'All right. Suggestions.'

She was drumming her fingers on the table and frowning. 'What about the woman?' she said.

'What about the woman?'

'We could talk to her. Get her to end the affair on her side. After all, she is married, and for a freeborn woman to have relations with a slave is an offence.'

I grinned. 'Blackmail, lady?'

She sniffed. 'In the best of possible causes.'

'Right. Right.'

'Do you know where she lives?'

'No, but it'd be easy enough for Alexis to follow Meton next time he jumps the wall and—' I stopped. 'Bugger. He's in Bovillae, isn't he?'

'What about Bathyllus?'

'Be serious, Perilla.'

'Yes, well, perhaps not. And not Lysias, either, he'd be worse than useless. One of the other slaves, then. Aunt Marcia's.'

'Lady, most of them can practically remember the celebrations after Actium. They couldn't follow a fucking *snail* without sitting down for a rest every five minutes. And I wouldn't trust any of the others to do the job because they haven't got brains enough among them to fill a saltspoon.'

'In that case—'

'Hi, Corvinus. Perilla. Did you have a nice day?'

I turned round. Marilla was coming up the terrace steps, accompanied by the slavering Placida. 'Oh, hi, Princess.'

'Clarus says he might have some information tomorrow for you on the dead woman. I left him having a look at her.'

'Uh . . . right. Right.'

'What's for dinner?'

'Veal with a caraway sauce and green beans in coriander.' Perilla was smiling. 'Or so Bathyllus reports. Marcus?'

'What? Oh. Oh, yeah.' I cleared my throat. 'I, uh, was wondering if you and Clarus would consider getting engaged.'

'Yes. Hyperion said. Of course we would.'

'Ah . . . fine.' I glanced at Perilla. 'That's settled, then.'

'Clarus says the stains on the back of her tunic are especially interesting.'

'Really?'

'But I won't spoil it for him.'

'Good. Uh . . . Princess?'

'Yes?'

'I've got a job for you.'

21

I rode over to Bovillae the next morning; largely to see how Alexis was getting on, but also to pick up a few loose strands. Such as Publius Novius, for example. That guy's name was cropping up far too often for comfort, and, besides, I wanted to see him and judge him for myself.

Bovillae's a lot bigger than Castrimoenium – most places are – but it isn't the hub of the universe, not even close. The records office was in the main square, with a statue of the Divine Augustus outside, arm raised and pointing commandingly in the direction of the public latrine across the way, his noble laurel-wreathed forehead striped with the recent offering of an irreverent pigeon. I parked the mare at the horse-trough and went inside.

'Yes, sir.' The clerk behind the counter looked up. 'What can I do for you?'

'I think you've got one of my slaves here. Guy called Alexis? He's looking for—'

'Oh, yes. You must be Valerius Corvinus. Yes, he's here. You'll find him rather dusty, I'm afraid, but that's only to be expected under the circumstances.' He lifted the counter's wooden flap. 'Come in and I'll take you to him.'

'How's he getting on?' I said as he led me down a gloomy corridor into the heart of the building. 'Any luck yet, do you know?'

'I'm afraid you'll have to ask him that yourself, sir. We don't have much call to dig into thirty-year-old trials as a rule, and

I've had to leave him completely to his own devices. Which I was happy to do, with Quintus Libanius's authorisation.' He stopped at a door, opened it and stepped back to let me through. 'Here we are. Dead records.'

The room was long and narrow, and it had pigeonholes all round the walls, all of them full. It was a sunny day outside, but the only light here came in dust-mote-clouded shafts from latticed clerestory windows high above us. Alexis was perched on a stepladder halfway along. He looked round and down as we came in . . .

Dusty was right; or maybe cobwebby would be a better word if the condition of the guy's tunic and hair was anything to go by. From the look on his face he wasn't exactly full of the joys of spring and goodwill to all men, either. To put it mildly. *Seriously pissed off* would just about cover things, if you didn't mind the gross understatement.

Uh-oh.

'Ah . . . hi, Alexis,' I said. 'How's it going, pal?'

'What does it look like, sir?' He blew a cobweb away from his mouth. 'One guess. Just one. Please consider your reply carefully.'

The clerk smiled nervously. 'I'll leave you to it, then,' he said to me. 'You can find your own way back, I expect?'

He exited.

Alexis rammed the bundle of record tablets he was holding into one of the topmost pigeonholes and came slowly down the ladder.

'So, uh, no luck so far, right?' I said brightly.

He gave me five clear seconds of eyeball. Then he said, 'Valerius Corvinus, do you know how many – *perishing* – trial records there are on these – *perishing* – shelves between the consulships of Lucius Aelius Lamia and Drusus – *perishing* – Caesar?'

'That's the length you've got, is it, pal? Drusus Caesar, eh? Wow, that is very, *very*—'

'One thousand, one hundred and sixty-three. And two-thirds.'

'Two-thirds?'

'Mice.'

I'd been edging back towards the door. 'Congratulations, Alexis,' I said. 'You're doing a sterling job, and I'm impressed. Don't worry, we'll get there eventually.'

'Will we now, sir? Marvellous, bully for us. That cheers me up no end.'

'Ah . . . good. Good. I'm glad.' I found the door-handle and turned it gratefully. 'Now if you'll excuse me, pal, I was just calling in in passing. I've got, uh, important business elsewhere. Don't work too hard. I'll catch you later, okay?'

I left, quickly, before he could unclench his jaw and answer, and made my way back to the counter. So where now? Publius Novius's, obviously. I didn't really have an excuse for calling on the guy, but if Quintus Libanius's name was enough for the records clerk it might just get me a hearing on its own.

'Finished already?' The clerk looked surprised.

'Yeah. No point in distracting the lad while he's working.' I lifted the flap and let myself out. 'You wouldn't happen to know where Publius Novius's office is, would you?'

'Novius the lawyer? Certainly, nothing easier. Only a couple of blocks from here, near the baths. Go out of the door, turn left and carry on straight ahead. There is a sign.'

'Great. Thanks, pal. I'll, ah, call in again this afternoon to see how Alexis is doing before I go back to Castrimoenium.'

'I'm sure he'll appreciate that hugely, sir.'

'Right. Right.'

I left the mare where I'd parked her and followed the directions as given. I hadn't gone more than the distance to the first side street when I noticed an opening twenty yards down it with a sign on the gatepost saying: 'Tuscius: Slaves'.

Had it been Scopas who'd said that Hostilius had bought Cosmus from Tuscius in Bovillae? I couldn't remember off-hand, but it probably had been. In any case, since I was passing it was worth a visit. Cosmus, and how he fitted into all this, still worried me, and if my memory served the kid had been reticent about where he'd been previous to joining the Hostilius ménage.

I took a sharp left and went through the gate . . .

'*Good* morning, sir! And how may I help you?'

Jupiter! That was fast! The guy must've been lurking behind the carefully trimmed topiary peacocks in the yard, like one of Alexis's spiders. He'd the look of an arachnid too: fat belly, spindly legs, greasy smile. Well, the metaphor had to break down somewhere.

'You Tuscius, pal?' I said.

'Marcus Tuscius, yes, sir. You want a slave, I presume? Or several slaves? Always a wide range in stock, sir, to suit every pocket and requirement, every one carrying the Tuscius personal guarantee.'

'Which is?'

'Totally sound in wind and limb when sold, sir. Should he or she drop dead within three months of purchase then we'll replace with equivalent or refund up to three-quarters of the purchase price, conditions apply, *mutatis mutandis*, acts of god and plague excepted. Male slave, sir? Female?' He leered. 'We've a special offer at present on flutegirls. Buy one and you get a Nubian contortionist half price.'

'Ah . . .'

'Or if your tastes run in another direction there's our Ganymede Special. Two luscious, peach-buttocked young—'

'Pal,' I said. 'Just shut up, okay?'

'If you insist, sir.'

'You remember selling a slave by the name of Cosmus to Lucius Hostilius? The lawyer over in Castrimoenium?'

The little piggy eyes narrowed. 'When would this be?'

'Uh . . .' I couldn't remember, exactly. 'A year ago? Maybe two?'

He beamed. 'Out of guarantee, I'm afraid. Even with our extended warranty.'

Gods! 'I'm not here to complain, sunshine. Even though he did murder his master.'

Tuscius blanched. '*He did what?*'

'Not off his own bat. He was put up to it.'

'Nevertheless.' Tuscius glanced nervously over his shoulder. 'Sir, I assure you . . . what's your name?'

'Corvinus. Valerius Corvinus.'

'I assure you, Valerius Corvinus, I would rather have gnawed my own arm off, this arm here, sir' – he held it up – 'than knowingly have sold a defective slave. We'll refund the full purchase price, naturally. If you're the next of kin then subject to your producing notarised verification of the claim and of your own relationship with the deceased—'

'Tuscius . . .'

'—there'll be no difficulty. I'll even throw in a flutegirl as a goodwill gesture, or a peach-buttocked whatever, at a specially discounted price.'

'Pal. All I want to know is where you bought him from.'

He stared at me. 'Really? That's *all?*'

'Watch my lips.'

'Then you'd better come into the office and I'll check my records.'

I did, and he did.

Cosmus had been sold to Marcus Tuscius thirteen months ago by Publius Novius.

Shit!

'You happen to remember anything about the kid?' I said. 'Or the sale itself?'

The eyes took on a guarded look. 'Oh, now, sir. You said very distinctly only a few minutes ago that you only wanted the name of the seller. Besides, I can't be expected to remember every—'

'No hassle, Tuscius. I promise you. On the other hand, when this business reaches open court, as it will, and if I happen to be asked which firm supplied the slave who so tragically—'

'Yes. Yes.' His hand pawed at my sleeve. 'Point taken. Now I come to think, Valerius Corvinus, I do recall something of the boy. Good-looking lad, not the sharpest knife in the drawer but well-spoken enough and with a nice manner. There's quite a turnaround for that sort of slave in the first-time-buyer domestic market. Easy on the eye without being too flash, no problems with temperament, cheap to run, keep their trade-in value well if you want to upgrade after two or three years to a more streamlined model with more between the ears or a bit more oomph in other departments. Of course—'

'Did Novius give you any reason for selling him?'

'Not that I remember offhand, sir. And I wouldn't have the effrontery to ask, not where an old customer like Publius Novius was concerned. He bought the first slave I ever sold, sir, when I took over the business eighteen years back, top-of-the-range, Greek-speaking accountant with all his own teeth and only twenty-eight years on the clock. Didn't quibble over the asking price, either. You don't forget something like that when you're a young man just starting up and have to watch your profit margins; it means a lot. And he's been a regular ever since, not one of the "nip up to Rome where they stack them high and sell them cheap" set, always dealt locally. Honestly, sir, it makes your blood boil when you see—'

'Yeah. Yeah, right. Did, uh, Hostilius buy Cosmus himself? Personally, I mean?'

'No, I've never met the gentleman. That was his wife, sir, and her brother, if I recall correctly. Them I *do* know, or know of, because they're Bovillans. Family has the wineshop by the Appian Gate, has had for years.'

'And this would be when?'

'You saw it in the ledger, sir. Two days after I bought the lad myself.'

Uh-huh. 'That usual, pal? Such a quick turnaround?'

'Not unusual. I said: that kind of slave's popular. They don't spend all that long on the forecourt, not like the really expensive specialist models or some of the two-a-penny agricultural workhorses. A real drag on the market, they can be, sometimes, especially in the winter months when they need more feeding and there isn't all that much for them to do.'

'They just walk in off the street? Veturina and Castor?'

'More or less. That isn't unusual either, sir. I've got quite a thriving business and the stock moves on quite quickly. Also there are the, well, the special offers, sir. So we get a fair number of browsers, and although I can't say the impulse-buyer market's all that significant it's a steady earner.'

'So they weren't regular customers?'

'No. Not per se, as it were.' Tuscius sucked on a tooth. 'Oh, I've sold a few slaves to the Hostilius household over the years, sir, and bought a few as well, but the gentleman'd always dealt through his major-domo up to then. Scopas, the name is, he's a Bovillan too.'

'How do you mean, a Bovillan?'

'He came with the lady as part of her dowry, quite a slice of it too because he knows his job back to front. Not that I sold him to old Veturinus myself, naturally, that was my predecessor in the business. Good eye for a slave, Scopas has. You know him?'

'Yeah, I know him. So Scopas was Veturina's slave originally? Not Hostilius's?'

'No. Technically he was the gentleman's. But old Veturinus
paid the bill.'

I frowned. 'Uh . . . thanks, friend. I'm much obliged.'

'You're most welcome, sir. While you're here you wouldn't
care to look over—'

'No. No, not today.'

'As you please, sir. Don't forget where we are, though.'

'I won't. Thanks again.'

Okay; onward and upward, to Publius Novius's. Like Acceius's
office in Castrimoenium, it was quite a swish affair, with a
prominent sign, a marble-columned porch and a smartly dressed
door-slave. A good business to be in, obviously, the legal trade.

'Good morning, sir.' The clerk was a younger version of
Fuscus, but with the same brisk efficiency. The anteroom was
impressive, too: marble and bronze statues seemed to be de
rigeur where law practice decor was concerned.

'I was hoping to talk to Publius Novius, pal,' I said. 'He
around at present?'

'I'm afraid not. He's in Antium until tomorrow. Was it
urgent?'

'Fairly urgent.' Damn.

'Then I'm sure I can help. Your name is . . .?'

'Corvinus. Valerius Corvinus.' Was that a flicker? 'Actually,
though, it's sort of private and personal. Could I make an
appointment, do you think?'

'No problem at all. Let's have a look at the book.' He
consulted a wax tablet on the desk beside him. 'The day after
tomorrow's relatively free, the morning at least. I can let you
have one first thing, or would you prefer later?'

'Later'd be better. I have to come over from Castrimoenium.'

'Really?' *Definitely* a flicker there. 'Very well. Shall we make it the fifth hour, then?'

An hour before noon. 'That'd be great,' I said.

He made a note. 'And you're sure you wouldn't like to give some sort of indication of what the matter's about? In the most general terms? Just so that Publius Novius can be prepared for you.'

Uh-uh; now that I certainly *didn't* want. 'I'd rather not, friend. Like I say, it's private and personal.'

'Just as you like.' He set the tablet aside. 'I look forward to seeing you then, Valerius Corvinus.'

'Fine.'

So. Just shy of noon, time for a bite of lunch and a cup of wine before I ran a last check on Alexis and headed back. There was a wineshop in the main square with a small terrace outside that looked inviting, but while I was in Bovillae I might as well mix business with pleasure and have them at Veturina's family's place. Next to the Appian Gate, Tuscius had said, so I must've passed it on the way in.

The mare looked quite happy where she was, by the horse-trough, it wasn't all that far and I'd have to come back anyway. I set off towards the gate on foot.

22

It was an old-fashioned wineshop, the sort that Gaius Marius might've sneaked his first underage drink in: stone-flagged floor, counter that was solid enough to have formed part of the town's defences, no tables, just stools at the bar, and a respectable selection of local wines on the rack. My kind of place, definitely: these days, with the influx into Latium of rich, holiday-home smoothies from the Big City, you're getting an increasing number of chichi winebars à la Tuscan Street and points adjacent, with carefully co-ordinated or themed decor and third-rate wine masquerading under a first-rate name and priced accordingly.

Old-fashioned clientele, too. The only other guy in the place apart from me and the barman looked like he could've bought the young Marius his second cup.

'Day, sir.' The barman was a close ringer for Castor, but a much older version: twenty years older, at least. 'What can I get you?'

'A half jug of the Bovillan'd be fine, pal,' I said. 'You do food?'

'Cold sausage, cheese and pickles. Nothing hot.'

'That'll do nicely.' I reached into my belt-pouch and pulled out some coins while he hefted the flask and poured. Big lad, and he'd worn well, late fifties or not.

'You from Rome?' he said.

'Yeah. 'Fraid so.'

'Holiday?'

'Yeah. My wife's got an aunt in Castrimoenium.'

'Really?' His back was to me, but I caught the tonic equivalent of the lowered eyebrows and the frown. The old guy at the other end of the bar lifted his head and stared at me. Yeah, right: I could see the family resemblance there, too.

'Understand you've got relatives there yourself,' I said. No harm in putting out feelers.

He turned round and set the filled half jug with a cup on the counter. 'Who told you that?' he said sharply.

'No hassle, pal.' I poured and sipped. It was good stuff, almost as good as Pontius's, in its class, and that's high praise. 'I was just making conversation. Maybe I've got the wrong wineshop.'

'No, you're right enough, sir. You know Veturina and Castor?'

'I've met them.'

'Yeah, you would have.' Then, when I raised an eyebrow: 'Oh, no offence, sir, none in the world, that's not the way I mean it. It's just that purple stripe of yours . . . well, Veturina and Castor move in higher circles than we do. Right, Dad?'

The old man at the end of the bar nodded. 'The girl made a good match, right enough,' he said smugly. It was like hearing a whisper through gravel.

'You don't see much of them now, then,' I said.

'Nah. Nothing since Castor left a couple of years back and moved in with her.' The barman sliced sausage and arranged it on a plate with pickles from the jar and a wedge of goat's cheese. 'Helping us to run this place wasn't good enough for him. Wanted to be a fucking lawyer.' He set two quarters of a loaf on to the plate. 'Sorry, sir, no call for that.'

'No problem.' I pulled the plate towards me and tried the sausage. That was good as well, smoked pork with cumin and lovage. A real find, Veturinus's. 'I'm not too keen on lawyers myself.'

'He was always ambitious, young Castor,' the old man said. 'Even when he was a boy. He knew what he wanted and he'd go right for it, whatever was in the way. Him and Veturina, they was a pair even though there was twenty years between them and they'd different mothers, always together when she came visiting. And close as—'

'Dad! Gentleman doesn't want to hear no ramblings, now.' The barman wrapped up the rest of the sausage.

'Oh, that's okay,' I said. 'Brother and sister. What would you expect?'

That got me a sideways look, but the guy didn't say anything more. I took a proper swallow of the wine.

'She'll be well set-up now, though, won't she?' the father went on. 'Rich widow with everyone chasing after her. You'll know the husband died, sir? Not long back?'

'Yeah,' I said. 'Yeah, I heard that.'

'They say he'd been ailing for a long time. A shame. He was a fine man in his day, Lucius Hostilius. Used to have a practice here in Bovillae, before he moved over to Castrimoenium. Lived just down the road, came in here a lot and sat just where you're sitting, sir. This was where they met, because Veturina used to help out sometimes when we were busy after her mother died and before I married again.'

'That so, now?'

The old man chuckled. '"I'll have him, Dad, just you wait." That's what she used to say to me, the minx, after he was gone of an evening. And why not? He was a bachelor, good-looking, rich enough but nothing special because he was just starting out and only half a dozen years older than she was. And she was a cracker, my Veturina. All the lads were after her, not that they got any encouragement after she clapped eyes on him. Hostilius, too: proper taken, he was, hook, line and sinker. Have him she did, in the end, and good luck to her.'

'So what's your business in Bovillae, sir?' Unasked, Veturinus Junior topped up my cup. Change of subject, obviously: I had the distinct impression that the big guy had had enough of gratuitous family revelations, but short of choking his blabbermouth old father off there hadn't been a lot he could do.

'Just a change of scenery, pal,' I said easily: I wasn't going to compromise my stranger-off-the-street pose unless it was really necessary, and if he hadn't seen hide nor hair of his sister or brother for two years then it wasn't likely I'd get anything useful. *Half*-brother, I corrected myself. Now *that* had been interesting. 'Castrimoenium's okay, but there isn't enough concrete around up there for my liking.'

'Not thinking of buying any property in the area, then?'

'Uh-uh.' I took a mouthful of wine and made inroads on the bread, cheese and pickles. 'Too many Romans. Besides, like I said, I've got a rooted aversion to lawyers.' I glanced sideways at the old man. 'No disrespect to your late son-in-law intended. My experience's mostly been with the big city variety, and your Bovillan guys are probably a different thing altogether.'

Veturinus Junior chuckled. 'Don't you believe it, sir! They're the same all over.'

'Yeah?'

'Take our local man for example, Novius his name is, been in practice here for, oh, forty-odd years and more. Now he—' The door opened and half a dozen workmen with seriously bloodstained tunics trooped in. ''Scuse me, sir, the hard drinkers from the slaughterhouse've arrived. Hello, lads, that's you for the morning, is it? The usual? Dad, give me a hand, will you?'

I went back to my sausage, cheese and pickles while the bar stools filled up around me with a gaggle of Bovillae's thirstiest, smelliest and rowdiest and the two Veturini busied themselves with filling jugs, slicing bread and swapping insults. Well, I couldn't fault the slaughterhouse lads' timing. Perfect; bloody perfect. No pun intended.

Bugger!

There was no chance to resume the chat, either, because the door didn't stop swinging for two minutes together until I'd cleaned my plate and emptied the half jug, and by that time the place was filled to the walls. I'd obviously hit the happy hour. Ah, well, it hadn't been time wasted, far from it. And it was always good to find a decent wineshop, barring the malodorous clientele. Still, the afternoon was getting on, I had to walk back to the town square, and after I'd checked with Alexis I had a fair ride to Castrimoenium.

I stopped at a pastry-seller's on the way to buy him a peace offering – Alexis is no wine drinker, but he'll kill for a nut and honey pastry sprinkled with poppy seeds – and carried on to the public records office.

He was waiting for me outside, and totally transformed from the snarling grouch I'd got earlier. The guy might still look like he'd been dragged through an unused hypocaust backwards, but he was grinning all over his face and brandishing a set of cobwebby tablets like they were the missing Sibylline Books.

'I've found it, sir!' he said. 'Just ten minutes since! At least I think I have. Twentieth of May, Tiberius Three, consulship of Statilius Taurus and Scribonius Libo. That's almost exactly, uh' – he did a quick calculation – 'twenty-one years ago.'

'Brilliant!'

'I can't give you any details – I only looked at the beginning, for the names of the accused and the lawyers, and the end for the verdict and sentence – but they seem to fit. You want them now?'

'Yeah. Yes, please.'

'Accused were two brothers, Brabbius Lupus and Brabbius

Senecio. Some sort of burglary and murder. The defence was Lucius Hostilius and Quintus Acceius, and—'

'Hang on, pal,' I said. 'The *defence*?'

'Yes, sir, that's right. Still, I thought you might want it in any case. It's all I've come up with.'

'Fine, fine. No problem, Alexis. Who were the prosecutors?'

'Just one, sir. Publius Novius.'

'Shit!' It *had* to be this one, it just had to be, whatever the explanation! 'Sorry, pal. Don't mind me, carry on.'

'There's just that, sir, and the verdict. The men were found guilty. Lupus was executed and Senecio was sent to the galleys for twenty years.'

Bull's-eye! 'Alexis, you are a fucking *genius*! Have a pastry.' I handed it over, and he gave me the tablets. 'Can I hang on to these?'

'For the time being, sir. Latro – that's the clerk – says there's no problem. Just be sure to bring them back when you've finished.'

'Great. How's your time in Bovillae been, incidentally? Apart from the spiders?'

'Not bad. I've been staying just round the corner, in the household of Agilleius Mundus.' Yeah, I remembered Mundus: Libanius's opposite number in Bovillae. 'Only they put me in with the coachman, and he snores. I'll be glad to get back.' He hesitated. 'Oh, by the way. I had a long chat with Latro yesterday when the . . . when I felt I needed a break. We got quite friendly.'

'Yeah?'

'It's just that . . . well, I admit I deliberately steered the conversation round to Quintus Acceius, sir. Latro's been working here long enough to remember Acceius before he moved to Castrimoenium, and although he didn't say so in so many words I got the feeling that the gentleman wasn't quite as . . . punctilious then as he is today. Or seems to be.'

'That so, now?' Of course, Bucca had said the same thing; but Bucca had an axe to grind, and, besides, he was just passing on what could've been a snide bit of backstabbing from Acceius's professional rival. Latro, being a disinterested party, was another matter altogether. 'Interesting.'

'Yes, sir, I thought so. Worth going more deeply into, certainly.' He finished his pastry and licked his fingers. 'Now, if there's nothing else you want me to do here I'll get over to Mundus's and pick up my bag and the mule.'

'What?' I'd been wool-gathering. 'Oh. I'm sorry, Alexis. Right, thanks, pal, you've been a great help. I'll stay on for a bit, read over this trial record and take it straight back to your friend Latro.' I put my hand in my belt-pouch and found a gold piece. 'There's no hurry for you. Buy yourself a new tunic, have a bath, see the town and pig out on pastries. Or whatever.'

He grinned. 'Yes, sir. Thank you. I'll do that.'

I gave him a farewell wave and moved off in the direction of the wineshop I'd spotted earlier. A smart cookie, Alexis, very smart: not many garden-slaves know the word 'punctilious' to start with, a hell of a lot fewer would go to the bother of finding out that a man their master was interested in didn't used to be it, and only one in a thousand of *them* would add that 'or seems to be'.

So when he practised in Bovillae Acceius wasn't as punctilious as he was today, right? Or seemed to be, rather.

Hmm.

The wineshop wasn't busy, despite its prime location, and when I'd tasted the wine I could see why. Still, all I really wanted was somewhere quiet to sit down for half an hour and see what we'd got here. I carried my cup outside on to the terrace, settled down at a corner table, opened the tablets and began to read.

It was fairly sordid, run-of-the-mill stuff: the two brothers, Lupus and Senecio, described as 'dyers from Bovillae', had broken into and started robbing a silversmith's shop near the precinct of Mercury. Unfortunately for them, the owner – a guy called Titus Vectillius – who lived at the back of the premises heard them furkling about and came through with the poker. There was a scuffle, Vectillius was knifed and the two of them fled, straight into the arms of a group of zealous but inebriated citizens further up the street who pinned them down and fetched the Night Watch. Lupus and Senecio claimed that they'd just been passing when the real villains burst out of the shop doorway and legged it in the other direction; that Lupus had found the silver bracelet he was clutching lying on the ground outside, and had had every intention of handing it over to the proper authorities in the morning; and that the knife Lupus was carrying in his other hand was used exclusively for the slicing of sausage and other edibles.

I had to hand it to the defence, Hostilius and Acceius, who'd evidently done their best to cast doubts on the reliability of a pack of witnesses who were pissed as newts and hadn't actually seen the two guys coming out of the shop. However, the facts that Lupus had a record of violence and petty thievery a yard long already and that he and his brother had been barrelling up the street like a pair of Phaedippideses after Marathon were pretty well clinchers. The jury found them both guilty as charged. Lupus, as the probable ringleader, got the strangler's noose and Senecio a twenty-year stretch in the galleys. End of trial, end of record.

I set the tablets down and took a large gulp of the sub-standard Signinan. Yeah, well, it added up, in general terms anyway: Senecio does his stint behind an oar, survives it against all the odds and comes back with a grudge to settle against the two guys who'd defended him. Or failed to, rather. None the less, there were serious holes in the logic that needed filling. It sounded like a fair cop, for a start: the two had been convicted on circumstantial evidence, sure, but as it stood that was pretty damning. Even if by some wild stretch of the imagination they had been telling the truth, Senecio couldn't complain that his advocates hadn't done their best with what they'd got. He'd a right to feel angry against the jurymen who'd returned the verdict, yeah, no argument, or against the judge who'd done the sentencing; but not against Hostilius and Acceius, not to the degree of hunting them down twenty years later. That took real hatred, and unless he was totally out of his tree – which was a possibility, I admitted, after twenty years in the galleys – I couldn't see he'd have a valid reason for it. Odd.

The second major hole was that with Lupus and Senecio both dead there should've been no one left. So who the hell had tried to put a knife into Acceius? Someone had, that was sure, and the chances there *wasn't* a connection were pretty remote. Oh, the probable answer was obvious: a relative, a third brother perhaps, here in Bovillae, that Senecio had been in touch with before the attack. He wouldn't've been in-volved in the affair, so naturally the trial record wouldn't mention him, but with two brothers dead now – the second killed by Acceius personally – he'd have a grudge in spades. I remembered the guy Trophius had mentioned, the guy who'd been hanging around the tombs when Trophius's lads burned Senecio's body. Right. That fitted as well. He'd've wanted to be there, at the funeral – if you could call it that – but if he'd been planning then, as he would've been, to pay off his brother's killer, plus the back-debt, there was no way he'd've come forward and shown himself properly . . .

It all made sense. The only question now was, how did I find him? I took another swig of the wine, the last, and emptied the cup.

Dyers. The record had described the brothers as 'dyers from Bovillae'. It was a long shot, sure, twenty years long, but at least I was lucky there. Dyeing's one of those professions that tends to go in families and stay there. Dyers, fullers and tanners largely keep to themselves, sticking to their own special area of town, because the raw materials of the trade can be pretty niffy when stored in bulk or put to use. In fact, there was a clear-cut dyers' and tanners' quarter in Bovillae. I could—

I stopped. Something was tugging at my memory; nothing to do with Bovillae or Senecio. Tanners' quarter . . . tanners' quarter . . .

Then I remembered. Acceius had said that the night he was attacked he'd been visiting a client in the tannery and slaughterhouse area of Castrimoenium, out by the Bovillan Gate. Shit! There had to be a connection! The guy could've moved, it was only four or five miles; *would* probably have moved, under the circumstances, with two of his brothers – we'd assume brothers – convicted of murder. He wouldn't've changed his profession, though, there was no need for that, none at all . . .

Still, if I was going to find him then I needed a name. There was no point starting afresh with Castrimoenium, not when I'd got a lead here. I could come back tomorrow and ask around the dyers' shops by the Appian Gate. If I was really, really lucky, then someone might just remember, and in that case we were in business.

Of course, there was that one, *other* possibility, that our mystery knifeman hadn't been a knifeman at all. But then, tempting to pursue as that line might be, before you can start faffing around with complications you've first got to check the obvious.

Yeah, well: enough for the present. If that was my day in Bovillae then I'd had it. I left the empty cup on the table, returned the tablets to Latro with thanks, collected the mare from her long stint at the water-trough and set off back to Castrimoenium.

23

I called in at Hyperion's in passing just in case Clarus was there – Marilla had told me the day before that he had something to tell me re the dead woman up at Caba – but he wasn't, so the odds were he was helping Marilla on Meton-dogging duties and I'd catch up on both of them later. Hyperion, though, had two interesting pieces of news: one, that Libanius had put Veturina under the gentlest form of house arrest he could officially manage; and two, that Castor had flown the coop for a second time.

'He has *what?*' I said. 'You're sure?'

'Oh, quite sure.' We were in Hyperion's workroom, and he was doing something complicated involving a lot of mixing and grinding of tiny quantities of dried herbs from stoppered pots. 'According to Scopas – and he sent word to Libanius – he packed a bag and left shortly after Libanius did, without saying where he was going, why or for how long. Veturina might know the answers to any or all of these questions, in fact she probably does, but she refuses to say.'

'Bugger!' That Veturina had killed Hostilius, or connived at his death, purely out of love I could accept, absolutely; Castor, however, was much more of a grey area. Oh, sure, in my report to Libanius it hadn't been up to me to make fine distinctions of guilt between them, and I'd been very loath to think along those lines in any case, under the circumstances: their motives – individual and shared – had been like one of these compact masses of underground roots that Alexis had shown me once, so tangled together that the plants and the weeds they belonged to were impossible to separate. All I could do, like Alexis, was dig the whole lot up, good and bad mixed, then hand them to Libanius to unravel as best he could. Even so, if one of the pair could be regarded as a proper murderer – and I wasn't forgetting Cosmus – then Castor was it, no question. And now the bastard had done a runner and left his sister to face the music on her own.

'It was to be expected, of course.' Hyperion added a little water to the powdered herbs in his mortar and began to grind them to a paste. 'He has very little to lose in any case, no property to be sequestrated, no family apart from Veturina herself. At least no family that he'd bother about, or who'd bother about him. No doubt he'll take ship from Puteoli for Gaul, or Spain, somewhere suitably remote, and that'll be the last anyone hears of the fellow.'

Shit, what a mess. 'Libanius isn't putting out the word on him?'

'No. Definitely not. To tell you the truth, Corvinus' – Hyperion used a tiny metal spatula to transfer the paste into a pill-mould – 'I suspect he was angling for something just like this. Libanius is a very astute man in the political sense. With Castor escaping from justice the whole business, or the more unsavoury aspects of it like Cosmus's murder, can be laid at his door unequivocally, and Veturina left out of the picture. He has become, as a Jewish colleague of mine would once have said' – he pressed the mixture hard down into the mould – 'a scapegoat. In the word's best possible sense.'

Yeah, right, I could see the benefit of that, even if I couldn't agree with it. Now Castor had gone – the guilty party fleeing, in admission of guilt – there would be no legal need for a trial, Veturina was off the hook and the whole sad mess could be shelved and forgotten. Like Hyperion had said, it was a politician's solution to the problem, ends justifying means, and if there's one thing I'm not it's a politician. Still, I couldn't complain: I'd handed the whole boiling to Libanius to do with as he thought fit, and there was no point in grousing now over how he'd managed things. 'What about Veturina herself?' I said. 'Did Libanius say she'd admitted to anything?'

'No. But neither did she deny it. In fact she said nothing at all, absolutely nothing. You've met the lady, Corvinus. You know, or you can guess, how stubborn she can be.'

'Yeah.' I frowned. 'How about Paulina?'

'Libanius has sent her to a sister of his own in Rome. With Veturina's knowledge and consent, of course. That side of things will be very difficult, I suspect. However, I'm sure it'll resolve itself in time.' He set the mould aside. 'Now. How are matters going otherwise? Libanius said you were still looking into that business of the woman at Caba.'

'Uh-huh. Among other things. Call it idle curiosity, pal, because I doubt if any of the strands I'm following will lead anywhere particularly profitable. Even so, I can't just let them go now the Hostilius problem's over and done with. It wouldn't sit right.'

He smiled. 'Oh, I can understand that perfectly, Corvinus. I hate to walk away from a puzzle myself, once I've set myself to solving it, no matter how unimportant I know the eventual answer will be. And Clarus would be very disappointed.'

'Right. Speaking of which I'd best be getting back, see what he has to tell me. You know what it is?'

'Oh, yes, indeed.' Hyperion wiped the spatula on a cloth. 'But I'll let him tell you for himself because it belongs to his field of expertise, not mine. You'll find it most interesting.'

I got back home just shy of dinner time. No sign of Perilla – the lady was up in Marcia's room, because the old girl was still bed-bound and she was keeping her company – but Clarus and Marilla were deep in conversation on the terrace. I cleared my throat and they sprang apart.

'Hi, Corvinus,' Clarus said. 'Any luck in Bovillae?'

'Yeah.' I carried my jug and wine cup over to the table. 'Chances are the tramp who attacked Hostilius was a guy called Brabbius Senecio. Hostilius and Acceius defended him in a burglary and murder trial twenty-one years back.' I gave them a quick run-down of events. 'So the next stage is to see whether we can trace the third brother, or whoever he is, who went for Acceius.'

'I've got some news too,' Marilla said.

Oh, yeah, right; Meton. Forget the case, this was important. 'Go ahead, Princess,' I said, steeling myself. 'Did you see her? Did they meet?'

'Yes, in the vegetable market. You were right, she is very good-looking, isn't she?'

Hell; I was hoping against hope that somewhere there'd been a mistake. 'You hear anything they said?'

'No, they were too far away, and we – Clarus was there as well, of course – we didn't like to get any closer in case Meton spotted us. They were . . . I know it sounds silly, but I think they were buying artichokes. At least, she was because she was the one who paid, but Meton was doing all the handling and all the talking. That's right, isn't it, Clarus?'

Clarus nodded.

Jupiter! Well, if it'd been anyone else then yes, it would've sounded silly. We were talking about Meton here, though: only our food-fixated chef could use the criteria for choosing a good artichoke as a chat-up line. Which I'd bet was what he'd been doing. If this seduction went through – and I'd guess, thank the gods, from what I'd seen myself and what Marilla was saying that we were only in the early stages here – then if they finally did get the length of going to bed together as far as a practical knowledge of culinary ingredients, their choice and preparation, was concerned the lady would be world class.

'Okay,' I said. 'So what happened then?'

'They bought some leeks.'

I sighed. 'Just skip the blow-by-blow account of the vegetable purchases, Princess.'

'Very well. When they'd bought the . . . artichokes, leeks, beetroot, carrots and dill, wasn't it, Clarus?' – nod – 'they walked back towards the town square. They stopped for a minute, then they split up. Meton went . . . where did he go, Clarus? You followed him.'

'To the meat market. At least, that was where he was heading, but I think he saw me and got suspicious because he gave me the slip before he got there. Sorry, Corvinus.'

Damn! If Meton knew he was being watched now, trailing him another day would be much trickier. Still, the woman was the important one of the pair. Meton we could always find. 'What about Renia, Princess?' I said.

'Oh, that was okay. I followed her to Ceres Temple Street. She's got a house about halfway along, next to the baker's. At least, that's what I assumed, because she went in there and didn't come out. *And* there's a locksmith's sign next to the door.'

Right, that seemed to be pretty conclusive. I'd get together with Perilla and we'd move on to the next stage. 'Great,' I said. 'Well done.'

'Let Clarus tell you about the body now,' Marilla said.

Oh, yeah; the Caba woman. I turned to Clarus. 'Go ahead, pal.'

'I think she was dumped.'

'What?'

'Corvinus, I don't believe she was killed where she was found at all. Of course, I haven't been up there myself, but I've talked it over with Dad, who has, and he agrees.'

'Hang on, Clarus,' I said. 'What leads you to think she was dumped?'

'The condition of her tunic. You wouldn't've had a chance to spot it for yourself, and neither would Dad, because she was lying face-up and the front and sides of her tunic are clear. But the back's covered with cement dust. At least, I'm almost certain that's what it is. And it couldn't've got that way where she was found.'

'Maybe she just had a dirty tunic.'

'Uh-uh. I told you, the front and sides were clean. Or clean of cement, anyway. And the back was caked in places to the depth of my fingernail, especially just under and level with the shoulder-blades, like she'd been pulled over the stuff. My guess is that she was loaded on to a wagon that'd been carrying cement, driven up into the woods then hauled out by her feet.'

'What about the cart they took her home in?'

He shook his head. 'That was the first thing I checked. Wood shavings, sawdust, sure, plenty of that, but no cement. Not a trace. Besides, the slaves left her on the stretcher so she could be lifted out easily. Her back didn't touch the boards.'

'So what do you think?'

'Like I say. She was killed elsewhere, loaded on to a cart with a good quarter inch of cement dust on its floor, probably covered over with a tarpaulin and taken up to Caba to be dumped. Caba's a sensible choice, and not just because it's wild country. There're plenty of carts use that road anyway, with the quarry being there. No one'd think anything about it. And Dad says you can see the road for half a mile in each direction from the start of the cart track. That's important. All it'd take would be for the killer to make sure there was nothing coming that might see him when he turned in and again when he left and he'd be perfectly safe.'

I whistled. 'You do anything for an encore, pal? Like pull live chickens out of hats?'

He grinned. So did Marilla.

'He's good, isn't he?' she said.

'He is bloody *brilliant*! We can take it further, too.'

'Can we?'

'Yeah. Horses, mules, donkeys, no problem, anyone can get one of these at five minutes' notice. But a cart? Uh-uh, that's tricky, not everybody has one of these, not in town, anyway. And you couldn't risk borrowing or hiring one, not if you were going to use it to transport a corpse, because later someone might just make the connection. On the other hand, if you'd got a cart already then—'

'Oh, gods,' Clarus said softly. 'Bucca Maecilius.'

'Spot on, pal. At least, one gets you ten. I'd take a small side bet on his brother, mind, because he's a farmer, but Bucca'll do nicely to begin with.'

'Why should Bucca kill the woman?'

I shrugged. 'Tell me who she was and I might have an answer. In the meantime, bring those eyes and that brain of yours round to his yard tomorrow morning and we'll sweat the bastard together, see if he's got answers of his own.'

'What about—' Marilla said; which was exactly when Bathyllus buttled in.

'Dinner, sir,' he said.

I stood up. Fair enough, sleuthing over for the day. Well, at least Meton was still alive and cooking, and after the ride into Bovillae and back my stomach thought my throat was cut.

I hadn't mentioned it to Clarus, but after what he'd told me that theoretical complication re the Brabbii had just moved up a slot and become a definite possibility.

24

I met up with Clarus by prearrangement just after dawn outside the gates of Bucca Maecilius's yard. No Marilla: if there was likely to be trouble – and trouble was a distinct possibility – then impassioned pleas, scathing sarcasm, tantrums and strident demands to be included notwithstanding the lady was *out*.

We went through the open gateway. No sign of the man himself, but like before there were a couple of carts parked next to the stables. I lifted the tarpaulin on one of them and Clarus took the other.

'Corvinus?' he said quietly.

'Yeah?'

'Come and have a look.'

I went over. The floor of the cart was covered in a thick layer of cement dust, like a bag of the stuff had burst and spread its contents over the width of the boards. The dust had been flattened and drawn in lines in a wide strip from the centre of the cart to the back, as if something big had been pulled out over the open tailgate.

Bull's-eye!

'Well done, pal,' I said. 'Full marks. If—'

'Wait.' He reached past me to where a splinter of wood stuck out from the tailgate itself, picked something up and held it out. I looked. A single brown thread. 'The dead woman's tunic was brown,' he said. 'It could be coincidence, of course.'

Coincidence nothing, that put the lid on it for me. We'd got the bastard by the balls. 'Let's go inside,' I said.

There were three horses in the stables, better-fed and healthier beasts than I'd've expected but no prizewinners. Bucca was lying in one of the empty stalls, snoring his head off. There was an empty wine flask in the straw beside him.

I went over, took hold of the front of his tunic and heaved him to his feet. 'Come on, pal,' I said. 'Rise and shine.'

His eyes opened, then widened. '*Corvinus?*'

'Well remembered.'

'What the hell do you want at this time of the morning? It's hardly—'

'Me and young Clarus here were interested in one of your carts. The one you used to transport that body up to Caba.'

'Never mind the—' he began; and then his brain must've caught up with his ears because suddenly he was very, very awake indeed. 'Oh, shit!'

I grabbed him by the sleeve as he turned to run and hauled him back, then ducked the roundhouse punch he threw and planted one of my own under his ribs. He went down gasping.

'Did you have to do that, Corvinus?' Clarus said.

I grinned. 'Uh-uh. But consider the bugger subdued.'

Clarus shook his head wearily. 'Let's get him outside,' he said.

We half escorted, half carried Bucca out of the stables to the cart and propped him against it. 'Now, pal,' I said. 'Let's have the details. Who was she, and why did you kill her?'

'I never!' He was still wheezing and clinging to the side of the cart for support, but he was getting his colour back. 'Corvinus, I never touched her, I swear it! You've got to believe that! I don't know who she is, either. Why should I kill a fucking woman I've never seen before in my life?'

'Bucca, watch my lips,' I said. 'In about ten minutes' time I am going to hand you over to the town magistrates to be charged with strangling a woman, name unknown, and taking her body in this cart up to the woods near Caba, where you dumped her. This will happen, friend, whatever you say, whether you deny it or admit it or opt to stay completely silent or whistle the fifth fucking Pindaric Ode through your teeth. What happens afterwards, though, depends totally on you, now, so you had better use those ten minutes wisely. Which means in telling me the truth, the whole truth and nothing but the truth. Because, sunshine, if you lie, or hide anything or even *think* of playing the smartass, and I find out, which I will, then so help me, Jupiter, I will see you nailed. Understand?'

He swallowed. 'Yes.'

'Good. Do you know who she is?'

'No.'

'Did you kill her?'

'*No!*'

'But you did transport the body to the woods near Caba and try to hide it?'

Another swallow. Then, very quietly: 'Yes.'

'Okay, pal. These were the only straight questions. You're on your own now. Let's have the story.'

He took a deep breath. 'I . . . found her three days back, first thing, when I got up. She was lying over there' – he pointed – 'behind that pile of rubbish. She was . . . I could see she was dead straight off because her face . . . oh, *gods!*'

'Yeah. Right,' I said. 'Never mind that. Carry on.'

'Can I be sick? Please?'

'Later.'

'I panicked. Corvinus, I fucking *panicked*! I told you about the people in this town and me, they wouldn't give my version two minutes' credence. If I'd reported her then a month down the road I'd be looking at the strangler's noose myself, no question. So I bundled her into the wagon, put the tarpaulin

over and drove up to Caba. I knew the road up there, I go up it
five, maybe six times a month, so there'd be nothing unusual
about me and my cart being seen. The bit of woodland where I
hid her, as well. I hauled a load of charcoal from there to
Bovillae once, three years back, I thought that'd be perfect. I
drove a couple of hundred yards up the track, well out of sight
of the road, pulled her out and covered her with what I could
find. Then I came straight back. That's it, that's all that
happened, I swear it!' He looked at me wild-eyed. 'I was
desperate, right? There was nothing else I could do!'

I sighed. 'Yeah. Yeah, okay.'

'You believe me?'

'I believe you. Only you'd better be telling the truth.'

'I am! I swear I am!'

'Fine. Let's go, then.'

'You're taking me to the magistrates?'

'Yeah. I said.'

'But—'

'Look, Bucca. Whoever killed this woman and dumped her
on your doorstep is no friend of yours. He's killed once, he
might decide to kill again, and you, pal, might be next on the
list. So, yes, I am taking you to the magistrates. Locked up safe
in the town hall cellars is probably the best place for you.'

He was staring at me. 'You think it was *deliberate*? I mean,
choosing here?'

I shrugged. 'Your guess is as good as mine, friend. The
difference is, whether I'm right or wrong it's no skin off my
nose either way. Whereas . . .' I left the rest of it hanging.

'Oh, *shit*!' He turned away abruptly and threw up. Most of it
was wine. Well, I'd told him he could, later, so I couldn't really
object.

I waited until he'd finished and had wiped his mouth on his
tunic. 'You any idea yourself who was responsible?' I said. 'Or
maybe why?'

'*No!* The only real enemy I've got is my brother, and Fimus wouldn't do anything like this! He's a stiff-necked bastard, true, but he's not that much of a bastard, and he's no killer, no way, never!' He paused. 'You don't think it was him, do you?'

'No,' I said. 'I don't think it was Fimus.'

'Then who?'

I took him gently by the arm. 'Let's go, Bucca.'

We dropped him off at the town hall, with a mention of the horses to be looked after in the stables, and I took Clarus to Pontius's for a cup of wine. This early not even Gabba was in evidence and the place was empty, but I wanted absolute privacy for the next bit, so we carried the wine cups – and some bread and cheese; there hadn't been much time for breakfast – outside on to the terrace.

'You didn't think Bucca was responsible from the beginning,' Clarus said as we settled down at one of the tables. 'For killing the woman, I mean.'

'No.' I took a sip of the wine.

'Then who was?'

'Quintus Acceius.'

He stared at me. '*What?*'

'I know why, too. And who she was. Not her name, just *who* she was.'

'Corvinus, I'm sorry, but you're not making sense.'

'She was Senecio's sister. Or his wife, or his girlfriend, or whatever. Senecio's *something*.'

He sat back. 'Ah.'

'"Ah" is right, pal. The bastard lied to us from start to finish. He wasn't attacked by a man at all; he was attacked by a woman. The attacker didn't run off; he killed her and dumped her body in Bucca's yard.'

'But Acceius wasn't attacked anywhere near Bucca's! He'd've had to lug the corpse all the way across town!'

'Who says where he was attacked?' I paused for the penny to drop. 'Right. Acceius does. No one else, there were no witnesses. Just like we've only got his word for what happened. Oh, sure, he'd have to cross town to get to your father's, bleeding like a pig all the way. I never said it was easy. But at least he'd have his story, and if the body was discovered and the whistle blown the Caba Gate would be a quarter of a mile off.'

'It was still a risk. A small town like Castrimoenium, with an attack and a death on the same night. The two would have to be put together.'

'You're not thinking, pal. Of course they would, they have been. Acceius couldn't do a thing about that; the killing was by no choice of his, it wasn't planned, all he could do was cover the best he could at the time, and that wasn't much. Me, I think he did bloody well, under the circumstances.'

'All right.' Clarus hadn't touched his wine: like Alexis, he wasn't a drinker. 'What happened?'

'The woman – we don't know her name, call her Nemesis – had been following him ever since Senecio died, waiting her chance; I knew that, he told me himself he had the feeling he was being watched. Now I don't know the exact circumstances – that's something we'll have to get from the bugger himself – but I'd guess he kept to the truth as far as he could, so I'd bet he was coming back from seeing a client. Only the client was somewhere up by the Caba Gate, not the Bovillan. Then things happened like he told us: Nemesis was waiting in ambush, she came out of an alleyway as he passed and stabbed him. The difference was, he didn't slug her – he couldn't've done, because her face wasn't marked – but he *did* catch at the necklace round her neck and strangle her.'

'Hold on, Corvinus. You said he was keeping to the truth as far as he could. So why not just say there was a struggle, the attacker dropped the knife and ran away? Why invent the punch?'

'Because Acceius is a smart cookie, Clarus. The guy *thinks*, even when he's desperate, as he had to be. Thinks on his feet, too; he has to, he's a forensic lawyer. If Nemesis's body was found – as it was – with no signs of a hefty punch to the face that'd be another reason for claiming she and the fictional attacker were different people. Not much of a reason, sure, but it'd help, and he'd need every edge he could get. Acceius was careful to tell us he'd really socked the man, remember, probably knocked out or damaged a few teeth. My bet is that after the woman was dead he bruised his own knuckles against the wall to give the story credence. Possible? You're the medical expert.'

'Possible. Dad might've seen a difference, sure, if he'd treated the damage, but he didn't bother. Not with that slice to the side and back to worry about.'

'Right.' I took a swallow of the wine. 'Then there was the real poser, the problem of the body. Now *that's* the really interesting part. The guy's been attacked, knifed. He's killed the attacker, fine, but he's a lawyer, he knows all about killing in self-defence. Like when he killed Senecio. And there'd be no question that he *had* been attacked and that the intention was murder, not with the wound he's carrying, so legally he's safe enough. But what does he do? He *doesn't* yell for help or hammer on the first available door. Instead, he lugs the corpse into Bucca's yard and dumps it, then drags himself all the way across town practically past his own front door just to pretend he was nowhere near the fucking place. Now unless he's got something major to hide, and I'd bet a rotten fig to a flask of Caecuban that he has, that is *weird*.'

'Yes.' Clarus chewed reflectively on his bread and cheese. 'He recognised the woman. That what you mean?'

'Yeah. And it was important, for some reason, that no one should realise that he had.' I stood up. 'You finished?'

'You're going to see him? *Now?*'

'As ever is. The bastard's got questions to answer, and the sooner the better.'

Clarus tucked the rest of the cheese inside the bread and stood up too.

We went to Acceius's.

25

They were at breakfast, Acceius and Seia Lucinda, when the slave showed us in.

'Corvinus! And Clarus.' Acceius put down his breakfast roll. 'What on *earth* are you doing here at this hour?'

'We've just been round at Bucca Maecilius's,' I said. 'Asking him about the corpse that he ferried over to Caba three days back.'

His eyes widened. 'Indeed? What corpse is this?'

'I was rather hoping you'd tell me, pal. After all, you dumped her on him in the first place.'

Silence. Long silence. Out of the corner of my eye I saw Seia Lucinda shoot him a look. Acceius dabbed carefully at his lips with his napkin and stood up, wincing as he did so. Yeah: the stitches would still be in.

'Perhaps we'd better go into the study,' he said.

I stood aside to let him pass, with Clarus tagging along behind. I could feel Seia Lucinda's eyes on my back all the way to the door.

We went in.

'Sit down, please.' He indicated the couches. 'I'd rather stand, if you don't mind. It makes things rather formal, but standing's more comfortable for me at present, and, besides, under the circumstances perhaps a certain degree of formality is called for.'

We sat.

'Now.' He took a breath. 'How did you know?'

'You admit it?'

'Yes. No point in a denial, is there?' He was frowning. 'I should've said I'd killed her – *her*, not *him* – straight away. Making up that story was silly. Worse than silly, stupid.'

'So why did you?'

He closed his eyes. 'Because I'm a lawyer, Corvinus, and because I'm a man. The first sometimes thinks too much, the second too little. Unfortunately the combination will sometimes act very stupidly indeed. As I did.' The eyes opened again. 'As far as the killing went, it followed roughly the same lines as I described, except that the struggle was more prolonged and of course ended . . . differently. She was a very powerful woman, you must be aware of that if you've seen the body. Also . . . well, she really, *really* wanted me dead. I managed to turn her round and get a tight grip of her knife hand about the wrist, but that was as much as I could do: she wouldn't drop the knife and I couldn't move the arm itself. I . . . got my left arm up to her throat and my fingers caught in her necklace. I thought if I twisted that and held on tightly, choking her, I could force her to let the weapon fall, or at worst render her unconscious. I . . . well, I simply held on too long and too hard. When she did finally go limp and I risked releasing her I found that she was dead.' He paused and looked me straight in the eyes. 'I swear to you I didn't mean to kill her. It was like the other time, an accident. I was so damn scared I just acted without thinking.'

I let that one pass for the moment. 'Okay. So why the story? You'd been attacked, badly wounded, you'd defended yourself and accidentally killed the attacker in the process. You're a lawyer, you'd know you were within your rights. So why try to cover things up?'

He smiled weakly. 'It was *because* I'm a lawyer, Corvinus. Or partly so. I told you, the combination of ordinary man and lawyer can give rise to acts of unbelievable stupidity. Thus far

I'd acted as a man. I was frightened, I panicked, I overreacted.'
He paused. 'No, I'm being unfair to myself, I didn't *over*react,
I simply fought as hard as I could to avoid being killed, which I
knew I would be if I gave the woman the smallest degree of
quarter. Once she was dead, unfortunately, the thinking
lawyer took over. I've argued cases, Corvinus, for the defence
and prosecution both, all my life. I know all about circumstantial evidence, and how damning it can be, how difficult it is
to get round. She was the second person I'd killed by "accident"' – he stressed the word – 'under identical circumstances
inside half a month. Suspicious? Of course it is! Besides, she
was a woman, I'm a strong man; why could I not simply have
disarmed her? And *strangulation*? A fatal knife wound could be
sudden and truly accidental; but strangulation is slow, and
therefore deliberate. Oh, yes: I could make a case myself, a
very good one at that.' I said nothing.

'So the upshot was that the lawyer made his points and the
man accepted and acted on them. Stupidly, as I say, criminally
so. I hid the body as best I could – yes, I suppose I did know it
was Bucca Maecilius's yard, but it was the handiest place at
the time and I was almost out of my mind with pain and fear –
and . . . well, the rest you know. Or I assume you do. When I
talked to you the next day, of course, it was as a lawyer trying
to make the most of a bad job, a nightmare situation. I'm sorry
about Bucca, very sorry: I will, naturally, go straight round to
Libanius, explain the whole business and take the consequences.'

'The bruise on your hand,' I said. 'You made that deliberately? After you'd killed her?'

Another weak smile. 'No. I'm not that devious, I'm glad to
say. I must've grazed my knuckles against the wall in the
struggle, although I didn't notice it at the time. But yes, you're
right, I did turn it to use later.'

'But you did recognise the woman?'

He looked at me blankly. 'What? No. No, of course I didn't! Why should I?'

'Come on, pal! She was a relative of the guy you killed, the guy who attacked you and your partner. Senecio.'

'No, Corvinus, I'm sorry, but . . .' He frowned. 'Hold on. Senecio . . . Senecio . . .?'

'You defended him, you and Hostilius. Him and his brother Lupus, on a burglary and murder charge.'

'Wait. I . . .' He was still frowning. 'The Brabbius brothers. Yes, by god, you're right. It must've been over fifteen years ago, in Bovillae, before we moved here. We lost the case, Lupus was executed and Senecio went to the galleys. The man was Brabbius Senecio?'

'Yeah. At least, I think so. And it was twenty-one years ago.'

'So it was.' He was staring at me. 'Why should Brabbius Senecio want to attack us? Yes, we lost and his brother died, but we did our best, it wasn't our fault. And I realise I shouldn't be saying this, but we never had a chance from the start because they were obviously guilty. You say the dead woman was a relative?'

'Yeah. My guess would be a wife or a sister. He have either of these, that you know of? Or anything like them?'

He shook his head numbly. 'No. I've genuinely no idea. Oh, I remember Senecio, yes, of course I do, although I'd never have recognised him in the man who attacked us even if I'd known who it was, certainly never made any sort of connection. But apart from Lupus I never met any of his family, to my knowledge. If they did exist then they kept well clear.'

I stood up. So did Clarus. 'Right,' I said. 'Thanks, pal. Very informative.'

His lips pursed. 'Yes . . . well. I'm sorry about all this, Valerius Corvinus. Sorry and deeply ashamed. As I said, I will see Quintus Libanius and make a full confession at the earliest opportunity. My apologies to your father, too, Clarus. I'll see you out.'

He did. No sign of Seia Lucinda now, but no doubt she'd be having a talk with her husband after we'd gone.

'You believe him, Corvinus?' Clarus said as the door closed behind us and we went down the steps.

I shrugged. 'I don't know,' I said. 'Jury's out on that completely.' He'd handled it well, though, I had to give him that. If he was lying, somewhere along the way, it'd be hellish difficult to prove. 'All we can do now is dig and see what turns up.'

One thing was certain: if I was going to get any more answers I'd have to do my digging in Bovillae.

26

I went back home and packed a bag. I'd got my appointment
with Publius Novius the next day, and if I was going
through to Bovillae now, with the likelihood of spending quite
some time there tracking down someone who'd known the
Brabbii, it'd be silly to shuttle back and forth to Castrimoenium. Agilleius Mundus would put me up for the asking, I was
sure of that. I just hoped I wouldn't have to sleep with the
snoring coachman.

I said goodbye to Perilla – she'd got her own job in the
meantime, setting up a woman-to-woman confab with the
elusive Renia re Meton – and headed off.

Mundus's was one of the older houses off the main square, a
big rambling place you could get lost in. The old guy was out,
but his equally decrepit major-domo assured me that there'd
be no problem about staying. I stabled the mare, dumped my
stuff in a guest bedroom overlooking the garden, checked on
dinner times – having Meton in your household gets you
twitchy about turning up punctually for meals – and set off for
the dyers' and fullers' part of town, up by the Appian Gate. A
handy locale, anyway: I'd give lunch a miss, especially if it
meant eating with the slaughterhouse brigade filling the place,
but no doubt a cup or two of wine at Veturinus's would go
down nicely in the run-up to dinner.

Okay. So off we went . . .

I was about a dozen yards from the front door when the

back of my neck started prickling. I turned round quickly, but apart from a harassed young mum dragging a squalling kid along the pavement and a couple of bored slaves kicking their heels against the wall of a draper's shop while they waited for the mistress to finish her business inside and load them up for the trip home there was nothing to see. Certainly no familiar faces, and any self-respecting mugger with designs on my purse would have more sense than to try it on in broad daylight, especially in the middle of a law-abiding town like Bovillae. I shrugged and grinned. False alarm. Yeah, well: maybe I was just getting needlessly jumpy in my old age.

I'd got to the tenth dyer's establishment, and got my tenth unequivocal and not-very-friendly brush-off, before I accepted the fact that this was going to be a real bummer of a job. Bugger! I should've used Alexis, even though he was still punch-drunk after his marathon with the spiders. It wasn't just the lapse of time involved – twenty-one years, for a lot of the people I talked to, would be three-quarters of a lifetime – it was the purple stripe: like I say, the dyers are a clannish profession, they stick together and they don't like strangers shoving their noses in, whatever the reason. Especially purple-striped Romans, who've always been about as popular generally in Latium as a cold in the head. I got the impression that quite a few of the older guys and guyesses – and some of them must've been tramping mantles when Tiberius was in rompers – could've helped if they'd wanted to, but one look at the stripe and an earful of the accent and their lips were zipped.

Shit.

The sun was definitely on the wane when I called it a day and trudged back to the Appian Gate and an unearned but badly needed half jug of wine. Trouble was, even if I did cut my losses now and send Alexis in, I'd queered his pitch good and proper. If someone else did turn up asking for news of the Brabbian family he'd get the bum's rush and the lifted finger.

Bugger, bugger, bugger, *bugger*!

Well, at least the wineshop was empty again. I'd hit the slot between the lunchtime rush and the evening binge, when the slaughterers would be croaking cattle and stiffing sheep. The only bodies in residence were the Veturini, father and son.

'Half a jug of the Bovillan, pal,' I said, heaving my weary carcass up on to a stool. 'And some of that sausage, if you've got it.'

The big guy hefted the wine flask and poured while I fumbled in my belt-pouch for coins. 'Hard day, sir?' he said, putting the jug and cup down on the counter in front of me.

'Tell me, friend.' I tipped the first of the jug into the cup and drank. Gods, I needed that! 'You haven't heard of the Brabbii, I suppose?'

'Nah.' He unwrapped the sausage and reached for a knife. 'No Brabbii around here for twenty years. That right, Dad?'

'*What?*' I almost spilled my wine.

Veturinus Junior lowered the knife. 'You okay, sir?'

'Yeah. Yeah.' Oh, gods! Please, please, gods! 'Ah . . . that'd be the two brothers, would it? Lupus and Senecio?'

'That's right.' He was looking at me strangely. Well, under the circumstances that was fair enough.

'Proper bad lots those two were,' Veturinus Senior said. He was still perched on his stool at the far end of the bar, but this time he had a wine cup in front of him. 'Specially Lupus. Got himself chopped for murder, did Lupus, and his brother went to the boats. My son-in-law defended them, him and his partner. Not that they could do much.'

'You knew them, then?' I said.

'The Brabbii? In and out of here all the time, from when they could lift a wine cup.' Old Veturinus grinned. 'And they lifted plenty of them, I can tell you. Senecio, he was sweet on our Veturina. I thought she might have him for a while, only she'd more sense. Then Hostilius came on the scene, and that was that.'

Jupiter! 'They, uh, have a sister at all?' I said.

Veturinus Junior was frowning now, and he'd set the sausage knife down. 'What's going on here?' he said. 'What's this about?'

Well, it was a fair cop. And I couldn't keep up the pretence of the barfly shooting the conversational breeze forever. On the other hand, saying that I'd been asked by the Castrimoenian senate to investigate Lucius Hostilius's death and that the two people currently being held responsible were the Veturinis' daughter and son and sister and brother respectively didn't seem such a sharp idea. 'Uh . . . my name's Valerius Corvinus,' I said. 'Quintus Libanius over in Castrimoenium asked me to look into the murder of a woman up at Caba. I thought she might be a relative of the Brabbii.'

'What, Habra?' Veturinus Senior said. 'Habra's been murdered?'

My stomach went cold. 'There was a sister called Habra?'

'Sure. Younger sister. Haven't seen her for years, mind, she left Bovillae after the trial and hasn't been back since, to my knowledge. So she was up in Caba, was she, and someone's done her in?' He chuckled. 'I'm not surprised. She was the worst of the three.'

'Yeah? And why was that?'

He made a sprinkling movement with his fingers. 'Doctoring. You know what I mean. No one ever caught her, mind, but everyone knew she did it. Girls who got themselves in trouble, they knew to go straight to Habra.'

Shit. 'She was an abortionist?'

'That's the fancy name, aye. That and worse, maybe, although if there was worse she was careful. She had the trade from her mother. A proper old witch she was, when she was alive. I remember—'

'Did she come in here? Habra? With her brothers, I mean?'

Another chuckle. 'Did she come in here? You hear that, Marcus? Oh, yes, sir, you couldn't keep her out. Habra could sink a half jug with the best of them. And she was fond of her brothers, I'll give her that. Stuck by them right the way through the trial and after all the way to the end, always back and forward to the lock-up seeing they'd enough to eat and drink. I couldn't fault her there, she was a good sister.'

'Your son-in-law's partner. Quintus Acceius. He ever drop in for a cup of wine?'

'Acceius? Course he did, along with Hostilius. I told you, Hostilius was no stranger, he liked his wine and he only lived up the road. Didn't come as often after he married my daughter, but until they moved to Castrimoenium the two of them'd be in here of an evening, the three of them some-times, oh, three or four times a month, easy. That was why the Brabbii boys went to them when they got into trouble. Who else would they ask?'

'So, uh, Acceius would know Habra, then?'

'Well enough. Not that they were friendly, mind.' Another chuckle. 'Not in that way. Habra'd no time for that sort of nonsense and Acceius wouldn't've looked at her twice, a good-looking man like him. But he'd know her, certainly he would. Specially come the time of the trial.'

I sat back on my stool. Bugger! The guy'd been lying through his teeth after all! And even if, for some reason, he hadn't recognised her physically when she'd attacked him he'd known of her existence. So *why* had he lied? It had to have something to do with the trial; everything came back to that . . .

Abortionist. Acceius's first wife had died in childbirth, round about the same time, and he'd married again, what? a couple of years later, was it? And Seia Lucinda had been quite a catch, financially, socially and probably sexually.

Convenient, right? Too convenient. And much too coinci-
dental to be coincidence . . .

Except that men who murder their wives, or have them
murdered, don't keep marble busts of them in their private
studies. And they don't break down – *genuinely* break down, as
far as I'd been able to tell – when a stranger refers to the
murdered woman twenty years on.

Shit! It didn't make sense! None of it! The only thing I knew
for certain was that when Quintus Acceius strangled Brabbia
Habra he knew exactly who he was killing.

'You want the sausage now, sir?' Veturinus Junior, with the
plate.

'Hmm?' I refocused my eyes. 'Oh. Yeah. Yeah, thanks, pal.
It's good sausage.'

'Real Bovillan sausage, that. You can keep your Lucanian.'

I turned back to the old man. 'You remember anything
about the trial?'

'Nah. 'Fraid I can't help you there.' Veturinus Senior sipped
his wine. 'I'd enough to do, keeping this place going, without
gadding off down to the courts. And why should I? I said: the
Brabbii may've been customers, good customers, but that was
just business. I wouldn't've trusted either further than I could
throw them, and I poured a full cup of my best to the Good
Lady Venus when my daughter split with Senecio and took up
with Lucius Hostilius. Proper peeved he was at the time, but
there wasn't nothing he could do about it. She had a lucky
escape, as things turned out. They were guilty as hell, and
good riddance to the pair of them.'

'The prosecutor was Publius Novius.'

'That's right. He was the only other lawyer in Bovillae, still
is; the old bugger'll outlast us all. Proper sharp he is, too, does
a roaring trade. You don't put much past Novius.'

'Just how straight is he? As a matter of interest.'

The old man gummed his wine cup. 'Oh, well, now,' he

said. 'We're talking lawyers, sir, they're another breed. He's straight enough by his lights, far as I know, but like I said he's sharp, and he knows his business backwards. Not one to let a chance slip, if you get me, so long as he thinks he won't be caught out. Hostilius was different, I'd a lot of time for him. That partner of his, mind . . . well, him and Novius had a lot in common. Smart as a whip, sure, but a pusher, desperate to get on, up to every trick he could get away with and too smooth-tongued by half. No, I wasn't too taken with young Quintus Acceius.'

'You remember his wife? His first wife?'

'Nah, I never met her, can't even remember the name, and the family wasn't from around here. Father was in the perfume trade in a small way down in Capua. She didn't keep well, died having their first.'

'He was fond of her?'

Veturinus shrugged. 'She was his wife, that's all I know, sir, and like I said I never met the girl. I never heard nothing to the contrary, certainly.'

'How about the second wife? Seia Lucinda?'

'Oh, now.' He chuckled. 'She was a different kettle of fish altogether. Big family around here, the Seii. Poultry breeders, supply most of the local butchers and send out as far as Rome. She was a catch, right enough, although word at the time was she'd done the chasing. A wild girl, young Seia was. They made a proper pair, those two.'

Yeah, that checked with what Gabba had told me. Interesting. 'Did—'

But that was as far as I got before the door opened and we got the Invasion of the Slaughterers, Part Two. Things got rapidly hectic, and I turned back with a sigh to my wine and sausage.

Ah, well; I couldn't complain, certainly not. I'd got a name for the dead woman, cast-iron proof that Acceius had known her, and possibly – *possibly* – the scent of a reason why he'd want her dead and burned. There were still some googlies in there, though, by the gods there were, especially with old Veturinus's description of the younger Acceius. Even if the guy was a liar to his boots – which he was – and guilty of *something* – which he also was – a lot of that didn't square. We'd just have to see what the chat with Novius produced.

I spent a leisurely half hour finishing off the wine and sausage and pushed the cup and plate across the counter. Veturinus Junior looked up from his conversation with one of the slaughterers.

'You want a refill, sir?' he said.

'No, that'll do me for the present, pal.' I stood up. 'You have a latrine I can use?'

'Out the front door and round the side to the back. Thanks for your custom, Valerius Corvinus. Give our regards to my sister when you see her.'

'I'll do that.' I left.

The latrine was a lean-to affair on the far side of a small yard full of the sort of junk you get in nine back yards out of ten; stuff that's either waiting to be thrown out properly and never will be or that someone thought might come in handy at some future date but wouldn't get round to using until the Greek kalends: empty wine jars, the remains of a cart that looked like it'd sat there providing a home for beetles and wood-lice for the past thirty years, a bedstead frame that was more rust than honest iron and a pile of nameless rubbish forming the remains of a half-hearted bonfire. The latrine itself, though, was relatively up-market, with cement flooring, a hole-in-the-floor toilet and a urinal slab with the guttering leading into a collecting bucket. I used the slab, adjusted my tunic and turned round . . .

'Hey, Roman.'

There were two of them, big guys, filling the space between the dead cart and the wall of the yard, blocking the entrance to the alleyway that connected it with the street. The one on the left was red-headed, and although I couldn't quite place him he looked vaguely familiar. On the other hand, I'd no problem recognising the two as a pair because I'd seen them both earlier that morning, propping up the wall outside the draper's near Mundus's house waiting for someone who obviously hadn't been their mistress to come out. Mind you, on that occasion they hadn't been swinging blackjacks and looking like they were just dying to try them out on me. Little details like that tend to fix your attention.

Bugger; so much for premature senility clouding the judgment. When the hairs on the back of my neck had prickled, I should've listened.

The guy on the left took a step forward. 'Broken arms or broken ribs, friend?' he said. 'Which is it to be? Your choice.'

Something clicked in my brain. Finally. 'You're one of the slaves from the Hostilius place,' I said. 'I saw you when I was over there last, three days ago. Who sent you? Castor or the widow?'

'Oh, now, then.' He paused, glanced at his pal, then back to me. 'Okay, so maybe you don't have a choice after all.'

Slowly, deliberately, he tucked the blackjack into the belt of his tunic, reached behind his back, drew out a knife and grinned.

Oh, shit. Nice one, Corvinus. I looked around for a weapon. Zilch. Whatever junk the Veturini, senior and junior, had thrown out over the past thirty years or so hadn't included lengths of two-by-four or useful sections of lead piping. Or not within grabbing distance, anyway. Of course, there was the collecting bucket . . .

They were moving as I turned, but I got a grip on the thing and swung it just as Blackjack was closing in on my right side.

Stale urine might not figure all that prominently in the military manual as an offensive weapon – not offensive in the army sense of the word, anyway – but a gallon of it in the face at point-blank range ain't something you can ignore, and Blackjack reeled back spluttering and cursing. The wooden bucket itself caught Red-head on the shoulder: not enough to do any real damage, but it threw him off-line. I moved in and made a grab for his wrist, driving my own shoulder into his chest.

He ducked under my left armpit and shoved hard. My heels met the concrete ledge of the latrine floor and I went arse over tip backwards, pinning the guy's head between the inside of my elbow and my chest, my right hand pushing down against his neck, forcing it lower. There was a dull thud as his skull hit the floor. He grunted and went limp.

One down and out, or hopefully so, anyway. I rolled sideways, letting go and trying to ignore the stab of pain as my elbow met the concrete; just as Blackjack came at me for a second shot. There was a flash of metal in his right hand: another knife. Fuck; we weren't out of the woods yet, not by a long way. I lashed out desperately with my foot, felt it connect against his shin and saw him stagger. Good, but not good enough; and I was still on my back.

The bucket was where I'd dropped it, just within reach. I grabbed it and swung it round, bottom up, as the knife came down straight for my chest. There was a *thunk!* as the point bit deep into the wood. I held the bucket steady for a split second, then heaved upwards and to the side, wrenching the knife from his hand, and tossed the whole boiling away from us as hard as I could. Blackjack swore and grabbed at my throat, thumbs pressing against my windpipe. I brought my knee up into his groin, and he gasped; his grip relaxed and I rolled again, forcing myself out from under him into clear space, scrabbling on to my hands and knees, then to my feet.

I was just in time. I'd scarcely got upright before he hit me again with a roundhouse punch that caught my shoulder, knocking me sideways. I managed a straight left that rattled his teeth but didn't stop him, and he came at me with both fists swinging . . .

'*Hey!*'

He turned his head; not by much, but the break in concentration was enough. I planted another left, then swung a punch of my own that met square with the side of his jaw and sent him sprawling against the latrine wall.

'What the hell's happening here?'

One of the slaughterhouse lads, latrine-bound himself; no quick thinker, obviously, because he was just standing at the exit to the yard like a bovine third actor in a play, but it was enough for Blackjack. The guy staggered to his feet, broke into a stumbling run, pushed him out of the way and hared off down the alley fast as a professional sprinter.

I moved over to the nearest wall and leaned against it, gasping my lungs out.

The slaughterer hurried over. 'You okay, sir?' he said.

'Yeah. Yeah, I'm fine.' I caught my breath, finally, and stood up straight. 'Thanks, pal.' . . . which was when he noticed Red-head, and his eyes widened.

'He dead?'

'Search me. I was too busy to check. You want to do it for me?'

He flashed me a worried look, then did, turning the body over. The forehead was a mess of blood and the eyes were closed. 'Nah, he's breathing,' he said. 'Just stunned.'

'Pity.'

That got me another nervous look, but I ignored it. I wasn't feeling too charitable at that point towards Red-head, myself.

'So what happened?'

'They jumped me. After my purse.' No sense in complicating things, not with Brain of Bovillae here, anyway. I was still in one piece, relatively unscathed, with all my bits attached, and that was enough to be thankful for. 'Do me a favour, pal, you and your mates inside.'

'Sure.'

There was a length of half-decent rope beside the remains of the cart. I picked it up, took it over to Red-head and used the two ends to tie his wrists and ankles. 'Keep an eye on him in case he wakes up, see he doesn't do a runner, while I nip round to the local Watch-house and have someone collect him.'

'You've got it. No problem.' He watched with slack-jawed fascination while I tied the final knot and pulled it tight.

'Great. Oh, and if you want to use the facilities you'd better replace the bucket.' Not that, with the latrine floor already awash with the best part of a gallon of fuller's delight, there was much point to that, really, but it's the thought that counts.

I left him staring and headed for the alley.

So: Veturina or Castor? One of them, certainly, and my bets were on the second: Red-head had been on his way to the east wing when I'd seen him, so he was probably Castor's slave rather than Veturina's, and a physical attempt to put me out of the game seemed more Castor's style than his sister's. On the other hand, I didn't trust Veturina the length of my arm, and I wouldn't be too surprised to find I was wrong. At least I'd got one of the murdering bastards alive, and this time I wouldn't object too strongly about what methods the authorities used to get the truth from him.

27

I was bang on time the next day for my appointment with Publius Novius. He must've been in his seventies, easy: a little guy with a face wrinkled like a prune whose pricey, well-starched mantle looked like it'd been meant for someone twice his size. There was nothing old about the eyes that considered me across the office desk, though. These were bright as a bird's, and sharp as a razor.

'So, Valerius Corvinus,' he said. 'How can I help you? My clerk said it was private and personal. The first I can understand, the second is a little more problematical. Oh, yes' – he held up a hand – 'I know who you are, you needn't bother explaining that. We don't have many murders in Latium, and word does tend to get around. Especially when the victim is a lawyer.'

Hell. Well, I couldn't reasonably have expected him not to've heard of me altogether. And it might actually make things easier in the long run. 'I've just got a couple of areas I thought you might be able to help me with,' I said.

'Yes?'

'The first is a trial twenty-one years ago, where you prosecuted and Hostilius and his partner defended. A burglary and murder. The two accused were brothers, Lupus and Senecio Brabbius.'

He'd blinked at the start, when I'd mentioned the trial, like he'd been surprised; but then his expression had settled into what I'd bet was careful indifference. Interesting. 'The Brabbii brothers,' he said. 'Oh, my goodness, now, that *is* going back! Just give me a moment to recollect.' His fingers tapped the desk. 'A silversmith's shop by the precinct of Mercury, wasn't it? The pair were interrupted by the owner, who got himself knifed in the process. Let's see . . . Vexillius, was that his name? No, Vectillius, Titus Vectillius. The jury found both men guilty, the elder brother was sentenced to death and the younger to the galleys. Is that right?'

'Yeah, that's it. You've a good memory, sir.'

'I'm a lawyer, Corvinus. Of course I have.'

'You remember the details of the trial itself?'

If I hadn't been looking for the slight flicker in the eyes I'd've missed it; but I was, and it was there. 'Not every detail, no,' he said. 'But in broad terms I think I do. It wasn't a difficult case, from my side. The pair were caught immediately after the crime, within minutes at most. Lupus had a silver bracelet in his possession, which certainly came from the shop, and also a knife, which was why he was the one to be executed. The defence tried to argue that he had picked the bracelet up in the street after the real perpetrators had fled in the other direction, and also that the arresting party were mostly drunk at the time so their evidence was suspect, but they couldn't get round the knife. Or the fact that Lupus and his brother were running when they were stopped.'

Check. 'So it was a unanimous verdict? On the part of the jury, I mean?'

Another slight flicker. 'Yes. Yes, it was.'

'You see, I was wondering whether . . . well, the word is that at that point in his career Quintus Acceius wasn't quite so . . . scrupulous as he is now.' I had to go delicately here; after all, it was only an idea, but it was one that fitted, and if I was right it'd go a long way towards explaining the whole boiling. Besides, Novius was being cagey over something; that I was sure of.

'Were you, indeed?' Bland as hell; but the eyes had sharpened. 'And?'

'I sort of thought that, if he couldn't do much about the strength of his case, he might've tried working on the verdict angle instead.'

Silence. Long silence. Novius was frowning and drumming his fingers again on the desk. Finally he said, 'It was a long time ago, Corvinus. People – especially young lawyers, just starting out – make mistakes, mistakes that they bitterly regret later. Quintus Acceius and I have had our differences over the years – we're frequently on opposing sides in court, for a start – but I have always had every respect for him professionally. Even then he was, not to put too fine a point on it, brilliant; much more capable than his partner. It would have been a shame to have ruined such a young man's career over a moment of idiocy.'

Bull's-eye! 'So he bribed the jury?' I said.

'No.' Novius sighed. 'He *meant* to bribe the jury. It never happened, because I got wind of it in time. One of the more honest members came to me privately and told me he'd been approached, and I had a quiet word with Acceius before things could go any further. He had no option but to drop the plan, of course: if he'd persisted I'd've taken the whole matter straight to the judge, he would've been facing prosecution himself and his legal career would've been over before it had properly started. I made that very clear to him.' He rubbed his temples. 'I need hardly say that this is totally confidential. As I said, it's ancient history now, no actual crime was perpetrated, and to my almost certain knowledge and belief it was an isolated incident. A single, stupid mistake.'

A single, stupid mistake. Yeah, that phrase, or something like it, had cropped up before, and it sent all sorts of bells ringing. The bribery aspect raised another question as well, but although it was important it had nothing to do with Novius and I didn't ask it. Finally, everything was beginning to fit together. 'Okay,' I said. 'Let's move on to the second area.'

'Second area?'

'Yeah. Castor. Lucius Hostilius's brother-in-law.'

Novius's face . . . *froze*. There was no other word for it. 'What about him?' he said.

'You were helping the guy out. He wanted to be a lawyer himself, but thanks to his brother-in-law he wasn't getting anywhere in Castrimoenium. You were . . . oh, I don't know, training him as an apprentice might be overstating it, but supplying him with books, talking him through cases, things like that. Yes?'

'I . . . took an interest, certainly.' He'd leaned back in his chair and put the tips of his fingers together, touching his lips. 'Although I can't think why that should be of any—'

'Cosmus. He used to be one of your slaves, didn't he?'

That got me a long, slow stare. 'I had a slave by that name, yes,' he said at last.

'You knew he was the one who . . . let's say poisoned Lucius Hostilius?'

Novius stood up abruptly. 'I think we'll have my clerk in here,' he said. 'If you're going to accuse me of—'

'I'm not accusing you of anything,' I said. 'Or not of arranging a murder, anyway. But if you'd like your clerk to hear the next bit then go ahead and call him, pal. It's no skin off my nose.'

He glared at me for all of five seconds. Then he sat down again. 'Carry on,' he said tightly.

'You sold Cosmus to Marcus Tuscius, the local slave-dealer, thirteen months ago. He was bought two days later by Veturina, Lucius Hostilius's wife, and her brother Castor.'

'Really? I wasn't aware of that, but if you tell me he was then no doubt it's so.'

'Now correct me if I'm wrong, pal, but I'd bet a gold piece to a kick in the teeth that the transaction didn't post-date the start of your association with Castor by all that much. And there's the question of what you were getting in return for your interest in him.'

'Corvinus, I do advise you that you're getting perilously close to slander here.'

'So call in your clerk, friend.' He didn't move. 'Castor's already admitted to me that he passed on the information about how high Hostilius's client was prepared to go in the offering price for the Lutatius property. And that it wasn't a one-off; you'd been running him as a mole for months, picking up what he could about areas you and the Castrimoenian practice shared an interest in until Hostilius caught on and pulled the plug. Me, I think the intention – the original intention – where Cosmus was concerned was to have someone else on the inside at the guy's home as well as his office, to run along with Castor. The problem was that although Cosmus was personable enough for promotion to an upstairs slave Hostilius didn't like or trust him, so that particular plan fizzled out in the end, but it was a sharp idea in principle. You're the lawyer, friend. Want to tell me how something like that would square legally?'

'I did nothing illegal.'

'No, I'm sure you didn't. Not as such, because you'd be very careful not to. But can you answer for Castor?' The lips formed a tight line. 'Over the Maecilius business, for a start. Colluding in the suppression of a will is definitely on the criminal side of the fence. Now I'll admit that that doesn't, on the face of it, seem to be to your advantage, quite the reverse, but—'

'Colluding in *what*?'

'Even though the chances are he was working on his own there you and he were definitely in bed together otherwise, and if it came out then you'd have awkward questions to answer.'

'Are you blackmailing me, Valerius Corvinus?'

I shook my head. 'No. Not at all. As far as I'm concerned you can play your lawyers' games until hell freezes. All I want to know is how Castor fits in with the deaths of Lucius Hostilius and Brabbia Habra.'

'Who?'

'The brothers' younger sister. Her body was found up by Caba a few days ago. Did you know her?'

'No. I knew there was a sister, but not her name. And I never met her.' He was frowning. 'Corvinus, what's this about Castor suppressing a will? Presumably you mean the one my client Gaius Maecilius – Bucca – says his father made shortly before he died, in which case if you have proof of its existence then you're legally obliged to reveal its whereabouts.'

'No proof, not yet, but I will have because I'm right. I just mentioned it to show you that covering up for Castor to save your own skin might not be such a smart idea in the long run. Oh, he's inoffensive and mild-mannered on the surface, sure, but his father said that when he was a kid if he wanted something then he'd go for it, whatever stood in the way, and I'd bet that sums the guy up neatly, especially the last bit. Believe me, pal, there is something very rotten about Castor, and it goes a long way past the games you're involved in.'

He was quiet for a long time. Then he said; 'What do you want to know?'

'When was the last time you saw him?'

'He was here perhaps seventeen or eighteen days ago.'

Uh-huh. That would put it – I did a quick calculation – just a day or so after Hostilius's conversation at the villa with Acceius, which I would bet that Veturina had overheard a hell of a lot more of than she'd told me, and duly passed on to her brother. 'For any specific reason?'

'He wanted to talk to me about the Julian law. Its precise terms and ramifications.'

Yeah; Veturina had mentioned a Julian law. 'Hang on, pal,' I said. 'This would be the Julian law on inheritance tax, would it?'

Novius chuckled. 'No, it wouldn't. At least, yes, there *is* a Julian law on inheritance tax – the Julia Vicesimaria – in fact there are several Julian laws. But the one Castor wanted to discuss – and before you ask, Corvinus, in purely theoretical terms – was the one on adultery and the punishment of adulterers.'

Everything went very still. 'You, ah, care to take me through that one, pal?' I said.

'Certainly. The gist of it is that if a man has proof that his wife is committing adultery he's legally obliged to divorce her forthwith. He then has sixty valid days – days when public business can be transacted – to instigate her formal prosecution, which, again, he is obliged by law to do. If the adultery is proved in court then, where the marriage is childless, as it was in Castor's theoretical scenario, the husband retains a sixth of the original dowry, the rest going in fines to the state; while the adulterer loses, again as a fine, half his property. The wife and adulterer are punished by exile to separate islands.'

I sat back. Sweet immortal gods! Unless I was really, *really* mistaken I'd just been handed the key to the whole case. The only problem was, which lock did it fit? *Wife and adulterer*, eh? I reckoned that if you stretched the definition of the second category a little we'd had four possibilities for that combination over the last few days, and they all made sense, of a kind at least. So which was it? You paid your money and you took your choice. 'And that's what Castor wanted to check up on?' I said.

'Oh, no. He already knew that much. It was the next proviso of the law that he wasn't altogether clear about.'

'Namely?'

Novius told me.

Jupiter bloody best and greatest. One possibility; not four. Just the one.

Shit!

Puteoli and Spain, nothing. He'd still be around, that I'd bet on, because he'd nothing to gain by running now. And I knew where to find him, sure I did; he'd told me that himself.

I left Novius and headed for the town granaries.

28

The girl who opened the door of the flat was thin as a whip, pinch-featured and, I'd guess, under her tunic, well-muscled. Yeah, he'd said she was a dancer.

'Stratyllis?' I said.

'Yes.' Suspicious as hell, and the hand on the door moved it forward an inch. 'What do you want?'

A stage name, obviously: you could've cut the Bovillan accent with a knife. 'My name's Valerius Corvinus. I've come to see—'

If I hadn't been quick and got my boot against it the door would've been slammed in my face. As it was, it bounced back hard against the wall and I shoved past the girl and in.

There was only the one room. Castor was sitting on the bed, a plate in his hand with some cheese, sliced sausage, bread and olives on it; the other, beside him, had mostly salad. Me, I'd've thought it was a bit early for lunch but maybe she had a gig that evening, and dancers don't eat before they work.

He set the plate aside and stood up slowly. I thought he was going to go for me because his fists bunched, but then he relaxed, shrugged and turned away. The girl sat down on a stool against the wall – apart from a clothes chest it was the only other piece of furniture – and folded her arms tightly like she was hugging something.

'So you found me,' Castor said.

'It wasn't difficult, pal,' I said quietly. I reached back and closed the door. 'Oh, and incidentally, those two heavies you sent after me? Red-head and his mate? We had a run-in yesterday, and they tried to knife me. The second one got away but Red wasn't so lucky. He's down at the Watch-house, charged with attempted murder and spilling his guts out.' True: I'd called in on the way to my appointment with Novius; not that it made much difference, practically speaking, where Castor was concerned because I'd got the bastard sewn up good and proper in any case.

He looked, suddenly, sick. 'Corvinus, I swear!' he said. 'I only told them to frighten you, get you off my back! Not—'

'Like hell you did.'

'It had nothing to do with Lucius's death! I'm no killer! Believe me!'

'No, you aren't,' I said. 'Or at least not yet, anyway.'

He hadn't expected that, and I'd kept my tone mild. He blinked and sat down again.

'Well?' he said. He was getting some of his bounce back fast, and there was an edge of truculence in his voice. I noticed he hadn't picked me up on the qualification, if he'd spotted it, but we'd let that pass for the present.

'You want to tell me about it?' I said. 'Or shall I tell you?'

Another shrug. 'Go ahead.'

'Your sister overheard a conversation between her husband and Quintus Acceius, the day after the attack in the street. Normally, she wouldn't've bothered to listen in, but your name was mentioned and so she did.' He said nothing. 'Hostilius was talking about the Julian law on adultery. Under its terms, if a husband is conscious that his wife is having an adulterous affair then he's legally obliged to divorce her and bring a formal prosecution. If he doesn't, or refuses to, then it's the right of a third party who knows of the affair to bring the prosecution himself. In which case the husband becomes technically a pander in collusion with the wife who has profited and is profiting, financially or otherwise, from the woman's immorality. Yes?'

He'd gone pale. 'Yes.'

'How did Hostilius know about your affair with Seia Lucinda?'

Silence. The girl – Stratyllis – raised her eyes and shot him a hard look, but she didn't say anything. Her arms still hugged her chest tightly.

'It . . . wasn't an affair,' Castor said finally. 'Not a proper one. And it was none of my doing. She was bored, she was lonely, she and Acceius hadn't slept together for years. I tried to avoid her as much as I could, but she's still a beautiful woman, and it just happened. She rode over to the villa once – *once* – about a month ago. Hostilius was at home – I didn't know that at the time – and he must've seen her coming in to my part of the house. He . . . sneaked in and caught us kissing. Kissing! No more! I swear to you!'

Yeah, right. Well, I reckoned I'd got the seriously edited version there, but it didn't matter, that side of things wasn't important. And I'd believe that Seia Lucinda had made the running, certainly: Castor might have playboy looks and be a lady's man through and through, but he wasn't a fool. If he started an affair it would be for what he could get out of it in other ways, and Seia Lucinda was just too damn dangerous to play around with. 'Okay,' I said. 'So Hostilius caught you. There weren't any witnesses, mind, or were there?' Castor shook his head. 'So if you'd been careful otherwise – and I'd bet you were – there wasn't any legal danger. We'll come back to that.'

'Corvinus, I swear—'

'You want to take over?' He shook his head again. 'Fine. Hostilius tells Acceius that if he doesn't divorce his wife and bring a prosecution against the pair of you then he'll do it for him.'

'But he'd've had no case! You said yourself if there were no witnesses – and there weren't – it was only his word against mine and Lucinda's. And the way my brother-in-law threw accusations around—'

'I told you we'd come back to that.' I leaned against the door. 'He didn't need a case, because he'd never have to bring one. Giving Quintus Acceius the chance to divorce his wife and prosecute her for adultery himself was the easy option, it was even generous, in its way. The alternative was for Hostilius to bring a charge against the two of them for murder, and that he *could* prove. Given time, which he wasn't. Acceius made sure of that.'

Silence. Total silence. Then Castor said, 'How did you know?'

'Working it out wasn't hard, once I knew about the second part of the Julian law. Oh, sure, having to divorce his wife would've hit Acceius badly, financially: if the charge had gone uncontested, which it'd have to have done under the terms of the bargain, he'd only be left with a sixth part of the original dowry, and the practice was built on Seia's money. But he could've weathered that, and so might Seia, although she'd've been the harder hit. The problem was, Hostilius being Hostilius, they could never have trusted him to keep to the deal.'

Castor shook his head. 'No,' he said. 'I meant the murder. How did you know that Acceius had killed his first wife?'

'I didn't. Oh, it was a possibility, sure, especially when I found out who the dead woman up at Caba was, but I didn't know for absolute certain until Publius Novius told me about Acceius's plans to bribe the jury in the Brabbius trial. That would've *cost*: it was an open-and-shut case, and he would've needed to buy at least half the jurors. The money had to come from somewhere, it sure as hell couldn't've come from the Brabbii themselves, and Acceius didn't have nearly that amount of gravy at the time even if he'd've wanted to spend it. It had to be Seia's. Which meant that the two of them were in it together.'

'Go on.' Now he was off the hook – or that hook, anyway – Castor seemed genuinely interested. Well, the guy was a lawyer, after all, or at least a wannabe lawyer. I shouldn't've been all that surprised. And he wouldn't've known all the whys and wherefores. I hadn't known them myself until that morning.

'*One stupid mistake*,' I said. 'Me, I think that's the phrase that sums everything up. My bet is that Seia Lucinda made the running, like she did with you, and Quintus Acceius made the one stupid mistake of his life by being tempted and giving in. On Seia's prompting he made a bargain with Brabbia Habra. She'd provide him with the poison that'd kill his wife in childbirth, leaving him free to marry Seia, and in return he'd bribe the jury and see that her brothers were acquitted. Only it went wrong: one of the jurors blabbed to Novius, Novius stopped the bribery and the two Brabbii went down after all. Acceius had welched on the deal, and Habra – and her brother Senecio – never forgot it. So when Senecio had done his stint in the galleys and came back—'

'Hold on, Corvinus.' Castor was frowning. 'You're going to say that this Senecio wanted revenge for his brother's death, right?'

'Yeah. Yeah, of course.'

'But why attack Hostilius? And what about Habra? She knew where Acceius lived, she'd known for twenty years. She'd've wanted revenge herself, surely?'

I shrugged. 'Habra I don't know about. Not yet. But Senecio thought that both the partners were in on the deal. He wanted both of them dead. If he went for Hostilius first, that was just chance.'

'You mean Hostilius didn't know at the time of the trial? About the bribery, at least?'

'Uh-uh. Not a thing. That's the whole point. If he had, he'd've blown the whistle himself. My guess is that Senecio said something, the day of the attack, just before he put the knife in, that gave the whole game away. Hostilius didn't say anything at the time – he was a lawyer, after all, he'd watch his mouth until he'd thought it through, especially round other people – but it would've registered. And he was an honest man, at root. When Acceius came round the next day he'd've worked out how he was going to handle things. Hence the ultimatum. It was beautiful: if Acceius stuck it out, then he'd track down Habra, subpoena Novius, and put together a case that his partner and his wife would find it difficult to answer even after all this time. Even if Acceius did manage to get off somehow a lot of the dirt would've stuck, because it was true, and he'd be ruined professionally and socially. On the other hand, if the guy agreed to the divorce and prosecution angle both he and his wife would get the punishment they deserved anyway. Hostilius had them both ways.'

'So he had to die.'

'Right.'

He was quiet for a long time. Then he said, 'What happens now?'

'With you? Or with Acceius?'

He tried a smile that didn't work. 'With me, for a start.'

'That's up to Libanius. You're an accessory after the fact. You and your sister.'

He glanced up sharply. 'Veturina knew nothing about—'

'Sure she did, pal. She had to. Almost from the start.'

'She thought I was responsible! She still does, even although I swore to her that I wasn't. She was shielding me, not Acceius.'

'Yeah. Yeah, I know.' I sighed; this bit was going to be difficult. The guy had a rotten streak a yard wide, sure, but he wasn't rotten in that way. 'Your sister . . . loves you. And I don't mean as a brother.' He looked away. 'There's nothing she can do about it, if she's admitted it to herself then she probably despises herself for it, and I'm not saying that you or she have taken things any further because I'm sure you haven't and wouldn't, ever. Still, it's a fact. I'm right, yes?'

He nodded, then said quietly, 'Yes. On her side, yes. She always has loved me.'

'She must've suspected that her husband's death wasn't natural even when it happened. It was too convenient, and she's a clever woman. She might even have thought of tasting the contents of the medicine bottle before Hyperion got to it.' He said nothing. 'Certainly she's lied and covered up the truth as far as she could all the way. That business with the two Julian laws. She's no lawyer, she couldn't've invented the confusion with the one on inheritance tax, and she knew damn well which one her husband was talking about. That had to come from you. And she knew all about Cosmus and how he fitted into your dealings with Novius. She thought – she still thinks – that you used him to poison her husband, to save yourself from disgrace and exile. Yes?'

He nodded again. His head was still turned away. 'I couldn't convince her that I hadn't done it,' he said. 'She said it didn't matter, she didn't mind, her husband was better off dead for his own sake anyway. What she couldn't've stood was to lose us both.'

'And maybe she had another reason for not believing you,' I said quietly. 'Because she knew just how much you were capable of, if it'd get you something you really wanted.' His head came round, and over by the wall Stratyllis, who had been sitting unmoving through all this, looked up startled. 'Fimus's wife Faenia. You're having an affair with her, aren't you? A genuine affair.'

'Why the hell should I—'

'Come on, pal! It's not because of her looks, that's for sure. Three million, isn't the estate worth, potentially, if it's kept whole and entire? As it would be if that missing will didn't turn up. Oh, sure, Fimus'd never sell, but that'd be all to the good, wouldn't it, because his widow might. If her new husband advised it. Of course, there is the kid, young Aulus, but if you left a decent interval after the accident to Fimus a couple more natural deaths wouldn't—'

He was on his feet and going for my throat, but I was ready for that. Castor may've been big, but he was no fighter, especially a dirty one. I kneed him in the balls and he collapsed gasping.

Yeah, well, I'd finished anyway. I turned to the wide-eyed Stratyllis.

'See that he gets that will to Quintus Libanius in Castri-moenium first thing in the morning, sister,' I said. 'No hassle, I promise you: I'll square things before then. And keep him out of trouble in future. Better still, ditch the bastard and find another boyfriend.'

I left. Well, it was nice to prevent a murder or three for a change rather than pick up the pieces afterwards. And you never knew: the shock might've done him some good.

Back to Castrimoenium myself, and a last talk with Quintus Acceius.

29

I went straight over there when I arrived. The slave who opened the door – Carillus, it was, I remembered – looked frightened as hell.

'Your master in?' I said.

'Yes, sir. In the study.' He swallowed. 'You're to go straight through.'

Acceius, when I got there, was sitting on the chair beside the desk dressed in his formal mantle. His face was like a death mask, and on the desk beside him was a basin and a knife.

'Hello, Corvinus,' he said. 'You got my message at last, then?'

'No.' I closed the door behind me. 'What message?'

He shrugged. 'It doesn't matter, you're here now in any case. But I've been expecting you since early this morning.'

'I was in Bovillae.' I sat down on the couch uninvited. There was something wrong here, very wrong, and the hairs were rising on the back of my neck. 'You wanted to see me?'

'Yes. Lucinda's dead. Upstairs. I smothered her with a pillow last night.' His voice was perfectly calm. I stared at him. 'She didn't suffer: she was drunk, as usual, and I'd crushed three of the sleeping pills Hyperion sent me into her wine. The slaves know, of course, but I told them not to report it until I'm dead myself' – a twist of the lips – 'which I will be shortly, now that you've arrived. I was only waiting to talk to you, to apologise, possibly to answer any questions you might have, before I slit my wrists and finish things.'

Gods! 'You, uh, know that I know you killed Hostilius, then,' I said cautiously.

'And the others, yes. Or rather no, I didn't know, not for certain. But you were getting very close, and my sympathies are with you rather than with me.' He cleared his throat. 'Corvinus, I'm not a natural killer, and yet I've killed four people. Five, counting Tascia.' He glanced at the marble bust. 'Do you realise how . . . *sick* that makes me of myself?' I said nothing. 'So I'll be very, very glad, when your visit is over, to make what little reparation I can. If you're good enough to grant me that licence.'

This was turning out all wrong. 'You admit that you and Seia Lucinda poisoned your first wife, then?' I said. 'Using a poison you got from Brabbia Habra?'

'Yes. It was the biggest, most stupid, most *evil* mistake of my life. Can I tell you about it now? Please?'

'Yeah,' I said quietly. 'Yeah, if you like. Go ahead, pal. Take your time.'

He looked at the bust again, but this time his eyes didn't shift. 'I never loved her,' he said. 'Not as much as she loved me, certainly. I don't think, at that stage, I was capable of genuinely loving anyone; certainly not Lucinda, that was a combination of lust, ambition and greed. Smugness, too, if that's not too small a vice to put beside the others. Fifteen-year-old girl or not, she made it perfectly clear almost from the first that she wanted me, even knowing that I was married already, and that she'd do anything to have me. Her father was no hindrance, she could wind him round her finger, she was beautiful and she was rich. And I . . . well, I had ambitions. Serious ambitions. I knew that with her as a wife I could get out of Bovillae, set up a practice in Rome, and . . . oh, but you know yourself. The only obstacle was Tascia.' He turned back. His cheeks were wet. 'A complete and utter fool, you see. So when Lucinda suggested at the time of the Brabbius trial that the obstacle might be removed I gave in without a struggle.'

'She knew about Habra, then?'

'Oh, yes. She'd used her before. A . . . young male cousin, she told me it was, but I suspect the man might've been one of the family's own slaves. Lucinda always was wild. She was certainly no virgin when we married, and she wouldn't've had any compunctions in that direction. It wasn't poison as such, just something to give Tascia when the time came that would . . . keep her bleeding, whatever the midwife did. Until she had no blood left. Then she died.'

I waited for a while, then I said, 'She started blackmailing you? Habra? After you married Lucinda?'

He shook his head slowly. 'No. Or not as such. Oh, she asked me for money, yes, but I gave it to her willingly, more than she asked, and I kept giving it. Call it a conscience payment, if you like. Lucinda never knew, I was careful of that, or that she'd settled in Castrimoenium, because it was part of my punishment of myself, nothing to do with her.'

'And another part was that you gave up the idea of moving to Rome.'

'Yes. Not immediately. It was no sudden conversion, don't think that. I told you, Corvinus, at the time I was not a very nice person. Even less nice' – another half-smile – 'than I am today. I was ambitious, I'd got – or thought I'd got – all I wanted. Only gradually it became not so important any more. I felt I had to *pay.* Do you understand that?'

'Yeah,' I said. 'Yeah, I understand.'

'So I stayed in Bovillae. And I . . . stopped sleeping with Lucinda. Then we moved to Castrimoenium and' – he shrugged – 'here we are. Still.'

Jupiter! Well, I had to admit the guy had paid, all right. Seia Lucinda, too. Twenty years! Gods! 'Then Senecio came back,' I said.

'I thought he was dead. As he should've been, because who survives twenty years in the galleys? He must've found Habra first, there would've been people in Bovillae who knew where she'd gone. Then he found us. Lucius and me. He thought we were equally responsible and, unlike his sister, he wanted us dead.'

'He said something, didn't he, when he attacked you?'

'Yes.' Acceius closed his eyes briefly. 'I can't remember exactly, but it was suitably explicit and damning: something about us having gone back on the deal with Habra over getting rid of Tascia. Lucius guessed at once who he was and what he meant, of course – however ill he was in other ways, he never lost his lawyer's sharpness – and that was that. I panicked. I . . . wrested the knife from Senecio and stabbed him. It was quite deliberate, and I'm sorry about that now. It would've been far better if I'd allowed him to stab me and finish things before they started.'

'Then, the next day, you went to confront Hostilius, and he gave you his ultimatum.'

'He was generous; very generous.' Acceius took a deep breath. 'But then Lucius always was, all the years I knew him. He offered me a simple choice. I would divorce Lucinda for adultery with Castor, which she would admit to, and prosecute her under the terms of the Julian law; you know, of course, that they'd been meeting secretly for the past seven or eight months in an empty house she owned in Bovillae?' I said nothing. 'Or he'd formally accuse the two of us of murder and start putting the case together. He gave me six days to decide.'

'How did you work things out with Cosmus?'

Another shrug. 'Oh, that was easy. A little judicious black-mail on my own account, plus the promise of a large sum in cash and help to disappear. I'd known for some time that he was acting with Castor in collusion with Publius Novius but . . . well, for various reasons I was reluctant to tell Lucius because – and I don't expect you to understand this, Corvinus, but it's the truth – I felt sorry for Castor himself, and it would've destroyed him, too.'

'You felt sorry for Castor,' I said neutrally. 'Even though you knew he was having an affair with your wife.'

He smiled. 'I said you wouldn't understand. Yes. Yes, I did. The affair was nothing. Lucinda wasn't a happy woman, no more than – for the past twenty years – I've been a happy man, and as I say we hadn't been properly husband and wife since Bovillae. Think of it, if you will, as another part of my punishment, and of hers. Besides, destroying Castor would've hurt Veturina very badly indeed. I didn't want that; I've never wanted that. Veturina has been hurt enough.' He paused. 'Arranging things wasn't difficult. Cosmus spent a lot of his time in the stables, so we were hardly strangers: I saw him practically every time I visited the house. I knew about Lucius's morning routine, of course, and about the medicine. I threatened Cosmus with exposure to Lucius – he would've sold him like a shot, and into a life that would've been far less pleasant than the one he had – and, as I say, added certain promises. Fortunately Cosmus wasn't the most intelligent of slaves, nor the most moral: he agreed almost at once. As to the actual killing . . . well, I won't defend that, I can't, but at least I tried to make it as merciful as I could.'

'Did Lucinda know?'

'Not immediately. But yes, I told her, shortly afterwards.' He frowned. 'She . . . again I don't expect you to believe this but I meant to play fair by Cosmus, originally. Lucinda persuaded me that perhaps it . . . was not a good idea.'

'So you killed him.'

'Yes. I went to the Bavius farm where we'd arranged he should hide with that intention in mind, and hit him with an iron bar while his back was turned.' He looked at me bleakly. 'It was a proper murder, for which I have no defence. There were no extenuating circumstances for Cosmus's death, none at all. I can't pretty it up by ascribing it to panic, like Senecio's, nor can I claim that the death in itself was a mercy from which other people benefited, as Lucius's was. I killed Cosmus out of purely selfish motives, and it was done intentionally, for Lucinda's sake and my own. I told you, Corvinus, we're not nice people. We're both better off dead.'

'What about Habra?'

'That happened exactly as I said it did. At least, I don't think I deliberately intended to kill her, although she certainly wanted to kill me. Understandably so. I'm sorry about Habra.' He shook his head. 'I'm sorry about it all.'

'Yeah. Right.' I stood up. I felt sick, and empty.

'That's all?' He was watching me. 'You've no more questions?' Again, that half-smile.

'No. I've no more questions.'

'Good. Then I won't keep you any longer.' He hesitated. Then he said, formally, 'Thank you for coming, Valerius Corvinus. Thank you for everything.'

I left him sitting. The marble bust's eyes were on me all the way to the door. I still felt them on my back as I closed it behind me.

30

When I got home after my long talk with Libanius, Perilla and the youngsters were already in the dining-room and the skivvies were serving the starters.

'Marcus, why on *earth* didn't you send word if you were intending to . . .' Perilla began. Then she must've noticed the look on my face, because her voice changed and she said simply, 'What's happened?'

I set the welcome-home cupful of wine down on the table and stretched out on my usual couch. 'Quintus Acceius is the murderer. By now he'll be dead. Him and his wife both.'

All three of them stared at me, Marilla with a stuffed olive halfway to her lips.

'*What?*' Perilla said.

I told them the whole boiling. I didn't feel much better by the end of it, either. He'd thanked me; the poor bugger had actually *thanked* me, like I'd done him a favour.

'It's not your fault, Corvinus,' Clarus said.

'No.' I sighed and took a swallow of the wine. 'He'd've killed himself anyway, eventually, even if Hostilius's murder had never come to light.'

'It would've done, or it might've, even if you hadn't got involved. Veturina knew who was responsible, right from the start. And Castor. Didn't they?'

I shot him a quick look. I hadn't been going to let that aspect of things out, not even to Perilla: it was too dirty. He was no fool, young Clarus: Marilla was lucky. If you could call it luck.

'Uh-huh,' I said. 'At least, I think so. For Veturina *not* to know, she'd've had to've stopped listening, that day of the conversation between Acceius and her husband. And she would've told Castor. I don't think she could've kept any secrets from him.'

'So why didn't she say?' Perilla was frowning. 'After all, he was her husband.'

'Clarus?' I took another slug of wine and topped up the cup from the jug. This was an evening I didn't intend to stay sober.

'She'd been planning to kill him herself,' Clarus said. 'A mercy killing. Acceius beat her to it, and whatever his motives were she couldn't bring herself to betray him. It could've been her; thanks to him, it wasn't.'

I nodded. 'Yeah. That about sums it up. Also . . . well, I'd guess she thought it could've been Castor, too. Although personally I think he preferred things the way they were. The chances are, a month down the line Acceius would've found himself being blackmailed; that is, if Castor hadn't already begun putting the bite on, which he may well have done because Acceius wouldn't've told me. And I doubt that Acceius would've stiffed him for it as he deserved, even if he'd lived, because the guy had had enough of killing. *Bugger!*' I slammed the cup down and the wine spilled. 'Why is it *always* the wrong person who dies?'

'Gently, Marcus,' Perilla said. 'Besides, it isn't.'

'I could've done without Castor,' I said. 'If there's anyone who deserves a place in a fucking urn just by existing it's that bastard.'

'It's over. Leave it. Change the subject.'

Yeah, well; she was right as usual. Not that that was any comfort. I refilled the cup and sank another quarter pint as the skivvies came in with the main courses. Meton had done us proud again. Which reminded me. 'So how did your meeting with Renia go, lady?' I said. 'You manage to see her?'

'Mmm. Chicken with chives and hazelnuts,' Marilla said

brightly. 'Corvinus, you *must* have some of this. Clarus, pass Corvinus the—'

'Yes, I did, Marcus. As a matter of fact.'

Uh-oh. There weren't any spiders to rush for cover, but I'd bet if there had been the little buggers would've been swinging on their webs as fast as their eight legs could carry them, because the atmosphere had just turned glacial. 'Ah . . . good,' I said. 'Good.'

' "Good" is not a term I'd use.' Perilla picked up her spoon. 'Not even close. I have never, *ever* been so embarrassed in the entire course of my life.'

'I forgot to check on Corydon,' Marilla said, sliding off the couch like it was greased. 'Come on, Clarus.'

They disappeared. Shit; for the princess to leave the table halfway through a meal this *had* to be bad. 'She, uh, denied it?' I said. 'Having an affair with Meton?'

'Renia, Marcus, is a perfectly respectable married woman who enjoys the complete and fully justified confidence of her doting husband and would not countenance having an affair with *anyone*, let alone a paunchy, middle-aged slave with all the allure and sexual charms of a warthog.' Perilla dumped a serving of carrots in cumin savagely on to her plate. 'Her words, not mine, in case you're wondering. Personally, I think the warthog comparison is over-generous.'

'But—'

'This when she saw that I was making a serious accusation, mind. Her first reaction to the idea, after I'd introduced myself and told her why I was there, was uncontrollable laughter involving a certain amount of rib-hugging. The stage that followed it consisted of a threat to call her husband's slaves and have me thrown out on my ear.'

'But—'

'Fortunately, she was and is by nature a very nice girl indeed, with a lively sense of humour and of the ridiculous.

After I had grovellingly apologised' – I winced; oh, *hell* – 'we got quite chatty and discussed the misunderstanding over a cake or two and a cup of honey wine. So' – she laid down her spoon with a snap – 'that is *that* little mystery cleared up. And, Marcus Valerius Messalla Corvinus, if you ever, *ever* again put me into a situation like that I will kill you in the slowest, most painful way I can possibly devise. And I have an extremely good imagination.'

'But I saw them! Marilla and Clarus saw them! Meton was all over the woman! And what about the way he was fucking dressed? Meton *never* wears—'

'*Marcus!*'

Oh, bugger. A chip of plaster from the ceiling fell on to the table. I clammed up, fast.

'Do you want me to explain or don't you?'

The hard ones first. Ah, well; best get it over with. I took another belt of the Alban as an anaesthetiser. 'Yeah, okay, lady,' I said. 'You've got the floor. Go ahead, tell me.'

She did.

Oh, *bugger*!

31

We took the carriage into town the next day, Perilla and I, about two hours shy of lunchtime. I got Lysias to park it just short of the market square – no point in giving the duplicitous bastard advance warning – and we walked the rest of the way to Pontius's. We'd timed it well: they'd all be inside already.

I led the way up the outside stair to the first floor and opened the door at the top. Perilla and I slipped inside.

The place was packed full of women. At least, there was one man there, apart from the major attraction at the front of the room, and he was standing two or three yards away. I edged over, grabbed his arm and twisted it up his back. He squealed, and a plump woman sitting on the bench immediately in front of him turned round and said, '*Sssh!*'

'Sorry, lady,' I whispered. 'Private business.' Then, in his ear: 'Gabba, you bastard! You set this up, didn't you?'

'*Corvinus?* What the hell are—' Then he saw Perilla, and swallowed. Yeah, well, I knew the feeling.

'How much are you getting?' I said.

'Just the usual agent's fee, Consul. Ten per cent of the gate. But it's a public service. You heard old Titus Luscius downstairs the other day, his wife feeds him on beans four days out of five, and the fifth it's chitterlings. I just thought—'

The plump woman turned round again. 'If you two don't shut up,' she said, 'I'll give you bloody chitterlings myself.'

'Right. Right.' I let go of Gabba's arm. 'Sorry, lady.'

'Sauce!'

'Sauce,' Meton said. 'Well, ladies, if you want to raise everyday braised meats like these' – he indicated the cutlets on the skillet sitting on top of the charcoal stove in front of him – 'right into the dinner-party bracket you can't do better than a fish pickle sauce. Here it is, very simple, I made it earlier. Grind the herbs and spice very finely, that's thyme, caraway, lovage and pepper, a good three-fingersful pinch of each. Me, I'd go for black peppercorns every time, but use white if you prefer a milder taste. Oh, and one small tip here: if you're on a very tight budget, or you want something more traditional, try using dried myrtle berries. They're not the same, but they're a lot cheaper, and a few juniper berries mixed in work wonders where flavour's concerned, especially with stronger meats such as goat, wild boar or venison, when I'd add them anyway. Lovage – well, I'd use the seeds here myself for preference, but I've nothing against the leaves, fresh or dried, or even the root, if you must. And if you can't get lovage for any reason, or again if you prefer something a little more subtle, then use celery, the seeds or the leaves, not the stems.

'Once you've done the business with the mortar and pestle, add the result to a mixture of finely chopped shallots and dates – again for you budget-watchers figs are a good alternative, but the taste'll be quite different – then stir in the fish pickle, Spanish if you can find it and afford it, naturally, but the factories in Pompeii are producing some pretty good stuff these days, so I'd give that a try if you see it in your local market. If you're in doubt I'd go for the mackerel-based version, the average quality tends to be higher, although anchovy pickle has a lot to be said for it if you know your source. Blend with some honey, a little of the meat stock and some olive oil, pour over the cutlets halfway through the cooking time – here we go – and—'

At which point, across the crowded room, our eyes met and held.

'Ah,' Meton said.

And dried.

Silence. Then three dozen other pairs of hostile eyes swivelled in my direction . . .

'But, Marcus, he was *talking*! Really talking, not his usual monosyllabic grunt-and-mumble.' Perilla steadied herself against the carriage's windowsill as Lysias hit yet another pothole. '*And* holding the entire audience spellbound. *Meton* was! Don't you find that interesting?'

'Personally, lady, I found it frightening. They'd've lynched us if we hadn't got out in time.' I wasn't exaggerating, either: when Meton had corpsed, and it became obvious why, the audience had turned distinctly nasty. Forget your stories of German Frauen wading into battle tooth and nail beside their husbands, a crowd of Latin matrons with their blood up'll have them beat six ways from nothing every time, and that plump woman had had fists the size of hams. 'It just shows you, where food's concerned you don't argue. Especially with a roomful of housewives caught in *compositio interrupta*.'

'Well, I think Gabba was right. Meton's performing a public service and we should encourage him. Not just live demonstrations, either: there must be a *huge* market out there for cookery books. If we could get him to write some of his recipes down and hire a few copyists—'

Gods! 'Watch my lips, lady,' I said. 'We'd be unleashing a monster. The world is not yet ready for a celebrity chef.'

She smiled and ducked her head. 'Perhaps just Castrimoenium, then.'

'Yeah.' I settled back into the cushions. 'I'll compromise on that.'

We drove home.

AUTHOR'S NOTE

A brief word, for those who might be interested, on Roman cookery.

The extant cookery book is the *De Re Coquinaria* – which just means 'On Cookery' – by Apicius. There are three historical candidates for authorship spanning just over a hundred and fifty years, between the times of Julius Caesar and the Emperor Trajan, although it's more than likely that no single one of them, if any at all, was actually responsible for the complete work as we have it (the source manuscript is late fourth/early fifth century AD, when 'Apicius' was long established as the gastronome par excellence). What is clear, though, is that all three took their food very seriously indeed, especially the second, Marcus Gavius Apicius: Seneca and the scholiast on Juvenal mention the fact that he made a written collection of his favourite recipes; Athenaeus tells the story of how he made a special voyage to Libya to compare the vaunted Libyan prawns in size to those of Campanian Minturnae (they came nowhere near, so he sailed back without landing); and both Martial and Juvenal use him as the subject of satirical epigrams (he is supposed to have spent sixty million sesterces on his stomach, then committed suicide because he reckoned the ten million he had left was insufficient to keep body and soul decently together). Interestingly enough, Tacitus also links his name – as a notorious debauchee – with the young Sejanus. Quite a character, obviously.

There are translations available. The one on my reference shelf (which may well be out of print, but is excellent if you can find a copy) is *The Roman Cookery of Apicius, Translated and Adapted for the Modern Kitchen,* by John Edwards (Century, 1984), and is where Meton's recipe for fish pickle sauce is taken from (Try it! For the fish pickle itself, Indonesian nam pla or anchovy sauce are good modern equivalents). Also, English Heritage do a very nice little book called *Roman Cookery: Recipes and History* by Jane Renfrew, which may be more accessible (the foreword is by Loyd Grossman). You might even like to stage a proper Roman dinner party, using mattresses for the three couches and a tablecloth spread on the floor, although if so it will hopefully not involve an incident such as occurred at one of ours when the Roman mantle made by a female guest from some old curtains embarrassingly and progressively disintegrated over the course of the evening . . .

My thanks, especially, to Harry Hine of the School of Classics at St Andrews University, and to his colleague Jill Harries, for their help with the Julian law. Any mistakes I've made over the interpretation of its terms and application are, of course, due entirely to my own ineptitude.